A
SCANDAL
of the
PARTICULAR

Steve Hamilton

Tellwell Talent
www.tellwell.ca

ISBN
978-0-2288-4873-8 (Hardcover)
978-0-2288-4872-1 (Paperback)
978-0-2288-4874-5 (eBook)

For all those that we can never hold that comprise the grains of sand,
and the brightest of all the stars,
for they remind us of the wisdom that we did not earn.

Maybe all one can do is hope to end up with the right regrets

—Arthur Miller

SOMETHING ABOUT THE West Coast rain makes him crazy—those dark, endless days of grey cold drizzle. It is then that Hyman Kazan would lose his sense of self-worth. *This weather*, he thinks, *invites depression*. He has to find a way to deal with it before it gets the better of him.

The Pacific Ocean is angry, rolling over in an emerald coral foam, as he walks the grainy salt and pepper beach. He feels abandoned by both time and light. He had attempted to escape, only to travel to Vancouver after the unexpected passing of a friend. The Globe and Mail obit was just a few scribbled lines about his friend, a man identified by his profession and the opportunities and dreams that he had left behind. Kazan wanted to avoid a similar fate. He knew it was a desperate move. He should have given it more thought. Now, he blames Briar for the move. She is the cause of his fractured life. He struggles to even partially recall how they met.

"If you are not committed, then you are addicted." A cereal box phrase that reminds him of his shortcomings. The passage of time has made it all so painfully clear. The ocean fog and grey mist paints an inky dark and unforgiving curtain to the canvas that has become his life. It also hides the luxury smokey glass-coloured homes dotting the snowcapped mountains that the locals call the "British Properties." The places that house doctors, lawyers and judges. He often looks eastward from downtown and wonders about the wealthy inhabitants of the homes across the bay, how their bankrupt lives are built upon the financial promise of tomorrow.

The damp Pacific air causes him to tug at the frayed and worn, soft rounded edges of the collar of his thick wool field coat, in a feeble attempt to find some warmth. Brindle-coloured seagulls screech and scatter, tearing holes in the silver-streaked plum-coloured clouds. The dense fog of his own uncertainty, and the northwest wind, exacerbates the cold. The dampness is unforgiving.

This is where he struggles with life, relationships, and the practice of law. He is forever uncomfortable with the rain, and that which is left of himself. All of it is washed in memories and regret.

Kazan, like Briar, is a reluctant transplant from Eastern Canada. He had made an unsavory pact with himself that he was going to stay with her until he got back on his feet. Solid ground is now in short supply. This makes him feel angry and defeated, a captive of a broken promise to himself and their relationship. The refuge and soft landing he had sought is nowhere in sight.

Briar had torched his vanishing ego by developing an annoying habit of introducing him as an empty shell of a man, one who spent the last half of his life getting over the first. He himself is an invisible cog in an overworked and broken justice system. She makes matters worse by characterizing him as an aging and out of breath runner. She will say he is running from both himself and his mysterious past, and with this description, she carefully crafts him into a social outcast. He just desires to be a survivor of the slaughterhouse because he is aware that he is treading water and he is getting tired.

She does not get that, nor does the local legal community, which had finally stopped calling for his overdue disbarment or separation from her. Clinging to both his career and her, provided him with no hope of escape. He now hopes to only survive his myriad of regrets.

The truth is that he can no longer feel himself eroding. She had once offered him a way out of the emptiness and the darkness, a time to reflect, an opportunity to change, and a chance to save that which remained of himself. Now, it has all but evaporated.

This is a whispered story from the vacant corner of the lawyer's lounge, the kind of tale that middle-aged men and women like to tell. It is about an unfortunate tumble. Hyman Kazan was fifty-six when he had just limped over one more judge and jury trial. Everyone knows the prose, the psycho knife wielding teenaged rapist who escapes overwhelming conviction based upon the trembling victim's incomplete description of how she had been penetrated by some angry adolescent person of colour. He knew this was the last time he would be able to harness his bottled-up rage. The obese Rotary Club members that comprised the judiciary had imbued all of his waking moments with feelings of despair, caused by their demonstrated total absence of humanity and empathy.

There had been a time when he would have been able to control his sadness and anger with large quantities of alcohol, but that time has passed. Yeah, there was a time when he could have gripped his opponent's cold reptilian hand and walked out of a darkened courtroom, but this time it is different. The demons are bubbling up past his anxiety-streaked heart. It is time to escape before it is too late. Time has become his most valuable and elusive commodity. He wants to recapture what is left of his evaporating life, and to embrace the possibilities of finding his own utopian idea of happiness. He convinces himself that it has nothing to do with the legal profession, but has everything to do with the slim, dollar store, razor's edge chance of finding some sense of meaning in his life.

At the start of their relationship, Briar attempted to understand him. His eager departure from life, and from friends, baffled her. She tried to get him to open up. It was a time of half consumed bottles of wine, and smoky beeswax candles. The scene was complete with a roaring slate-coloured fieldstone fireplace, and the 70s sounds of Joni Mitchell's voice, etched with cigarette smoke, being played on a warped turntable. The rain never stopped falling.

Once, after way too many glasses of a straw-coloured wine, Briar placed a muted silky scarf scorched with deep forest greens and blues over his tired and bloodshot eyes and led him into their minimally decorated bedroom. She then instructed him to remove all his clothes, but to leave the scarf over his eyes. Suddenly, she placed her icy long fingers on the small of his back and pulled him down on to her.

"We are going to fuck away the bad," she quipped.

When they had ended their love making, he took off the scarf, just in time to get a boyish glimpse of her walking back toward their dimly lit kitchen in search of another glass of wine.

HYMAN KAZAN

2

BRITISH COLUMBIA

LIVING IN VANCOUVER during this time is unparalleled. The lower mainland has changed, becoming the landing spot for greying hipsters, self-proclaimed actualized gurus, and real estate profiteers. It is changing him too. Perceptions, memories and reality, can be altered in a moment. Life is thrown upon a misaligned potter's wheel, where lives can be easily changed forever. Still, the wind appears cacheable.

Their wobbly emotions are constantly in a frenzied motion. Their seldom beach walks together are often interrupted when she pulls him close until the edge of his unshaven chin shelters her from the salt stinging Pacific cold. The meditative sound of the waves crashing against the timber lined shore roar in his ears and cause his mind to wander. She walks without direction, further down the abandoned beach, turning around with every third half step, to seek shelter from the northwest wind. These calculated mid-steps are interrupted by moments where she will turn back and smile at him.

It is only then when he will suddenly realize how alone he is. When he does venture out without her, he will sometimes make his way to a nearby beachside restaurant, where a twisted bleached driftwood fire crackled out a much needed welcome. He will search out a quiet table in the back, overlooking the abandoned beach. The sound of the wind is soon muffled and replaced by the blue chords of Coltrane.

Habit often causes him to order a bottle of a Napa red and two glasses. Loneliness provides the reasons for bouts of drinking alone. Misfortune finds the moment.

A slender middle-aged woman with chestnut coloured hair smiles at him from across the room. Her introduction is launched without warning.

"Are you okay?"

An impossible question to answer truthfully, he thinks. He responds with a hesitant smile and a gentle nod of his head. She is attractive. *Waiting for someone?* He wonders. Disconnected from himself, he fumbles with what to say.

"He would have to be a fool to keep you waiting," he offers up, glancing away while awaiting her response.

"He has no sense of time!"

And with that, she pushes her chair away from the heavily starched ivory-coloured tablecloth and floats toward him. He feels his heart turn over like a rogue wave, while being fully aware that sharks and stingrays swim below the murky surface. A welcoming and richly warm smile greets him. She wears dark blue square Warby Parker reading glasses and an Italian tailored mocha-coloured suit. She extends her hand.

"Lucia," she offers.

"Kazan," he responds.

He slowly stands up from his bleached pine curved chair as she crosses over to his table. Drawing back the heavily knotted chair beside him causes her smile to grow larger across her face. She looks at him as if they have met before, a whimsical but loving glance. When his eyes meet hers, he feels a passion and an energy between them erupt. The electricity grows as the space between them evaporates. For a second, he forgets about his problems at home.

And then she asks him about his absent drinking partner. His loneliness is underlined. It is so odd to hear someone who he has just met sum up his life so easily. Foolishly, he attempts to explain this unfolding scenario, the unfinished script that has become his life.

"I am working on finding a workable solution," he scoffs. "Or better yet, attempting to find a better life here in BC."

She takes hold of the empty chair beside him, and places her long slender fingers around one of the empty wine glasses on the table. She tips the glass toward him and smiles as he raises the bottle up to meet her goblet. The garnet colour of the wine is highlighted by the remaining sunlight streaming through the window beside her. He pours out the wine, and unlike his life, a prism of colour splashes across the creases of the cotton tablecloth through the sunlit stemware.

"What does that mean?" she says.

He searches his scattered mind for an accurate response. *Awareness of a thought is not a thought*, he ponders, and he struggles with finding a contemporaneous explanation for his situation. There is none.

It seems like a calendar, where the pages of the months, like the hours of a day, are being torn off by a gust of a hurricane wind, before he breaks the awkward silence with his response.

"I . . . I am sorry," he says. "We just met and I have already treated you like someone who should be warned to step no further!"

He places the palms of his hands on the edge of the tablecloth beside their glasses.

"I have regrets, you may understand, about situations where I should have walked away, instead of pulling the pin from the grenade."

"We all have, my dear, we all have," she answers.

This unexpected game of truth or consequences intrigues him. Why he has made such an honest disclosure escapes him. He has peeled away the orange and exposed the fruit. He has revealed that which is left of him. He rubs his exhausted eyes and looks at her.

"Oh, I am sorry," he says. "Not the kind of introduction you were likely expecting. I get carried away sometimes, caught in what might have been, rather than what is."

She counters with, "Are you really expecting more?"

"Not really," he says. She forces a reluctant smile and then slips into the chair beside him. "I don't want you to think I am too forward, but I would love your company."

He is amazed at how easy the words come out.

The waiter then surfaces, holding two aged and weathered open black leather bound menus.

"Lucia, I would love the company, but you need to know that I am just . . ."

His explanation about Briar falls short, but then again, so does his relationship with her. His heart skips with the excitement of escape.

Before he can explain, she says, "I only have about half an hour, and then Ivan will be looking for me."

"Ivan, thirty minutes? What have I gotten myself into?" he quips.

She responds, "I guess, I could ask you the very same question."

VANCOUVER IN THE emerging fall is a very drab and grey place with brief splashes of deep forest greens and sunsets the colour of yellow tulips. It is all about dressing in layers. Seeking out what can be placed on, and what has to be left behind, in order to stay comfortable. Comfort comes in degrees.

Kazan watches as she tumbles into her mocha-coloured Burberry raincoat and walks across the stressed caramel-coloured pine floors to the front of the dimly lit restaurant where a tall dark-haired man attempts to embrace her. It appears to be all wrong to him, but it hardly matters now, he is stepping toward her as she is walking away from him. How is this happening? Why does she plunge into his life, only to be washed away by a past forgotten tide? He takes a cautious step toward her and to that which might have been, only to be abandoned like a misplaced note in a familiar song.

Scenes like these play out in restaurants every day, he thinks to himself. A place where couples first meet, or where they decide to extinguish a tumultuous relationship in the protective custody of inattentive strangers. He attempts to make some sense of the feelings he has for this woman he has just met.

When he returns to the apartment, Briar has let down her hair. He feels the air escape from his tight diaphragm as he crosses over the Rubicon.

The apartment is awash in the watercolour golden hue of a late Pacific early evening. Despite the fact that both of them are strained against the imaginary borders of their unspoken journeys and their pending questions, they both look upon each other with a patient hesitation, as if they both know where the other has been.

He attempts to recall the contract he had made with himself. That he would never fall into the snare that his father had fallen into. That he would never let the easily swallowed opioid of routine dissolve his lost and fractured soul.

In the corner of their living room, he struggles to find the calm that rests between day and night. He seeks out the margins between rest and sleep. When Kazan was a teenager, coming home after a night of drinking with his buddies, he would seek out the silence of the night in an attempt to avoid the sounds of traffic and late night voices from a nearby apartment. Now, the sounds are muffled by a wave of electronic sounds, televisions and game systems, operated by unemployed husbands or wayward kids in search of an escape from the day.

Kazan and Briar's place is a contrast, a small condominium on the North Shore that was built in the late sixties. Of the several places he had called home, this was the only one Briar would even entertain, given its proximity to the beach and the North Shore Mountains. He loved the mixture of the dated architecture and quirky inconvenience of old. Still, when left alone, he loves the light and view offered by their place. The presence of a snowcapped mountain or a shore view, mixed with the presence of younger residents, offeres him a sense of hope. A place to start something new.

Before moving to Vancouver, Kazan lived in an old west end apartment in Montreal. It was a collecting depository for all his past lives and misspent energies. It was an unplanned home. It was a place to drop and go, a safe place where memories would be harvested whenever needed. For a while, he found that his move west had been in search of something he was missing. By the time he had moved in with Briar, he was negotiating with her for those things from his past life that would be allowed to remain.

She had become entirely focused on a new residence that would resemble their relationship, which meant throwing out the old and replacing it with something only she treasured. His life needed an upgrade, a new coat of paint on a condemned building, even if no one else was able to see it. Kazan was kept off balance by the ever-shifting art and photographs of people and places that held no significance to him. He had always made it a point of decorating his home and office with those things that meant the most to him. This space housed neither.

At the end of the day, this was about him finding his way into her life, while giving up his own. Compromised solutions were never discussed. All that mattered was Briar being happy with this place she called home. What he had wanted then, would have to fit into those things that would make her happy, someplace where she could find refuge from the dark forbidding storm clouds that was the climate produced by his job and former life.

This is a constant source of friction between them—the sense that Kazan has a past, and his constant complaining about his lack of a positive future. She does not understand the stress and anger he is feeling. She is only focused on indulging her love of wine and the meager successes that the little money they have will acquire.

And in the beginning, he loved that about her. He welcomed her sense of wild adventure and fun. And of course, it wasn't that he did not enjoy the extravagances she embraced. When it came down to it, Briar had offered him a new and exciting life—an endless supply of unexpected gifts to be unwrapped, and a long hallway of doors that led to incredible adventures he had never conceived of. Not in decades had he felt such love and turbulence. Briar had offered him a welcomed escape from all those demons and empty feelings that plagued him. But like the West Coast, winds, temperatures, and moods can shift without notice.

HYMAN KAZAN
BRITISH COLUMBIA

4

SAFE INJECTION SITES and drug clinics are a unique paradox. Six nondescript gay men arrived at the province's cascading failure of an answer to the overdose problem, all in a few days of each other in mid-October. They all ended up dead. Their deaths were chalked up to a risky lifestyle or a sexual misadventure. They all ended up alone, and they all ended up having overdosed. But those exhausted health care workers that knew them, all said they were not the type to risk their lives so carelessly, and that their blood work showed no indication of something beyond the usual consumption of recreational drugs. The only thing that those six men had in common was their sexual orientation and desire for safety. Questions and rumours were raised by the nurses. Those who occupied the much larger offices turned a blind eye.

Months later, Simon Westfall, another migrant from the West End neighbourhood, was rushed to Vancouver General Hospital, as another victim of an alleged overdose. This time, a young nurse named Ashley Shultz contacted the police.

There was no rational explanation for his untimely death, and his blood work did not show any levels of the toxins that might have led to his cardiac arrest. Shultz had gone home, and had called her mother back east, later that evening, saying she was bothered by the indifference that was being shown toward these men. Together, they decided that the police had to be forced to investigate the situation. Threats of contact with the media during an election year finally prompted a response. Police were instructed to become interested.

Kazan and Simon Westfall are soon to have their problems intertwined. The outdated black anvil sized Bell telephone on his oil stained oak desk that late afternoon is ringing unanswered. Investigators want to talk and to find some direction for their investigation. They are upset that he is nowhere to be found. They are eager to make an arrest, but want to wisely seek some advice on how to proceed. Kazan is at home, unaware of the urgency of others, still focusing on Briar.

Unaware of the role he will soon be cast in, Kazan feels like a nonunion line worker in a forgotten mill that chews up the disenfranchised. A handicapped factory worker in a place that is filled with asbestos. Like Simon, he is on a path of destruction, since in a way, they were both addicted to things that would kill them, whether it was drugs, or the need for approval or the fanciful admiration of those closest to them. Their paths to destruction were hidden by the political landscape and their own lack of foresight. The search for love is not without its pitfalls.

From the assortment of international students that recreationally occupied the adjacent low rise apartment building, Briar and Kazan appeared as aging insignificant roommates. There is nothing that would indicate that they have anything in common. They are nothing like the two former passionate adventurers that had first created the surging electrical storm that shook every inch of a room. He can feel it too—there he is, still wearing his damp overcoat, as if an overdue bus or empty train will suddenly appear and pull him back. Back to the stormy beach he has just left. Back to the safety of his daydreams. What if he had not returned home? He allows himself to contemplate the thought, like a runner who stops to catch his breath after a long hard run up a hill. *There will come a time,* he thinks, *when I will return home to an empty apartment, and the other frailties of my misfortunes.* He lacks purpose and concentration. He is still focused on how it was when they first met. He remembers how they used to laugh, and how he crashed through doors and hallways into her never-ending embraces. So long ago. Time has a habit of slipping away.

He had, against the odds and the sage advice of those who loved him, returned to BC. He almost didn't return. His friends had strongly warned him against it.

"You can never go back to the ways things used to be."

"You will be throwing any chance of finding happiness into the ocean."

He can't recall what it means to be carefree. It is like he has been stripped of all those things that had once given him a reason to smile or laugh. He has to break free—he is running out of energy, oxygen, and time.

He thinks back to his late night, half empty Air Canada flight from Quebec, accompanied only by a small tan leather bag and twenty-five thousand dollars. Now, he is held up in Briar's apartment, devoid of both. Now, he has nothing, and wants nothing.

Still, her western exposure beach apartment had magically transformed the lives of several young men, offering them a much desired escape from their mundane partners or unfulfilled occupations. It offers him no escape. Others can feel the presence of his overwhelming sadness. It is manifested through the sideways glances he receives when they run into colleagues outside of work hours. It is as if they have struggled to feed each other's unfilled dreams, always drawing up short, leaving the other one more hungry than before. She was greedy in those days, trying to quench a great and salty thirst, and she was prepared to deal with the consequences later. He had largely given up. Kazan was void of the emotional energy needed to challenge her. In order to move in with her, he was going to have to set some emotional ground rules. He had to steal away a few unpacked emotions from his past, or stay elusive in other ways.

The sound of a questionably mechanically safe seaplane can be heard outside of the apartment as it swoops in and then is suddenly gone. The sounds of the wind blowing and the tide rolling in accompany the silence of the moment. Briar appears beside him, cradling a glass of wine in her hand. She tilts her head back and drinks half the glass down. It seems to pour out of the glass and cascade directly into her much travelled arteries. She is very good at becoming numb.

"You always make me nervous when you are so damn quiet," she chirps.

"Sorry?" he responds, accompanied by a sideways shake of his head.

"I always wonder where the fuck do you go?" she says, raising her voice.

He is thrown off balance by her comments, but it also causes him to find his footing. It comes to him that it is better to jump than to fall.

"I have been here all the time. Can we just have a nice night, for once?"

"Nice night?" her voice begins to get louder.

"Yeah! You know, one where we are friendly, no more attacks, Christ. Can we just give it a break tonight, Briar, for one fuckin night?"

"Sure, whatever you want, whatever you want. Why don't you please just join me in a glass of wine? Maybe it will take the edge off. Maybe we can talk, you know, like we used too?"

"I would like that. Is there anything left?"

"In the bottle or the relationship, Kazan?" she responds.

He feels like he is teetering on an overstretched piano wire, high above an emotional canyon, and he is at risk of losing his balance. He readies himself for one more ball to be juggled, aloft the taut wire as she drains the last glass of wine into her glass. His glass remains empty.

He takes one last hopeful look outside, the errant yellow seaplane is nowhere in sight, and seagulls can be heard all along the strand, beneath the purple dark rain clouds that hang over their lives. Briar's voice reaches him from the bedroom as she starts to shed her hidden outside persona. He hears the sound of her voice but cannot make out the words she is saying. Kazan is absent again, from both Briar and himself. The promise of a restful night at home is now a mirage. She appears beside him, holding a single half empty wine glass.

"This is fucking exhausting."

He can feel the temperature in the room start to lower, a cold rush of air shears off any thought of relaxation. Her voice is hollow and sounds like it is coming from a cellar or a cave. The apartment feels like it is closing in.

"Do you ever think about how this is killing me, Kazan? Just tell me what to expect, for Christ's sake? Just be honest with me for once, is that too much to ask for?"

Briar has now stepped back into the ring in search of a fight. He offers very little resistance to her aggressive attacks. The truth is something that has escaped them both. If only she could give him a chance to catch his breath once in a while. If he could turn back the clock on their lives to the time when they first met, he would have done that in an instant, but the time was too late for that. He is sad by what remains. The thought of arguing with her sickens him.

Kazan is now getting angry. He feels a tightness going down his arms into his hands. The evening has rapidly deteriorated. The hope of a relaxed evening is gone.

The evening will come to an abrupt end. The moment of salvation when they might have been able to talk to each other has passed. The fires are now burning out of control, fanned by winds of past memories and the lies that have surrounded their relationship. The dry kindling is now primed by their past indiscretions, feeding the firestorm.

They are both angry now and the shouting has started. Kazan has managed to fan the flames with his emotional indifference to her concerns. All the nice moments of the day seem to be built like a child's sandcastle caught by the tide, a rehashing of the same old lies, failed excuses and misplaced expectations. How fragile everything feels to him at this moment. His whole life becomes vulnerable like a piece of antique glass—nothing that a well thrown baseball sized stone won't shatter into a million fragments.

The television is on in the background. All this time, it has shown the grainy pixelated image of a forgotten Simon Westfall. It is like he is an unwelcome house guest looking in, or one more lost sideline participant in a battle which only Kazan will be summoned to solve.

5

HYMAN KAZAN
BRITISH COLUMBIA

LIKE ANY OTHER Justice dinner, it is designed to bring together members of the community in response to the many issues that plague center ice. That's what Justice Craig Donald Smith and his judicial cronies call the intersection at Main and East Hastings. Smith is new to Vancouver. He has left Eastern Canada and is now looking to make a name for himself. This area of Vancouver is ripe with problems: AIDS, crime, indigenous issues, and the opioid crisis have overtaken the streets.

After the speeches and the empty promises have been made, Smith throws on his dark blue topcoat and makes his way down East Hastings Street and over to Granville in search of a drink. The rain is falling, making the streets aglow from the mixture of water and oil. Many of the businesses are closed and the streets are largely empty except for the usual vagabonds and panhandlers. They are huddled in storefronts and bank entrances and after-hours clubs.

Smith knows the landscape and seeks out a watering hole where he is unknown, or at the very least, unrecognizable to himself and others. Every time he goes into these places, bars frequented by young gay men, he is putting himself at risk. There is always a chance that he will be discovered or questioned about his surroundings. The risk is great, but the temptation is greater, and he is drawn in by the opportunity to meet someone.

The last time he had done so, he became trapped in a seven month pathetic relationship with a bespeckled tight jean wearing pharmacist. He had promised himself that there would be no more clandestine long-term relationships of any kind, that they were far too risky. Or, at least, that's what he told himself. He is ill-equipped to handle the temptation presented on this night by Simon Westfall. His strong body and sense of humour melts away any chance of not going further. A drink and some conversation is all that Simon is looking for, but Smith attempts to seduce him with his money and undisclosed position of power.

Smith knows too well that it will take many more informal meetings like this to get Simon into his bed. Simon is all too trusting of his new friend, and agrees to meet up with him again in the future for a chance to get to know each other better.

Simon thinks that Smith could be a valuable asset or partner in assisting the community in finding a way to lessen the myriad of issues that led to the over hospitalization at VGH or the early passing of many of his friends. Simon thinks that judges can get things done that others can not.

They agree to meet again. Simon leaves the bar first, later followed by Smith, who crosses the road in the grey drizzle and makes his way back to his home near the University of British Columbia. There, he jumps into the shower and attempts to wash away his well-hidden persona. He is excited about his time with Simon, and feels relieved that he is undiscovered in his new home, free to shuffle between two lifestyles. *This time,* he tells himself, *I will be free to love who I want, as many times as I want.* The problem that escapes him is the lack of realization that he is incapable of loving anyone other than himself.

6

HYMAN KAZAN

BRITISHCOLUMBIA

IT HAS HELD a long and mysterious history. Names like Nat King Cole and Errol Flynn were once guests at the Hotel Georgia. It was, at one time, the tallest building in Vancouver. The shine has come off the old building, but it still provides a meeting place for pilots arriving late into YVR and young gay men in search of a hotel for the night. A stack of luggage greets guests rather than a well-dressed doorman who once traversed the twelve floors that make up the hotel.

Simon arrives late to find that Smith has already checked in. Their plan to meet in the lobby bar had given way to something a bit less tactful. Simon is already questioning why he has decided to meet Smith there, after only knowing him for approximately three months. He looks around the run-down lobby and thinks, *fuck it, I should have never agreed to this.* He goes in search of a house phone to locate Smith. He feels out of place and wonders why he agreed to meet up with Judge Smith like this.

Simon checks his cell phone and realizes that he has received a text from Smith, indicating that he is waiting in room 907 with drinks on ice, and something special to get him in the mood. As Simon rides the old elevator up to the ninth floor, he feels trapped by the confined space and is nervous about their meeting. The elevator shudders and stops at a couple of floors before reaching the ninth. When the doors open, he pushes his way through a middle-aged man and his wife who are lingering in front of the elevator doors, waiting for a ride to the lobby. The hallways are dark and the carpet is well-worn as he walks past the line of rooms leading up to 907. Muffled sounds are heard as he passes by each of the occupied rooms.

Smith greets him at the door. He is dressed in a blue denim shirt and blue jeans. He leans in for a kiss, but Simon pulls back. He attempts to make conversation in the dimly lit entrance to the hotel room. He offers Simon a drink from the hotel's minibar, and both men can feel the tension in the room. Smith is both awkward and clumsy and time drags on as Simon sits on the far corner of the bed, facing Smith who has turned around one of the chairs from the room's workstation. Simon consumes the vodka and ice quickly and it burns his throat and brings about the realization that he should leave before things get out of hand.

Simon gets up from the bed and gets ready to leave. Smith knows that he is losing his chance at romance and reaches into the pocket of his jeans and retrieves a small sugar sized packet that he had secreted away during a drug trial held earlier in the day.

A small portion of exhibit number 1176, he chuckles to himself. *This is the little boost that is needed to get us over the finish line,* or so he thinks.

He places the packet between his nicotine stained teeth and tears a small opening in it and then sprinkles a small dusting onto the space between his thumb and forefinger. With his other hand, he takes hold of Simon's hand and dumps the remainder of the packet on the back of his hand between his buttery soft leather bracelet and his knuckles.

In an instant, Smith has taken in a small amount of pixie dust he has given himself. He assures Simon that he is about to feel the best he has ever felt. If that is what it will take to be allowed to leave, Simon is prepared to venture down this unfathomable rabbit hole. Smith has begun to sway and dance around the room and to remove his pants. Simon hesitates and tells himself that this first attempt at using coke will provide him the key and the reason to leave. *Fuck it,* he thinks, as he snorts back the powder off the back of his hand. He feels an electric shock surge through his nose as the drug surges toward his brain.

Simon is staggered by this jolt of lightning. He is both energized and disoriented by the powerful shock felt throughout his body. The hotel room's door and ceiling are now being propelled away from him as if they have been shot through a cannon or shotgun. He has stepped on a land mine and God damn it, it has gone off.

Simon is blindsided with how quickly it has hit him. He is shaking from the electric shock created by the drug. He is overwhelmed by this feeling of euphoria and loss of control. Simon sees that Smith is beginning to show signs of panic, but finds it difficult to talk or think. *What is happening?* He thinks he must find a way to make it back down to the lobby and find help. He has become short of breath and feels a crushing weight on his chest, and his left arm has suddenly become numb. He staggers a few steps and then collapses. The room has become dark and his breathing has stopped. Smith searches for a way out of this catastrophic explosion of circumstances.

Like Errol Flynn, Simon is later rushed to VGH, another victim of multiple sex partners and a myocardial infarction due to coronary thrombosis. Both men suffer the same fate, yet only one of them will be remembered.

HYMAN KAZAN

7

BRITISH COLUMBIA

DANIEL CHMURA IS a veteran of the Vancouver Police Department, and he has become tired of picking up and stepping over the bodies of the discarded, those that are found near rusted out dumpsters, or piss stained steps that lead to and from the entrances to safe injection sites.

On this drizzly morning, he rolls out of bed at 5:30 a.m. The lack of sleep and motivation to go to work is self-evident on his face. He tossed and turned most of the night, despite the two doses of diazepam he had taken along with multiple shots of bourbon.

Chmura drags himself out of bed and makes himself a coffee. He makes the mistake of checking his messages from the night before. He hopes for some overnight arrests of the usual dirt bags because that will reduce his workload. Instead, he is greeted with the discovery of a body downtown that requires his attention.

"Looks like a shipment must have come in from Shenzhen."

"No time to waste, looks like all hell is breaking loose again. God, I hate this job."

Paula, his wife, offers no response.

It is Friday and he should be making plans to go to Whistler, or maybe the island, to get away from this shit. What happened? The bodies keep piling up and the politicians keep begging for more resources to clean up this mess. *And I have to deal with yet one more life squandered in the hopes of finding an escape from the suffering,* he thinks.

"Fuck it," he scoffs.

His second wife of fifteen years, hears the ranting from their bedroom, but has decided to avoid any engagement on the issue. She has heard these complaints, time and time again, and has chosen to try and find an additional couple of minutes in bed rather than to debate the issue with him this morning.

"I got to get going. See you tonight, don't wait up. It is likely going to be a late one!" he shouts.

Farley, their basset hound, looks up from his warm soft bed in front of the fireplace, but decides to also catch up on his sleep this morning.

Chmura has never rushed to a crime scene. He found that if he took his time, the confusion of the hyper moment and early unanswered questions, had a way of floating to the top, and was often dealt with by some patrol guys who were already on scene. Better yet, sometimes his tardiness paid off with one of his uptight superiors finding another eager recruit or a climber on scene, holding his hands out, waiting to be given that one case that will define his position or offer a gateway to that overlooked promotion. At times, he found himself not caring about the outcome of an investigation one way or another. He had been told for years now, that it is all "pensionable time" and he is starting to adopt that view.

As he starts his car, he considers calling the station before going to the crime scene, but instead he wrestles with whether to stop for another cup of coffee. *Fuck it*, he thinks to himself, *the dead guy is not going anywhere*, but in the end, he drives directly toward East Hastings just around the corner from Cambie and Alberta Street.

Traffic is thick for a Friday morning, even at this hour, as he makes his way through the drizzle toward the Burrard Street Bridge and heads downtown toward the flashing red and blue lights that highlighted the location of the investigation.

"You look like you have been up all night, Chmura."

"Jesus, when are you ever going to quit this job?" chirps a twentysomething patrolman.

Chmura walks over to where a ratty old Hudson Bay blanket is covering Simon Westfall who is face down on the pavement. He bends down to take a closer look at the body. He pulls back the blanket which reveals a well-dressed young man, fit and strong, not your usual addict or junkie.

"Who put the blanket on him?"

"One of the staff from inside, found him on her way to work."

"This guy looks a bit out of place here, don't you think?"

"Yeah, we kind of thought he might be a tourist or something."

"Is this the extent of what you know? Can you get a media release together and follow up with whoever found John Doe? Can you stick around and see if there are any witnesses willing to answer to the Beyond the Call bumper sticker slogan that is attached to everything the VPD says or does?"

Constable Nyugen has already taken up a seat in the nearest cruiser, but yells out his answer. "Sure, we can do that, and then it is all yours, Chummy!"

And with that, the few lost sheep of college-aged officers assist EMS who have now arrived with the removal of the body unit. After that, a crime scene officer tosses his cigarette on the ground and begins to carefully photograph the scene.

"Beautiful British Columbia, yours to discover," chirps one of the younger officers as they lift Simon into the back of an ambulance marked Coroner's Office.

The death is a mystery, and so is the victim at this point. Chmura thinks to himself, *no matter what the others think, all suicides are murders, something leads up the point where a life is taken or lost.*

"Why investigate this? Could it be a homicide? Who was this guy?"

Little was known at this point. The staff nurse who worked at the clinic, told them she found the body shortly before 4:30 a.m. on her way into work. Chmura lights up a cigarette and thinks, *what causes someone this young to be this reckless?*

Chmura follows the body back to VGH where an autopsy will later be conducted to explain why this young man had become the latest lower mainland crime statistic. Naive drug users meant there were bodies stacking up all over the city like driftwood on an abandoned beach after a storm. Just one more young man was a victim of an over developed taste for drugs, likely opioids laced with fentanyl. These types of scenarios were not uncommon to this part of town, but why it occurred outside this clinic puzzles him.

Hours later, this misadventure will be explained by a drug screen that will show very little "fenny" and the death being more likely caused by a weak heart. A tragic case of an opioid user going one too many occasions to the wrong buffet. An insatiable hunger that feeds on more and more, leading to a lethal final dose. But there is something different about this one. Something odd, it is kind of like he was a slumbering child left at the steps of the orphanage to wake up, but just didn't.

Chmura considers it for a second, contemplating the absence of drug paraphernalia found at the scene, and the healthy appearance of the victim. He grips a styrofoam cup of coffee that one of the attending physicians had provided him.

"So what if he died somewhere else?"

"Who would want to deposit the body here?" Chmura asks himself.

He takes a sip of the lukewarm Coffee-Mate concoction, twirls the half empty cup, and stares into it, searching for answers.

Looking up, he swallows a mouthful of the cold coffee and asks the coroner, "What happens to someone when they overdose?"

"They usually just pass out, you know, stop breathing," the coroner responds. "That often leads to cardiac arrest. Whatever drugs your friend here was using, he must have gone out with a bang! You know, he was likely sky high."

"When?" asks Chmura.

"You know, before they pulled the oxygen cord from him. Before it all went black."

"You are saying that he may have not known he was dying? That he likely did not have a clue that this was going to be it, the big one, the last ride. He just passed out. Would you not agree with me, it is highly unlikely that he would have died here, steps away from the clinic. I mean, this is not Studio 54 around here."

"Yeah, I kind of see what you are getting at, he may have ended up here afterwards. Who knows?"

"I guess we just have to find someone who does."

The thin greying coroner shrugs and tells Chmura, "Wait and see what the tox report indicates."

Both men nod, indicating to the other they are anticipating the same likely results.

HYMAN KAZAN

8

BRITISH COLUMBIA

CAL MARKS LOVES working outdoors, whether it is raining or not. He moved to Vancouver from Calgary. He still remembers that day when he crossed over into British Columbia from Alberta, how the sun was shining and the snow was gathered on the mountains rather than on the highways. It was the beginning of December when he arrived in Vancouver looking for work.

He had never been to British Columbia before moving here, and he was eager to start a new life. He had left a crummy job at Alloy, a high end restaurant in downtown Calgary. He had been a waiter there. Soon after his arrival, he found employment at Bridges, a restaurant located on Granville Island.

He was lucky enough to find an apartment in an old craftsman style house located on Blenheim Street in the Point Grey area. It was an older home that had been broken into two separate apartments, an upstairs unit and a main floor unit. The lower level housed a two bedroom apartment. The previous tenants had been a pair of Australian doctors who had chosen to return to Australia to practice orthopedic medicine rather than fight for a BC billing number. The house was an older style of home with a large front porch that had been carpeted with a dulled green indoor and outdoor carpeting, but offered a wide set of wooden steps from which he would often drink his morning coffee or his late evening glass of wine. The upstairs was occupied by a tall good-looking man who worked for Euro Canadian, a local construction company. He would ride his CCM bicycle to and from work and would be gone for days at a time.

Cal would sometimes sit on the steps and light up a pipe filled with marijuana, and after a few deep inhales, he would explain why the BC government was so inept or why the province was so far behind Europe in terms of accepting the use of recreational drugs. He was also committed to helping out with those who were in need. That is how he came to know Simon.

Simon shows up, walking down the street and greets Cal with a wave and a smile. He is eager to tell him about the rich socialite he met at a bar downtown.

"He works in justice, and wants to meet you too," Simon says as he places one foot on the paint worn bottom stair. "It's nothing serious, we are just good friends. And besides, my new acquaintance indicated he is prepared to offer some help to some of the residents in the neighbourhood. Such a good man, community minded and wanting to help . . ."

Cal had heard this too many times. Simon was so trusting and the type of person who saw only the good in others. Cal, having worked in the service industry, was a bit more skeptical.

Cal smiles and listens to Simon describe his new fiend. He drinks his coffee and then reaches into his back pocket and removes a small plastic baggie filled with marijuana. He leans forward and extends the baggie toward Simon.

"One of the cooks gave it to me," he says. "It's really good shit. He got it when he got back from Hawaii."

Simon holds up his hand, and tells his friend that he is not interested.

"Ah, c'mon," responds Cal. "If you can't trust me, then who the hell are you going to trust?"

"It's not you, Cal. You really don't know what kind of shit they are putting in drugs these days."

Less than three weeks later, Cal will receive a phone call from an unknown male, telling him his roommate has overdosed.

HYMAN KAZAN

9

BRITISH COLUMBIA

MICHAEL MCQUEEN GRABS the coal black battered payphone outside of Abode, a restaurant off of Robson Square, and feverishly calls his older sister, Briar.

"He was too young to die!" he screams. "This doesn't make any sense, he doesn't even do drugs!"

The patrons on the street look down at their eggs benny and side of bacon, hoping to escape this tirade. It is Saturday morning, and the street is packed with both shoppers and the usual brunch crowd.

Briar glances up from her cell phone and looks outside. The rain is still gently falling from the night before. She cannot find the words that will provide any comfort to her younger brother, who never knew love until he had fallen for Simon. She wants to provide some sort of comfort to him.

"What happened?"

"I do not know yet, they just said he likely overdosed, and was found outside a downtown clinic."

"Seriously, maybe that is a mistake, this does not make any sense! You know, maybe someone stole his ID and there is a mistake?"

Michael responds, "No," and went on to tell about a meeting he says he had with a Detective Chmura who had come over to the house to give him the bad news.

"Oh, I am so sorry, Michael. If there is anything I can do, just mention it. I know you must be hurting right now, but you need to hold yourself together."

"I just don't know how I am going to tell his parents. They are very old and this will likely kill them."

"Have you been up all night?"

"I have not been able to sleep, there is so much to do and I do not know where to begin. Do you think Kazan could help me?"

"I don't know, Michael. You know he has been a bit distant lately, and he is God knows where right now. But I will tell him when he gets back and ask him to call you. Where are you? Are you going to be at home later? What do you want to me to tell Kazan?"

"He's got contacts at VPD, doesn't he? Maybe he can tell me what the cops are saying?"

"I doubt that, but I can get him to call you later if you want?"

"Sure, have him call me."

"When are you going to be home?"

"I don't know. I just needed to get out of the apartment for a while, go for a walk. Maybe over to Jericho or Kits, for some air."

"Okay, call me if there is anything I can do or if there is anything you need. Promise?"

"Okay. Promise. Please have Kazan call me when he gets in."

"Sure, Michael. I will make sure to tell him."

"Okay, goodbye."

"Okay."

The phone then goes quiet. Briar is confused as to what to do. She decides that with her world falling apart, she does not need to tell Kazan this latest news. *It's just all too much*, she thinks.

She decides to call the man she is seeing, to seek some comfort and some advice on what to do given this bad news. She dials the number, but only reaches his answering service who promises to pass on the message or return the call. Without thinking, she dials the number for Kazan. She clears her throat and squeezes the phone between her shoulder and the side of her face. Kazan answers the phone, but is already engaged in a conversation with someone else. As usual, Briar will have to wait for her turn at his attention.

"Good, good, yeah, I have to go. I have another call waiting, can we talk about this at the meeting next week? Sure, sure," and with that he is now saying, "Hello" to Briar.

Briar can't help but think of how she will get over to Michael's later to check on him. She tries to remember why she has called Kazan. She wants to tell him about the bad news, about Michael's partner, but chooses to avoid bringing up the subject.

"When are you coming home?" she asks.

Kazan is preoccupied with his previous conversation and tells Briar that he will be working late as VPD has been calling about somebody they found outside of a clinic. He switches the call to the speaker.

"Why are you calling, Briar? You know I am trying to get some work done."

Briar slams down the phone and stares blankly outside, troubled with the fact that she will have to come up with some other plan on how to deal with this alone.

She runs down the hallway and into the bathroom. She jumps into the shower, and lets the hot water cascade over her. It helps to hide the tears and frustration she is feeling. The bathroom is littered with the usual bottles of lotions and perfumes. She pushes them aside, tosses her wet hair back, and goes to the bedroom in search of something to wear. She tries to find something that will hide her insecurity, something that will shield her from hearing any more bad news. She calls for an cab to take her to his Point Grey condo.

Briar shows up unannounced at his door, her eyes red rimmed from crying. A middle-aged man with greasy grey hair makes his way down a flight of stairs toward the glass front door of his condominium. She had been bouncing back and forth between Kazan and him for the past few weeks, trying to find some resemblance of happiness, and a diversion between her everyday life. And now the tragic death of Michael's partner has caused the winding staircase into the darkness to engulf her. She wonders why she has ended up here, instead of seeking out Kazan as requested by her brother.

The man approaches the door, dressed in an untucked white tuxedo style shirt and dark striped pants. He looks like he is dressed for some formal occasion. She is unexpected. Smith pulls the door open and invites her in.

"I did not expect you, why didn't you phone first?" he says as he takes her hand and leads her into the front landing.

She reaches into her purse and shuts her phone off before speaking to him.

"I just needed to see you. I got some bad news this morning."

"Oh, I am sorry to hear that. On a Saturday morning?"

She rubs her eyes.

"What happened? Are you alright? Did you tell Kazan about us?"

"No. My brother called me from downtown to tell me that his partner died."

His reaction to such heartbreaking news falls between merely housekeeping and banal. Briar had never shared anything about her family before, and she expected some type of empathetic response. She found it difficult to imagine herself mourning alone, she wanted to be comforted and loved. She wanted him to help her make some sense out of the death. It is at that moment, and his strange response, that she feels the loneliness surround her, but the feeling of being unequipped to deal with this tragedy allows her the ability to come to terms with the feelings of loneliness and abandonment. Kazan would have wrapped his arms around her, but this man just stands there with an awkward smile on his face.

As she takes a seat in the living room, Briar considers getting up and leaving and calling Kazan, but in the end she decides to stay and have a coffee in front of the fire.

"Are you able to stay?" he asks as he emerges from the kitchen.

"I really should get going. I am sorry to have just dropped in. I just needed someone to talk to."

He chuckles. "You are welcome anytime, just call first."

"Yes, of course," she says. "I wouldn't want to catch you in an awkward moment."

She runs her eyes up and down him, giving careful examination to this man she has fallen for.

"Ok," she says, and she stands up and places her half empty coffee cup on the table beside the sofa as she gets ready to leave.

"If you would like to come back later, just call," he says.

Briar is both bewildered and a bit insulted by his response.

"Thank you for letting me in."

He walks her to the door and holds the door open for her.

"Would you like a ride home?" he asks.

"No," she says. "Kazan will be waiting for me and I can find a way home, thank you for the coffee."

They step out on the grey brick landing outside of his condo into the light rain that is falling. The day is dreary and cold with the temperatures ushering in the fall. Briar sees her unmarked Black Top Taxi, a dirty black Toyota Prius is parked a couple of houses down the street with its flashers and wipers running. Briar steps away from the landing, and waves her hand, catching the eye of her driver. As Briar steps toward the car, she takes one more look back toward the condo, but he has already gone back in. She glances down and is mystified by his lack of concern. Just another death of someone once removed from her.

What did it all mean? Why was he so cold?

Why did her search for comfort just lead to the downward winding staircase into hell?

What was real? What was not?

The bruised sky opens up to her and it is impossible for her to feel the ground beneath her feet.

Was time running out on her, and the people she loved? Did anyone care?

The dark haired Middle Eastern man who is slumped behind the wheel of the cab asks her if she is alright, and then asks her where she wants to go. She ponders the question for a second and then tells him the address for her home. As she sits in the back of the Prius, she digs around her oversized purse in search of her cell phone. After a couple of attempts, she finally locates her phone and places her index finger on the bottom of it unlocking it. It flashes a picture of her and Kazan laughing in front of the Pan Pacific hotel. Happier times, times gone by. She unlocks her phone and taps the number for Kazan listed at the top of her screen, and after three rings, she hears Kazan's slow melodic voice over the phone.

"Sorry I missed your call. Please leave a message."

Briar turns and looks out the back window of the car as it passes the tree-lined boulevard en route to her home. The car swerves to the right to avoid a car that has suddenly slammed on its brakes to avoid a collision. A few more blocks pass by, and then with a grunt, the car stops and the driver opens the driver's door and steps back to open the rear passenger side door of the car. Briar is sad that the motion of the car and her daydream have come to such an abrupt end. She gives the driver two twenty dollar bills and thanks him for the ride, and takes a second standing outside of their building, not knowing whether to go in or not. She has arrived back, but does not feel like she has arrived home. The black taxi accelerates away.

THERE ARE BRIGHTLY coloured tulips placed strategically all around her contemporarily decorated office, highlighted by dimly lit photographs of powdery lemon limestone buildings from both Prague and Northern Ireland. Alexandra Elliott, the Senior Crown Attorney for the lower mainland, is looking at herself in the rain-streaked reflection cast by her corner office window. She is attractive, with translucent skin. Her eyes are a deep turquoise and she has a soft sensuous mouth. Razor straight blonde hair cradles her face.

A large coffee-coloured banker box with scribbled black magic marker labels was dropped off by the VPD that morning and sat on the edge of her desk. It held the notes from a lead investigator and some patrolmen who had been called to deal with a body found outside of a clinic downtown. The case is in its infancy, and much work will need to be done before indictments are sworn or arrests are made. At the urging of the police, she will be delivering this ticking time bomb to Kazan. She wonders if it is more advantageous to have it just left on his desk after hours, so as to avoid his endless questions as to why he is getting assigned this case, or his desire to have explanations provided for the many holes in the evidence presented.

Kazan is a problem for Elliott. He can be both cynical and abusive, and he has seen far too many ill-prepared cases during his long career. Still, this case seems well suited for him. The synopsis of the case reads like a crime novel: a young good-looking man is found dead at a safe injection site after being a guest of a judge at a Justice dinner. It makes no sense, and is a potential political and media nightmare. A hard drinking, no nonsense, Montreal expat will be perfect for the job.

Hyman Kazan's troubles are more immediate. Last month, the Regional Director for the Ministry of the Attorney General had visited him at his office late one evening. He came, as you would expect, offering yet one more difficult case to his endless supply of non winnable cases.

He was handed a case involving a historical sexual assault that took place in a residential school setting. Kazan questions how he has time to do the case, but is offered the promise that he can hire a local per diem lawyer to assist him if need be. The director knows. He knows Kazan will not say no. He also knows that Kazan is getting more and more frustrated by the lack of support being offered from his office.

The case involves a blemish on the province's woefully bad record involving indigenous affairs. Trinity Rivers Residential School was a Canadian aboriginal residential school in New Westminster, British Columbia. The school operated to reform incorrigible and delinquent girls. The facility housed an average of ninety girls aged twelve to eighteen. The girls who were sent there were described as in need of reform and integration into Canadian values, largely due to their chronic truancy, drug use, and perceived sexual immorality.

On April 16, 1972, authorities discovered that two of the residents had been repeatedly sexually abused by their headmaster. After the passage of several years, the accused was charged with two counts of sexual assault for a series of related incidents in which he sexually assaulted two young aboriginal women over a number of years.

The RCMP became involved when the two young women, Kingston McCraw and Connie Dawson, who had met up on the streets of Winnipeg, Manitoba, described suffering physical, sexual and emotional abuse at the school and were referred to a psychologist, Jocelyn Evans, who reported the pattern of abuse to BC authorities.

Ms. McCraw and Ms. Dawson having survived Trinity Rivers proved to be an issue for the Manitoba Justice System, so they were soon transported back to Vancouver to be questioned by staff lawyers for the Ministry of the Attorney General for the province.

Kingston McCraw, a former student who attended Trinity from ages sixteen to eighteen, gave evidence of being raped by her principal on a weekly basis. Both her and Ms. Dawson were labelled "trouble makers" who could not be trusted. After one of the times she was sexually assaulted, she began to bleed and sought medical attention. When she described what had happened, the doctor gave her pain medication, and told her she was fabricating a story just to get a prescription for opioids, and she was told that she should never bring up the subject again.

Hyman Kazan is now being tasked with the challenge of bringing up the subject again. Connie Dawson was unable to deal with her suffering, and after several failed suicide attempts, was able to finally silence her critics and herself, shortly before the case was transferred to Vancouver. Now the race is on to prevent a similar way of ending the pain for Ms. McCraw.

As Jocelyn Evans had tried, he is also faced with the herculean task of convincing Kingston that none of these events were her fault, that it was the headmaster or the system's fault. But like Connie Dawson, she is convinced that if the fault lies with her, then she has a chance to correct things. If it lies elsewhere, she is likely to have the same unfortunate and inescapable outcome.

The judge to be assigned to this case is from out of town. Now, Kazan has a couple of weeks to review the mountains of disclosure, not an easy task given his already overly packed list of assigned cases. Endless days and sleepless nights provide a prescription for disaster.

It is the edge of fall, near the end of year, and the leaves have started to evolve, but not the way it happens in Eastern Canada. Burnt oranges and crimson reds are nowhere to be found. Instead, the colours are muted by the lack of sunlight. When Kazan is en route to his downtown office that afternoon, he notices that crisp white sugary snow that has now covered the mountain tops at Grouse and Seymour. It bathes him in memories of his troubled childhood in Europe. The sienna-coloured sun is slowly draining behind the mountains. He can feel the strong lure of fresh snow and the pull of starry night skiing.

"Careful, Kazan. Nature can be unforgiving. Take time to enjoy the momentary glimpses of this beautiful land," that is what his adored uncle often preached, especially when they took to the slopes together.

The sound of his recognizable inner voice is carved into his subconscious, causing him to be aware of his own shadow. He can sense his own inability to break free from the shackles of dependency, preventing him from confronting the chaos that haunts him.

The combination of the lack of sunshine and the harsh northwest wind causes a glistening cold tear to form at the corner of his dry tired eyes. He is reminded of his younger days when he was free. The mixture of pharmacology and neurology gave way to bouts of alcoholism, leading to a degradation of his consciousness.

By the time he had moved in with Briar, he had become objectionably possessed.

Don't let yourself get carried away! Stay focused. Don't run away. Try not to become the angry man. It is only midafternoon and he is already tired of all the bullshit.

Visions of his kindly faced uncle sometimes appear in his lucid daydreams, often as an old man holding a diamond speckled snake. In his mind's eye, he can see a faceless tattered crowd around his uncle who is holding the twisting snake. He fears both the crowd and the snake, but forces himself a bit each day to move slowly toward both. The goal is bit by bit to become close enough to touch the archetype of his fears. To caresses the slithering reptile with or without the crowd's approval, while his kind uncle struggles to reassure him of his decision. The dream's meaning is to triumph over his deepest fears. It is only a hope, shattered by the self imposed limitations of his reality.

Returning to his cramped government office, Kazan sits down on the torn, cracked, weathered, brown leather couch that is jammed into his workspace and closes his eyes, breathing deeply, trying to recapture that which is left of himself.

He knows all too well how this plays out, and he faces the loneliness of how he ended up in the city, suffocated by this urban office cave. The fragment of a building beside the rundown graffiti etched bus terminal.

He feels the need to venture to the water's edge, reuniting his sense of adventure. He thought he would never be the type of guy to get caged.

The kind of guy who watches others live the type of life he longed for. The kind of guy who blames others for his misfortunes. Sadly, he has become the orphaned puppet who gets entangled in the strings of life. Now, he struggles to perform for others.

Kazan fingers search out his lined and warm forehead, and he gets up from the couch to stretch. He rubs his wrists, aware of his shackles. His disappointments and psychological pain are real.

The entrance hallway to his office is covered with unfocused black and white photographs of indigenous children. Many of them feature young girls looking straight into the camera. Their eyes are captured in an arm's length lens. They remind him of a younger version of Briar, her soft plump lips and sensual mouth. He misses the warmth and wetness of her calculated kisses. He adored the taste of her; she had a sweet salty taste to her mouth and body that reminded him of the soft caramels he would suck during a long boring lecture at university. He had attempted to forget about her from time to time, but it never worked out. He would close his eyes and remember the softness of her mouth.

He sits down at his paper cannoned desk. The reflection of the hunched over male sitting in the chair captured by the darkened computer screen, reminds him of his father. He reaches for his tangled office phone, but catches himself. How did he let his life slip away? What stopped him from slaying his demons? How can he absorb the power, and overcome the experience of failure? A surfer who can successfully navigate the raw power of the Pacific. The need to go into the darkest of places in search of the light, this is the gateway to what he needs, and what he needs to know.

It has been a thankless impossible transition, becoming a prosecutor in Vancouver, mostly because he despises the other lawyers in his office. The accused make him feel worse. They are a collection of misfits. Drugs, violence and a sense of entitlement have produced a new breed of criminal, and lawyer, and they both disgust him. He shares a conspiracy of unhappiness with his colleagues, that make him both popular and a puppet of the crowd.

It has been an arduous court day, mostly because the freshly appointed judge is a complete egotistical bastard. Like most days, the evidence is lacking, or the nervous witnesses who shows up is going to be irrelevant to the outcome of any trial. He is a vegetarian forced to go into a slaughterhouse buffet to find his redemption. Exposure to this bloody waste is killing him. He has to remind himself to keep both feet on the ever-shifting sand, and swallow slowly to prevent him from gagging en route to the voyage to the other side of the darkness. There are dragons to be slain and hurdles to be cleared.

Verbose opposing counsel quickly sum up the problem.

"Who the hell does this guy think he is?"

"He hasn't a fuckin clue what's going on."

Still, the afternoon will linger on, and despite the abundance of judicial beatings he has suffered, he marches on, attempting to find a scintilla of justice in this psychological charade. A day of complete suffering, in search of one single crystal of light in the darkness.

Common sense will be further compromised when his balding overweight lead investigator keeps parroting his own mantra: "This is an overwhelming case here, you've have got to be fucking kidding!"

This only causes Kazan's mind to wander more. He can almost feel the seaweed infused mist from his earlier beach sojourn. He tries to breathe deeply, letting the air travel in his nostrils and fill his entire rib cage, while allowing the stress to magically escape with every timed exhale. It isn't working. Calmness is in short supply. He can feel the jagged edge of a shard of regret in his closing throat.

Kazan stammers out the obvious, "Remember, this is all about making this fool understand the evidence! One witness at a time, one piece of evidence at a time. Don't ever lose your cool!"

His pleas fall on deaf ears, including his own. He cannot convince himself or anyone else in the room of the priority of his message. Their interest, and frankly his, has gone cold.

His head starts to spin with every foggy memory of how it had been. Justice was an unattainable construct, a mysterious fiction, created by those that were out of control seeking some form of control where there was none. It was unfair, it wasn't even close to being fair.

On days like these, he discovers that it is even harder to throw punches than it is to receive them. It takes everything he has, to hold back to the last minute, and then deliver a calculated knockout blow with every ounce of his being. He had been an underweight boxer in his early adulthood, and it had served him well. It was like he had never left the ring, finding himself again and again, throwing punches at an opponent who was always beyond his reach. He soon discovered that while he loved the game, he was totally disgusted by the participants.

He would knock himself out before submitting to a technical loss from a lesser opponent. It satisfied something deep within him. The love of striking his opponent, or fending off a pounding. It more often than not, left him consumed by the alchemy of irrational thought and shattered by the conspiracy of agreement among the dishonest.

When he prepared for trial, he did so like no other. He was preparing for battle. In that vein, he would always gaze directly into the judicial officer's vacant eyes. He had to, otherwise it became this imaginary play. This mockery of a judicial system, bound together by years of legal fictions.

The legal texts are now fraying, and the trick, he thinks, is to not allow the whole bloody mess to unravel around you.

As the day comes to a close, he can't recall how the whole thing has become so damn frustrating and funny: incompetent judges, ridiculous defense counsel, and inept police officers. Frustrated by the whole damn useless scenario, he starts to joke with the frustrated minimally paid court staff. They can find no fault in this legal morality play. They have nothing to gain or lose.

Later, when he returns home, he finds Briar in a steamy hot bath. Her oil-coloured shiny dark hair is held back by a thick green rubber band, the type that holds his legal briefs together. Her smooth soft skin glistens with a youthful shine and her rounded breasts dance upon the top of the soapy bathwater. He reaches for a warmed towel, overcome by her beauty. The curve of her back arches as she struggles to find the warmth of the bathwater against the rush of cool air from the bathroom door he has left ajar. He pushes back his rain soft hair from the creases of his forehead, and contemplates removing of his wrinkled suit and joining her in the tub. The corner of his thumb finds the edge of his soft leather belt, and he tugs at it as he makes a feeble attempt at conversation. There is no doubt that he wants to draw her wet and warm body close to his.

HYMAN KAZAN

11

BRITISH COLUMBIA

THE BODY OF Simon Westfall is laid out on an icy cold stainless steel autopsy table. The government has no idea what clues will be found with a close examination of his body. The scandalous truth is that no one cares. He came to Vancouver in 1986 from Northern Scotland. He secured a job with a local construction company, and quickly became very popular with the after-hours crowd. In 1987, he met his partner Michael who gave lectures at the University of British Columbia. Together, they developed a circle of well-meaning friends who wanted to serve and improve their community.

It was hard to find information about Simon Westfall. He is still relatively new to Canada, and largely keeps to himself and his small circle of friends. Friends describe him as one to speak his mind and to have a short fuse. He is tanned and calloused from working outdoors, and spends what little he earns on risky travel adventures. With an absence of fear, he maintains a level of confidence, and yet is very approachable and likeable. When asked about his drug use, most describe him as a drinker rather than a serious drug user.

His death is unexplained. The summary of the dog-eared coroner's report will be Kazan's first introduction to Simon, and it will raise more questions than answers.

Elliott has given him a copy of the coroner's report: twenty-seven pages of statistics and primary school drawings of the human body that for days Kazan had resisted putting the time into reading. He doesn't want to plant another victim into his crowded and neglected soul. Now, with every tick of the clock, he begins to inject every fact into himself. He has been embarrassed at how little he has known about the gay community given how much it dominates the lower east side of the town. One thing is for sure: it is more emotionally and psychologically complex than he had imagined. He has always thought that victims came in all shapes and forms, and he found it very easy to develop a respect and affinity for those overlooked by others.

Out of this crash and mosaic of emotions, a structure or outline of the case is formed. It is as if the board game becomes alive with different characters looking back at him across the checker boarded legal landscape, becoming hardwired into the slow moving cynical fatigued lawyer he has become. These characters will worm their way into his subconscious.

When he feels the walls closing in, Kazan likes to put on his oversized shiny aluminum headphones and stare out the window of his downtown office. He wants to escape the pressure of his job and the disappointment of his home life. He thinks about a nurse he once dated in college. She had walked away from emergency medicine after seeing one to many of her patients torn from operating tables so as to preserve the statistics of those who survived surgery. The deck was stacked, and like the justice system, too many people were being dealt losing hands from the bottom of the deck.

The windows of his office run down the entire side of the wall, and except for the decorative stones on the window's ledge, it offers him a unobstructed view of the North Shore Mountains. He loves watching the planes fly over the mountains toward the glass-like waters of the harbour. The music helps to accentuate the view. High above the street, he can see for miles. Often, when forced to stay late, he will take out a bottle of scotch from his lower left side desk drawer and pour himself a drink while listening to Pachelbel and focusing on the golden starburst lights leading up to the summit of Grouse. The amber glow of the lights reflected on the snowy landscape present a floating mythical stage where life is enjoyed.

Kazan loves the view, and the scotch helps to numb the pain or disappointment of the day. He allows the moment to find him, until there is a loud knocking on the glass partition outside of his door. Kazan steps away from the window and hides his glass behind a mound of criminal briefs. Lauren, the office manager, can be seen outside of his office, holding her right hand up against her ear, mimicking a telephone conversation.

Kazan hurries over to his desk and notices that he has placed his flashing office phone on hold so as to not mute his escape. He grabs the phone and punches the clear tab at the bottom of the phone, allowing a call to be placed through. He pushes the stack of paper from the corner of his desk and tosses his briefcase onto the sofa in the corner of his office. He walks around his desk and falls into his scuffed red leather office chair, which is pulled back from his desk. Lauren watches as he gathers himself in preparation for taking the call. Like an air traffic controller, the message is communicated that a call can be put through.

The Centre of Forensic Sciences working with Poison Control and VGH found that there were trace amounts of carfentanil found in the blood samples taken from Simon Westfall. The initial blood work had only revealed a small amount of fentanyl, and for some unknown reason, further tests had not been conducted. It was only after some nurse had called a number of times to report her misgivings about the death, that the police took a closer look at the blood screens and tox reports.

A gruff Detective Chmura had told Porter Radley of the Centre, that he wanted the tests to be run and rerun. His promise of lower bowl Canuck tickets and a bottle of single malt, had provided the force behind the need for a closer examination of the tox workup.

"Jesus, how could this have been overlooked?" Kazan asks Chmura over the phone.

"I will be damned if I know," answers Chmura. "You know, everyone is up to here with the drug problem in Vancouver! It has become an everyday event. Nobody can keep up. We are lucky they agreed to run the tests again!"

"I know, one more junkie, but this kid, by all reports, was no junkie. If there is more of this shit on the streets, we will all need to do something or we will be running out of body bags," offers Kazan on the other line.

"You don't have to tell me. I had a half dozen bodies last month that I now have to check up on due to this blood work, to find out why the hell this could have been missed," chirps Chmura. "Great. Why do you always have to drop the bomb on my shift?" Chmura is now taunting Kazan.

"I guess we should be investigating this thing as a possible unexplained death or homicide. At least that is what Porter is saying," responds Kazan.

"Unexplained? We know what killed him, don't we? But what if he did not take the drug by himself? What if there were others who took the drug and survived?" adds Chmura.

"Survived! Then they are not our problem," says Kazan.

An inappropriate chuckle is heard muffled on the line.

"We can't prosecute everyone who holds the hand of another kid who uses, can we?" adds Kazan.

"Why not? What if the person who provides the drug is aware it is laced with carfentanil? What then?" asks Chmura. "It would be like giving antifreeze to your mother-in-law, wouldn't it? It is sugary and has a nice colour to it, but fuck it, it can give you one hell of a hangover," Chmura adds.

"Well, I don't know, I guess it is curious how this kid ended up outside of the clinic. Maybe the boys over on Cordova Street can find out how he ended up here, and from there, we can figure out how this junk got into his system?"

Chmura thanks Kazan for taking his call and promises to think of him when the Canucks play next. Both men end their conversation the way it started, with a math equation that does not make any sense.

The thought of working on another case with no hopes of success sickens him. Before he can even get up from his desk, his cell phone is ringing. It is Briar, asking him when he is coming home, and if he can stop by a liquor store and pick her up a bottle of wine. He laughs and tells her he is on his way.

"I need you, Kazan," she tells him.

Surprised by her lingering desire for him, he responds, "Sure, everybody does right now!"

IN BETWEEN A heavenly bite of his sweet soft-shell crab and crustless
avocado sandwich, and her third glass of chardonnay, Briar tells Kazan
that there will be no more questions about what she wants, and how she
hopes to quench this burning sense of misplaced desire. That is how she
is. He laughs, telling her he is fine with it. However the evening is going
to play out, he just wants to be with her. As soon as he says this, she craves
him. It keeps shifting back and forth between them. It is like being at an
overpriced art auction with no money. She looks so attractive to him, and
when she gives him that look that it isn't going to happen, the surging
energy becomes unbearable.

What she really likes is that feeling of being in total unbridled control,
and yet, without any consequences. She is intoxicated with his sex. It has
been a long time since she had been drunk and had a night of reckless love
making. She likes having the upper hand, or at least the illusion of holding
all of the cards close to her chest. The melted butter harvest moon is fat
and illuminates the oily rain washed streets, as hip hop music thumps in
the starless night air from a passing SUV. She slips her damp cottony white
bathrobe off and walks ahead of him.

In the dimly lit bathroom, she glances at the pond like reflection in the
mirror, and becomes startled by how much she has aged. She is no longer

that young girl who would enter a room and immediately become noticed. The passage of time has exaggerated the fine lines that surround her aqua blue eyes. She splashes a warm drizzle of water on her face in an attempt to erase her anxiety. She crosses over her soft cotton terry cloth robe with a dancer's agility that has fallen to the hallway floor.

When she returns to their bedroom, she finds him lying on his side, naked on their bed. She walks over and draws the thick white canvas curtains, so as to block the moonlight that shines into their room. A single prop float plane skips over the mountains en route to a crowded harbour below.

The wine she drank makes her relaxed, and she feels the warmth of his strong angular body as she lies down beside him. He reaches out for her hand and places his arm around the small of her back.

"I love you, you know that, don't you? I miss us and the way we were," she says.

"I'm right beside you," he replies so as to confirm his presence.

She hesitates and swallows an unspoken painful moment.

"I need to tell you something. We need to face the reality of our situation," she says.

"Reality, hmm, okay. You should tell me anything you feel comfortable talking about," he replies.

"Damn it, this isn't easy. I did it because of you," she says.

"For Christ's sake, Briar! Don't confess anything to me you can't live with. Because of me? Here we go," he replies, unaware of what is to come next.

The unforgiving circle of their past begins to shrink rapidly.

"I'm not . . . I have not been honest with you."

"Now is the time then, Briar!"

He feels a throbbing knot form in his tensely held stomach, a reaction to the anticipated arrival of emotional upset and conflict. She is now seated upright and she begins to nervously twist her dark hair, pulling it back and forth, and then finally into a bun. He hates these late evening cage match conversations, as there is no easy way of surviving them. It is far more prudent to admit defeat early, and get on with the evening. Still, she persists.

"Remember that time we spent in Taormina? Jesus, I loved Sicily, you know, the beaches, the people and just time together. I wish we never left, Kazan!"

This is a quick escape down a side street away from the epicenter of our argument, he thinks.

"Taormina, I never knew how much you loved it there. I thought you hated it there and couldn't wait to get back to Rome," he says.

Taormina was a magical place. A jewel of an ancient village that had been dug out of the side of a mountain overlooking the crystal blue azure while resting on the shoulder blade of Mount Etna. It was spectacular. Lemon trees dotted the smooth stone Roman streets, framing the decaying roads and sun drenched stone churches amidst hard water stained gothic fountains. They had escaped to Sicily, abandoning the cold damp winter, the previous year.

"Taormina! Strange, what made you think about that?"

"Happier times, I guess. We were so free there, weren't we? We were ourselves again," she says.

He finds that this trip down memory lane is masking the hurt that is about to reign down on him.

"Are you alright? I really don't know where this is going?" he asks.

Suddenly, she blurts out her bottled up confession.

"I am seeing someone else, Kazan!" she cries.

The air is suddenly sucked out of their room. He sits up and watches as she swallows her act of contrition, and he attempts to take in what she has just disclosed. He struggles with what to say.

"When, when did this start? Why? Why, Briar? Don't you love me?"

"About three months ago."

"God damn it, Briar! Are you in love with him?"

"It was because of you," she replies. "I thought you would understand."

The words fall from the dark skies overhead.

"Oh, Briar! You don't have to do this if you want out?"

He can't believe what he is saying. He struggles with his lack of ability to run downhill. *Here it comes,* he thinks, *the understatement, the invitation to the execution.*

"And what about you, Kazan?"

He attempts to look away, drawing his right hand and long slender fingers through the edges of his hair that rest just slightly above his forehead. Then, she suddenly offers up the knock out punch to his exposed throat, sparking off an incendiary explosion.

"He is a judge and I think you might know him."

What? There it is, out from left field. A judge, a God damn judge. Can it get much worse?

"What the fuck?" he utters.

"Yes, what the fuck!" she responds.

He asks her, "Is this some kind of sick cruel joke?"

She says that it is something that just happened.

He asks her again, "Do you love the guy?"

He struggles with how to be relative with the inevitable. She has been preparing him for this moment for some time now.

And she says that everything is up in the air. He thinks for a moment, but avoids the obvious question as to the identity of this cad.

It was like a thunderous Alaskan blue iceberg calving. Jagged pieces of ice and rock falling into the emerald ocean. He thinks, *how am I going to learn to go on without her? How to imagine my life, after being promised a life together.* He had painted her into every blurred line and incomplete scene of his ill-constructed shaky West Coast future.

He grabs hold of his frayed emotions, and thinks, *you have to live your life by holding something back.* He thinks he needs something to hold on to, something that will allow him to carry on. A readiness to survive the hurricanes and torment that life can serve up. What now?

And, just before he can again ask who is this man who is tearing up their lives, she says, "I need more passion and love. I feel like time is running out. He is a good man, Kazan, and he is new to Vancouver."

He says he knows what she is saying, and that he too has felt alone so many nights, and the thought now of living alone, makes him feel both stupid and lonely. He decides right then and there to just say no more.

She laughs like a great weight has been removed from her hyperventilating chest and lies back down on their bed, sliding her body away from him.

"I am glad you understand. I guess you will be moving out. That's the best thing for both of us, don't you think?"

It is like she has just delivered a punch line to a joke that he can't get. Her words and actions appear so incongruent to him. He stumbles with what to say, what to do. Seconds tick before he can reply.

"I guess," he replies.

It finally occurs to him that it is a very bad habit to continue to lie to himself any longer. His mind is swamped with his mounting problems. Trinity Rivers, an unexplained homicide, a new judge to contend with and her desire for a life without him. There is nothing left to say, so he says nothing. There is darkness and peaceful quiet after that. They have reached an unexpected and unspoken truce. They both lie there motionless in the dark. The silence is then broken with unneeded comments about nothing.

"I need to get some sleep. I just don't get it," is all that he can get out. Words escape him.

"You never have, and you never will," she responds.

"I guess sleep would do us some good, but what happens when I wake up? Even if I can sleep, I doubt it is going to be possible. What will I do without you?" Kazan asks.

He is caught between the sides of persistence and letting go.

"Kazan, you will land on your feet, you always do."

She can't sleep either. The wine, like everything else, falls short.

"What about us?" he asks. "What happened with all of our plans and dreams?"

The room falls silent again. *I have betrayed my promise to not ask foolish questions,* he thinks. He doesn't want to be the only person in their relationship, that would be running an emotional deficit. He wonders if she feels any of his pain. Her answers demonstrate she has already moved to an emotional space void of his feelings.

"He is a great guy," she says. "He wants the same things as me."

Something or some aspect of time and space shifts again in the room when she says that. *This is an unexpected nightmare,* he tells himself. *I must be dreaming as this shouldn't be happening to me.* Still, she appears oblivious to how her words are affecting him. He props himself up on his left arm, and moves a bit closer to her, but can't recognize her anymore. She is waiting to see if he will touch her again, given her disclosure.

"I should go," he says.

He coughs and begins to get off the bed, his feet searching for the floor.

"If that is what you want," she sputters.

She gathers herself in the entangled bedclothes and turns around to face him.

"I miss the good times," she says.

Why can't she just shut up and let things go, he thinks.

"I miss the excitement of feeling like you want me with all of your physical and emotional heart."

"Jesus, Briar. What do you want from me? Why are you doing this?"

"Nothing. I sadly don't want anything more from you," she says between a slight showing of some concern for him.

He places his hand on her shoulder, and she smiles. *Oh my God,* he thinks, *don't ask her anything more and don't beg for her to change her mind.*

This is what he remembers every time he closes his eyes, the way in which your life can change in a second. Suddenly, the chapters that make up your life are torn from the book, forgotten by time and circumstance. Sometimes, when he is walking alone on the beach, he daydreams about that night. He tries to find the words to change things, to rewrite a fading history, but finds himself mute.

Then the loneliness sets in.

HYMAN KAZAN

13

BRITISH COLUMBIA

THE FLICKERING WHITE tubular fluorescent sign on the fake wood veneer courtroom door says: Court is in Session. The charge through the doors is led by Mathew Stirling. He carries a black Italian leather briefcase with gold locking clasps. He thinks it is mandatory that he appears successful, or at the very least, as being in demand. That's what the paying public expects, they expect him to look the part. As a senior lawyer, he will put on the required costume and carry the props that will fulfill that expectation. His billing practices demand it.

But not today, today he is clad in aged and faded blue jeans, more appropriate for attendance at a farmers market or some trendy coffee house than the courthouse. He has also brought the young and attractive Marianne Cummings to court with him as he can't keep his hands off her. Her cinnamon-coloured hair cascades down her shoulders as she checks the dog-eared laser printed green and white striped computer generated docket that takes up a horizontal position on the scratched and worn counsel table. It takes him a second or two to gather some resemblance of self-control and to move beside her and not bring his arm around the small of her back.

"I forgot Devlin was sitting," he says as he watches her crossing her shapely legs while taking a seat at the table reserved for counsel.

He snatches a moment to glance down at her tanned legs as they disappear under the table.

"You know him, don't you?"

"I appeared before him a time or two when he was in Thunder Bay," he says.

She looks at him and he is a bit surprised and amused by the crooked grin and smile that has come across her face.

Of course, he has forgotten about his time spent in Northern Ontario. He can barely remember the number of gas bag judges he had appeared before. But he doesn't want to immediately display his disdain for everyone who has placed a red sash over their rounded shoulders, especially in front of the impressionable Marianne.

He wants to savor the excitement he feels from being around her. He feels so good when he thinks about what she said over coffee earlier that morning. Something about his presence in a courtroom, something flattering about the way he carried himself. He can't recall exactly the way she put it, but he recalls how her eyes widened and her smile became more broad when she spoke, and how beautiful she looked when they had first met outside of Bean Brothers, a popular coffee shop downtown.

Today, the courtroom is jammed. The large rectangular room is mostly occupied by members of the struggling unemployed middle class.

An annoyed Stirling spies a gaggle of particularly young police officers occupying chairs in the corner of the courtroom, beside the row of windows overlooking the parking lot. The roar coming from them reminds him of an opening night at some type of after-hours club, or a sporting event. Next, there is a row of empty scratched and worn, barrel back wooden chairs, reserved for counsel. Most of them spend their time digging in their briefcases or ushering fearful clients in and outside of the courtroom, providing them with last minute instructions, or allowing them a moment to think about the stupidity of the defenses they want to be advanced.

As the lawyers keep coming to the front of the courtroom, one well-dressed lawyer asks one of the young junior lawyers if the seat beside her is taken. She waves her arm across the chair, indicating its vacancy. Like pistons in an old car, counsel rises and falls until all the chairs at the front are now occupied.

Marianne's paper jammed leather briefcase takes up a strategic position on the empty chair in front of her. She leans over to speak to Stirling, with the edges of her hair brushing softly against the side of his face.

In a hushed tone, she asks, "Who's that?"

"Justice Smith!"

"Pardon?"

"Craig Donald Smith! What the hell is he doing here? I thought it was Eddie Devlin?"

He barely gets the words out when he suddenly feels embarrassed by his lack of professional dress. His dark navy blue suit spills over on a chair at his home, failing to provide him the much needed shield against any of the personal attacks he might face from Smith. He feels naked and ashamed. Unarmed and ill-prepared for what is about to unfold.

He will later recount the story for months to come. Yes, Smith. A simple name, the kind you use when you don't want to use your own. Little did he realize that this name would be subjected to gross speculation and gossip for so many months to come. Gossip will spread through the legal community like an Alberta prairie fire in August, destroying everything in its way, and now his raven like eyes are burning a hole through him.

Smith is a former defense lawyer from Northern Ontario, or some sketchy law office in Campbell River. He is in his early fifties, or maybe younger, no one is quite sure. There is an element of scandal that follows him wherever he shows up. He is rumoured to be gay, but it is soon discovered that he had fallen madly in love with a much younger court clerk, causing her to leave her court reporter husband and public school aged children. His newest acquisition is young and very attractive, and is said to have often been mistaken for his daughter rather than his spouse. Time and time again, it is proven "beyond a reasonable doubt" that people are objects to him, both privately and professionally.

Stirling does not care much about his rumoured past. He is just another egotistical bastard who fucks over people for his own cruel amusement. Still, the young lawyers admire him, and wish they had a mysterious past like him, full of sex and scandal. The female members of the bar are excited about the power that comes from his position, while they privately condemn him. Both of them bow dutifully before him, and laugh at all of his jokes right on cue.

The story now centers around Carol Edwards, his long suffering spouse. The rumour is that she has thrown Smith out, and that he had been living in Southern Ontario before coming back to BC. He had left Edwards penniless and in a drunken tailspin. A spectacular illustration of gas lighting. This had set up his judicial move. Months later, after being sheep dipped, he had landed on his swollen feet in the Emerald City, absent Edwards, with no alimony to pay. A feat unheard of.

And now, he is perched high above the clouds, looking down upon all those who appear before him. The gossip river is overflowing its banks. Rumours circulate both from his fellow judges and lawyers alike, who both fear he will be bringing his dystopian brand of justice or indifference to their community.

His greasy salt and pepper hair is swept back as he peers over top of his dark Barry Goldwater glasses, constantly checking the clock on the wall and the rear doors to the courtroom. He resembles a cat burglar who is just waiting for the security alarm to go off. He can both smell and instill fear, and the legal waters are chummed with blood.

"Cummings!" he bellows.

"Yes, Your Honor," her voice breaks with anxiety and anticipation.

"Why are you here with Stirling? And why is he dressed like a bum? Oh, are you charged with a criminal offence, Mr. Stirling? Finally? This is going to be fun!"

A small controlled scattering of laughter erupts from the back of the court. No one can be sure where it is coming from. Stirling's face is flushed with rage and embarrassment.

"What matter do you two appear on? Why are you here?" Smith bellows. "Why do you waste the court's time?"

"We are here on the Russell matter," Marianne speaks out.

"What is happening on this matter?" Smith grins, reminding himself that he is in full control of how this situation will look to the nervous client who is standing before him with a smug look on his face.

"We are seeking an adjournment to October 23rd."

"October 23rd and bring a real lawyer with you next time, Ms. Cummings, for both you and your client, or I will hold both you and Stirling's tailor in contempt!"

Stirling is angry now, but knows better than to take the bait. They both pack up their briefcases and head toward the door.

The courtroom is very crowded now, and the audience is more restless. Stirling catches a glimpse of a young man walking into the courtroom from over his shoulder, looking for his client. He is carrying a tabbed criminal code tucked under his arm, and wears his black court robes in an off the shoulder or reckless manner.

"Jack Pescet."

That's who it is. He too had been counsel in the North before moving to Vancouver. Great, he is now a spectator to this attack. What is he doing here? Gossip suggested that he is there to get even with a judge who had caused his marriage to disintegrate.

Stirling closes his eyes in an effort to fend it off. He grabs Marianne's hand, holding it tightly as if hurricane winds are about to erupt, throwing them and everything in the room into a tailspin. There is a lump in his throat, a sudden dryness. It is the beginning of his day in court. It is familiar to him, but still causes his stomach to ache. *Don't let this egotistical bastard get to you,* he thinks. Need not make matters worse, or lose control in a world without any real rules. The players present try to hide their individual biases and prejudices, only to be outdone by the oceans of a lack of empathy demonstrated by Craig Donald Smith. Before leaving, Marianne stares straight at Judge Smith, strategically looking just slightly above his rounded face. Within seconds, she has unknowingly become his newest target or anticipated conquest.

"We were just here seeking an adjournment," she speaks up, without taking a second breath.

Through gritted and grinding teeth, and an under the breath "fuck you," they are both on their way out of the courtroom.

Smith is a completely bad draw as a judge. He is totally ill-equipped to hear any case, be it a case involving a homicide or a dog bite. A person like Simon Westfall would never meet someone like Smith if he was lucky, and now with a change of wind, both men will become involved in a postmortem dance. Now, with the strangest of coincidences, Kazan is going to become the linchpin between both.

Kazan's personal and professional problems are growing each day as agents of the VPD make repeated unanswered phone calls to both his office and home. They know that he is the only Crown that will work around the clock to secure a conviction. Kazan is the man for this job. They know that out of the forty lawyers downtown, he is the best. Everyone loves Kazan, except his coworkers. The court reporters and special constables who walk the corridors of the courtrooms are his only allies, and they will advise him of what the others are saying behind his back.

"It is good that someone has my back," Kazan often says to them.

He laughs when they disclose the latest rumour or complaint made about him. He does not ask or seek out what cases come his way, he is just tasked with taking the garbage out, or finding a way to block the turnstile. He is the guy that is called in to clean up the mess. A janitor, a fixer, the one lawyer you can count on to get you out of a jam. The problem is that there is a log jammed up river and nothing is floating through to the saw mill.

It is fitting, in a strange way, that he will inherit this case about a man no one cared about. It is predictable. He has long become accustomed to setting up his temporary residence upon the twisted dumping ground of troublesome cases. It is no coincidence. In fact, it is by design. It is a plan by his bosses to bring him down a notch or two. It is a tangled web designed to betray all that he believes in, and it is working.

WHERE IS SHE? *Where did she go now?* Kazan thinks. He is dead tired, and his wool coat is soaked from the sudden and unexpected downpour. He had walked from the crowded market at Granville Island, where he was supposed to meet her for a drink at Bridges, a popular waterfront restaurant. He can hear the nonchalant reaction to their non-meeting in her whispered voice, saying to him, "I waited as long as I could." And now the afternoon is ruined. He looks around the crowded restaurant and searches out her face from among the plastic reserved signs placed upon empty tables. *Of course,* he thinks, *everyone is looking at me, the fool, searching for someone who does not care about me or my time.*

His stomach is now hurting. He is both frustrated and angry. The roar of the diners is finally drawn out as he grabs the handle of the oversized wooden front door and rushes back into the wind and rain.

He makes his way back to their apartment. The building is warm and dry. The emptiness from the restaurant is still with him as he turns the brass-coloured key to their unit. Like a domestic animal returning to his cage, he removes his rain soaked coat, and falls into a chair. Exhausted by both the walk back and the disappointment he feels, he makes his way to the kitchen area, where he grabs a wine glass from the back of the cupboard. Within seconds, out of character, the wine glass shatters and slices open his index finger. He spends the next hour trying to stop the bleeding both physically and emotionally.

It draws him into himself as the pain shoots through to his heart. His blood is thick and bright red. He grabs an errant dish towel in an attempt to stop the flow of blood. He mistakenly places his hand into his rear jeans pocket. The tightness of his pants makes his finger sting and the bleeding stops from the pressure of the lining of his pocket. No choice now but to remove his pants and crawl into a hot shower with his glass of wine.

His return home has been anything but restful, and now he is feeling both the pain in his finger and the effects of the wine on his empty stomach. When he finally sits down, he examines the wound, very careful to not disturb the jagged cut that has oozed blood for the past twenty minutes. He adjusts his reading glasses and examines his finger. It would appear that the wound has finally begun to close.

The feelings of loneliness do not go away.

He has been pushed into a puzzling set of circumstances he had not chosen. It is dangerous now that he has started the process of thinking about his life and the missed opportunities. But soon she will be home, and there will be some idle conversation about what had led up to this mishap.

Jesus, doesn't anything go right? Take it easy. He attempts to find calmness or a reasonable excuse for a day that is rapidly evaporating. He sits down and takes a deep breath. He will have to wait for her return, whenever that happens. He hears the echo of footsteps in the hallway outside of their apartment, a clicking of heels on the dark wooden floors outside of their unit. He rises from his chair and makes his way to the hallway bathroom to have a look in the mirror. He catches a glimpse of the dark circles under his eyes, and thinks he sees the reflection of his father staring back at him, shaking his head in a scolding fashion, filled with questions.

The door finally opens, and after a few misspoken lines, she asks him about his finger. Not a mention of her absence at Granville Island. He places his finger into the corner of his mouth and tries to calm down, the taste from his throbbing cut does little to make him relax. What prevents her from asking about their missed meeting? Why doesn't he go into a rage and demand an explanation? He asks her if they have any disinfectant for his wound.

The back hallway is dark. He makes his way into their walk-in closet and removes a inky black handgun from his dresser drawer. He checks to see if the chamber is empty. It is a well-worn Beretta handgun and Kazan wonders when it must have been fired last. He also wonders who was the target when the gun was fired. He is not comfortable around handguns, or any guns for that matter. He wonders why he has kept the gun in the first place. For a brief second, he lets his mind wander, and recalls if he hadn't been drinking with the police that night, he might have never brought it home. Nobody should bring a gun into a home he had thought. He had wrapped it up in an old United Way T-shirt and placed it in the back of his top drawer.

In that awkward moment, he turns back and sees Briar walking toward the bedroom. Her eyes are glassy and red. Hurt eyes. *I'm sorry. I'm sorry.* He thinks the words, but he does not speak them. His thumb traces the edge of the drawer where the gun had been secreted away. Hey, he thinks, he is so grateful for the few seconds that have elapsed before she has entered the room. It gives him the chance to collect himself, to draw that thin line that separates him from the moment and his repressed feelings of hurt and betrayal.

To look into Briar's eyes and see the upset he has caused hurts him deeply. She has been the love of his life, the reason for him uprooting and going to British Columbia in the first place. Kazan embraces her and attempts to calm things down a bit. Now it is her turn again, to find the correct combination of words that will cut him emotionally to the bone. He grows depressed by the absurdity of the evening's events.

Outside, an ambulance blares its siren. He never liked the sounds of the city at night. His hallow eyes picture another victim like Simon Westfall, going to the hospital, the cops screeching down a rain slick coastal road. It is like bearing witness to the tearing of the social fabric or the removal of muscle from bone, again and again, diminishing the hope offered by the misty mountains or the greenish foam of the sea.

His mind bounces back to the handgun, its coolness and blackness. He thinks about looking down its dark thick barrel and pulling back the trigger, blasting away all of his troubles. It sickens him, and his body begins to shake in the way it would if he was actually holding the weapon, while confronting an unexpected intruder in the middle of the night. He reminds himself not to think like that, take a step back, and gather yourself. His thoughts scare him. He must not give in to such craziness.

HYMAN KAZAN

15

BRITISH COLUMBIA

STIRLING REMOVES HIS tortoise-coloured glasses. Marianne is staring at him, and he realizes that he had been daydreaming. The beautiful thing about it is that he is so relaxed in such a tense situation. It isn't like the courtroom, instead it is like being at a spa or some new age meditation retreat. Seconds later, he is back on the taut high wire, and there is no one there to break his fall, to catch him, to put him back together. The room is a bended prism of confusion and tension. The daydream is over.

The scratched brass-coloured combination lock on her litigation briefcase clicks, breaking the silence of the moment. Stirling leans back in his chair, moving his legs toward Marianne's legs placed under the counsel table. A feeble attempt to get closer to her and make it a more comfortable situation, but when the side of his leg touches her knee, he thinks he will melt. It feels amazing. He has never felt that before. Not with Kathleen. Not ever. His relationship with Kathleen ended badly.

Kathleen desired a public or stage like relationship, and had used him to get ahead. He just held the ladder for her as she attempted to climb higher to the top. That is all behind him now, she had found happiness in the arms of another aging lawyer to move in with. The last time he saw her, she was walking up the narrow steps to the courthouse hand in hand with another victim. His name was Tony, tossing her head to the side in an attempt to ignore him.

"I am happy now! You didn't know what you had."

Who was she trying so hard to convince? Relationships between lawyers are like that, he thinks, *random plays acted out before the local legal community, eager to be entertained while they wait for the curtain to fall on their own interpersonal failures.* And then, in an ironic way, he caught a forced smile forming on Tony's face. He looked like a golfer who had been found to have done an illegal drop after taking a mulligan. And after that, he felt both empty and alone. Perhaps, this was the way in which things were meant to be.

The sound of the sardine packed prisoner van backing up can be heard around the corner. It is true that Kathleen's departure made him feel lost. He detested her desire to get ahead by using others. Everyone was classified as what they could or could not do for her.

A water taxi ride away from the courthouse, Kazan is attempting to get his life back on track. Kazan looks up at the snow covered mountains on the North Shore and then back at Briar, recalling how things were when he first relocated to the West Coast. He had asked her for dinner, and at first, she had said she was busy, but after some awkward pauses, she'd said yes. And at dinner, she'd said she was somewhat taken back by his invitation. A mere moment that would set in motion the whole set of events that led up to this point in his life, the first domino to fall, setting off the chain reaction of events that comprised his life.

He has reached the point in his life where he has come to the realization that one's identity comes from within rather than being dependent on what one owns or what one achieves. The opinion of others does not define him. In coming to this revelation, he holds steadfast to the belief that everyone is divine, or worthy of respect. That is, if you start out with the concrete or the particular, then and only then can you find the elusive doorway to the universal. This is a truth that shapes every aspect of his life. It is a one way street that causes him to shift away from the futile journey of trying to discern why some fit in, while others do not. It helps him understand the life or lifestyle of Simon Westfall, and reject the dishonesty of the values held by judges like Craig Donald Smith.

His caseload, as far as caseloads go, is horrible. It is like working in a slaughterhouse and the cases are piling up on the killing floor without a break. Most of the accused are struggling blue-collar workers who have abandoned their comfortable lives through the ingestion of too much alcohol or drugs. The types of folks who build the railroads and infrastructures that we rest upon. The usual scenario goes something like this: the husband works long hours and comes home to find his home in a state of complete chaos, and when he arrives at the front door of his residence, he is usually drunk, often with a beer in one hand and a cigarette in the other.

"How was your day?"

The question is usually followed by a harsh list of expletives.

Allan Richardson is one such client. He had aimed his deceased grandfather's unregistered nickel tarnished shotgun at his second wife, and cocked back the hammer. After several moments of yelling and feet shuffling, he snapped, the gun was tossed on the front lawn and the police were on their way. Tears fell from his and her eyes as the cops placed him into the back of a waiting cruiser.

"How was your day?"

The sound of sirens wailed in the distance.

Kazan shuffled the neglected stack of papers on his home office desk, a glass of scotch cradled in his left hand in a feeble attempt to numb the day. The amber liquid from the Hebrides worked in the past, but now it can't touch the pain. He just wants to feel whole again, his thoughts drift back to the 9mm Beretta in the bedroom. It is his passport to escape.

The quietness of the room makes him feel safe. He worries that maybe he has taken too much time to sort out his life. He recalls the feeling he had when he was climbing the coastal mountains and was caught in a rainstorm, caught between the rock face and a steep fall onto jagged rocks below. He placed his hands at his sides and felt the smooth rock face behind him. It made him both worried and comforted that he could feel the safety of his position, and yet, one false step or slip would send him to his death. Maybe life is like that: a combination of near life ending events, a tourniquet of responsibilities tied around his main artery. Kazan thinks it is very lucky for him to have survived this living with Briar; he can share his burden of his chosen occupation.

He is surprised to see that Briar has arrived home again, searching the apartment for him. He feels even more alone, abandoned by circumstance and preoccupied by the moment. *The gun,* Kazan thinks to himself, *it can end all this frustration, once and for all.*

Why must she always come home at the exact moment in which he has just caught his breath. The next few days' events will culminate in a fantastic fireworks show of inarticulate melodrama. Where was his home? Where was that place of safety and rest? Kazan feels the temperature in the room begin to rise. An ambulance screams out in the distance.

"God, where were you? I was worried about you," Kazan says as he gets up from his chair and goes to put his arms around her.

"What have you been up to? How long have you been sitting here?" she replies.

Kazan fumbles for his damp raincoat. "I have to go out," he stammers.

"Now?"

"Yes, I have to prepare for tomorrow. How about joining me for a drink later?"

"How long will you be?"

He looks at her, her dark brown hair catches the light from the hallway, her face looks kind and for once hopeful. He imagines that she still wants him, like before.

"You go. I just got home, and I will catch up with you later."

They both know that she will not be going out to be with him, but both of them let the statement rise and fall like the empty response it is to an ill-intentioned invitation. Briar sticks her thumb in the waistband of her jeans and tugs at them, sending them to the floor. She brushes her hair back with her other hand and goes off in search of a glass of wine. He makes his way out of the apartment in silence. He hears the door shut behind him. No goodbyes, just the promise of some time together later.

HYMAN KAZAN · 16 · BRITISH COLUMBIA

"YOU LAWYERS! THAT arrogant prick is waiting!"

It is Kenny James, the 140 pound blade of a court officer who had just stuck his head through the ante doors that are outside of the courtroom and everyone is ignoring him.

"You better get your asses in there," he says. "The judge is getting steamed!"

Stirling looks at Marianne and takes a gulp of a God awful cold coffee. He will get there in good time. Robert Valley is feverishly smoking a cigarette outside of the courthouse. Stirling has only been told about this aging playboy, and his "fuck it" attitude. Stories abound about his enthralling jury addresses and cavalier attitude. Robert hates the practice of law, and yet, he still is addicted to the admiration and rush of adrenalin that comes from winning. A crooked smile forms on his face which translates to "nobody gives a shit about you unless you win your case." He smiles and gives a nod to Stirling, and Kazan, who has finally arrived at the courthouse.

"Loser clients, fucked up judges, and nobody gives a shit!" spouts Stirling as he reaches into his navy blue jacket, pulls out a cigarette and hands it to Kazan.

He lets go of a long exhale of smoke like he is unlocking the stress that has followed him the entire day. Kazan welcomes the Players plain smoke, cracks the wooden match against the cover, and tosses the package back to Stirling while tugging at his raincoat and blowing smoke away from the front doors. This trilogy of counsel looks like Hamlet, Horatio and Claudius of Denmark, all marching to their inevitable demise.

"You are God damn right! Sons of bitches everywhere you look, everyone looking to become a judge of something other than themselves. They are mere tourists to the trials of the middle class," responds Kazan.

"And the opioid addicted," cracks Stirling.

Kazan looks away only to catch a brief glimpse of Marianne, who is looking young and sexy, much like his travelling partners when he was eighteen years of age travelling through Southern France in search of love and adventure. She reminds him of a young local woman he had met on the train leaving Toulon, dressed in a white blouse and short pencil black skirt, smiling at him whenever he looked in her direction. Now, she is accompanying Stirling. *What are you doing?* he thinks. She seems a bit out of place, but she is a welcomed change to the usual cast of characters. She is unexpectedly good company.

And so, it is just another day at the courthouse, a gang of misfits looking to earn a few dollars or escape their own failures or responsibilities. Clients and witnesses stumble about, attempting to find their seats in this most awkward of theaters. Kazan is here to earn a living. He has had enough. He just wants out. He will drink away the day later, and throw himself back into the insane world of Briar. He just needs to catch a break. The odds are insurmountable.

Briar does not go into the office that day, but goes straight up to the courthouse's cafeteria in search of coffee, and to see if she can get a sight of Craig Smith. She has told herself that she likely will not, but has failed to keep any such promise she made to herself. She wanders the halls until she comes upon Stirling and Marianne.

She asks Stirling, who is looking for a quiet place to get away from his client, whether he has seen any sign of Smith. He tells her he has last seen him on the "perch" in courtroom number 103, so she sits down and sips her Tim Hortons coffee, checking her cell phone for any text messages that might explain when he might become available. She passes the time, scanning through her junk mail and rolls through the countless emails from insurance companies and dating sites.

She stays there beside the thick wire reinforced glass windows, long enough to hear Smith laughing as he makes his way to the Tim Hortons stand in the south east corner of the courthouse. His deep sounding voice echoes in the hallways.

"Did you see that client Matt Stirling had? And did you get a chance to see his new young associate?" he asks one of his judicial friends. "She was one of the poorest liars I have ever heard," chortles Smith.

"Not as poor as Stirling," one of his pear shaped colleagues responds and they both laugh.

Kazan can be seen about twenty yards away with his foot up on a chair, looking down at a young police officer seated outside of the courtroom.

Smith grabs his coffee from the aging Asian woman working the cash register, and then sees Briar. He looks for a reaction from her, and then makes a slight detour before ending up in front of where she is seated. His presence makes everyone uncomfortable.

Smith grins and speaks first, "Are you looking for Kazan?"

Briar replies, "Not really, no. I was hoping to find you."

"Are you sure?" he quips.

The awkwardness of their attraction and the location of where this is all playing out, leaves both of them a bit off balance. Stirling and Marianne stare into their coffee cups, not knowing how this awkward moment will end.

"Up to your usual games?"

Kazan suddenly appears beside Stirling and Marianne who seem happy to see him.

"Just ran into your lovely Briar, Kazan," says Smith. "You know, you shouldn't always ignore her. She might surprise you."

Kazan just looks away in disgust. After some more awkward small talk, Kazan excuses himself and makes his way into the men's room. In the washroom, he splashes some grey lukewarm water on his face and looks at his tired and lined face in the cracked and worn mirror. He is both upset and filled with disgust at this chance meeting of Briar and Smith.

The problem is that it is so difficult to remain in the profession without running into the two of them. He wants out of his relationship with Briar, and he has tried to leave her on countless occasions, but to be seen as somehow endorsing this coupling was beyond him. He feels both impotent and subservient to the corrupt judiciary, leaving him nauseated.

The idea of judges hooking up with other lawyers' wives and girlfriends wasn't a new concept. Kazan himself had become involved with one of the senior partner's wife when he was a junior partner. It wasn't really a relationship, it was benign. Once upon a time, he had been eager to fall in love with someone who understood the nature of the legal game, because it allowed him to be fully and completely lost in the profession. He had loved arguing the law and by being before a jury with everything to lose, the adrenaline produced from such moments surged through him like a runaway Japanese subway train.

Time and the constant dealing with the intellectual dishonesty wore his enthusiasm away; the demands of the job and corruption had made him depressed, but the love and moral value of the profession still burned deep inside his psyche. His anger and bitterness were developed from the level of dishonesty and betrayal of the truth that was on display everywhere.

Still, Kazan was often held in high regard and confidence by most of the local legal community. Those with the intellectual capacity and desire for honesty yearned for his friendship. It was starting to occur to him that many of his colleagues secretly shared the same view from the gallows as he did, and perhaps that was the reason they liked him. Perhaps, they all thought they would end up in the same place someday.

"Hey, Kazan, where did you go?" Stirling asks.

Smith has left the group, and a sense of comfortableness has returned to the moment.

"Briar was just talking to me about South Beach."

"Where do you stay when you go to Florida?" he asks.

"Oh, she loves Miami, especially the beach," responds Kazan who is trying to look interested.

Briar laughs and rubs her bottom lip with her flickering tongue while holding her coffee cup. Smith can be seen a short distance away, walking down the long crowded corridor, coffee in hand. Kazan's mind wanders as he thinks about Smith and his reputation for chaos.

It is mid-morning, and the courthouse is full of older lawyers who wear navy blazers and mismatched ties. It hardly matters what they look like, nobody of any accord really sees them. And their female counterparts wear skirts that are too tight for their aging misshaped bodies. Store clerks, most of them, weathered mannequins wired to briefcases, depressed egomaniacs, recently released from hospitals, sales jobs, or offices. The oldest of the group are those referred to as "senior counsel," most of them tumbling down the corridors in search of their clients after years of service, as they navigate the deep end of the judicial system pool.

"I am no joke!" Joseph Fera says.

"Fera has got his finger in everyone's pie," Kazan says. "Too bad he should be eating salad."

Fera is a fifty something old lawyer who has a reputation for being a loud, straight forward son of a bitch who looks more like an extra from a Hollywood mafia movie than a member of the bar. He is often mistaken for the accused by out of town counsel or by visiting judges.

"Fuck you, Kazan," Fera says, adjusting his glasses. "As if you get this bullshit!"

"I get this circus as much as you do, Fera," Kazan answers. He then turns to Briar and says, "This is a madhouse. Shall we get the hell out of here?"

Kazan has had his fill for the day, and he is eager to get out of the building before something else goes terribly wrong or demands his attention.

"I am definitely ready to go," she says.

He is both angry and aroused at seeing her with another man, and his mind wanders back to that 1995 Barolo that sits on the top of his dresser, housing his Beretta.

He thinks of her plum rich lips and the sweet smoothness of the wine and then misspeaks by saying, "Let's go, Lucia."

Briar suddenly stares at him. "Who is Lucia? Why did you call me Lucia?"

"What?"

"You said, let's go home, Lucia." She tilts her head and then shakes it slightly from side to side, showing her disapproval. And then says, "Jesus, Kazan. I never know what or whom you are thinking about."

He stumbles for an explanation. "I will get the Saab," he responds.

"It's fine, Kazan! I would rather walk. I will see you when you get home."

"C'mon, Briar, it is still raining," he says, adding, "Are you sure? I am just parked behind the building."

"I am sure the walk will clear my head," Briar responds.

"Sure, but if you can just wait a second, I can get the car and drive us both home."

In the awkward silence, he thinks, *she isn't promising anything, she is not delivering anything, and she may not be going anywhere.*

The car he drives never works properly. The wiper mechanism never operates smoothly, so you are always looking through smeared and rain-streaked glass, obscuring the things that are right in front of you. It was not a comfortable means of transportation, but allowed them some quiet time alone. She sighs and then tells him he can pick her up in the front of the building. When Kazan has finally been able to retrieve the car and park it in front of the courthouse, she steps from the building into the pouring rain and toward the car. The window wipers on the aging Saab beat out at a frantic rhythm. The car is warm and dry inside.

She closes the creaking passenger door with a loud thump. He drives for a bit before looking over toward her, gathering his damp hair with his other hand while clutching the steering wheel. He has suffered a terrible day. He wants more out of life, just a little more.

I NEED TO *get into my office.*

He weaves his way through a line of zombie like smokers and mentally ill homeless men. This is the path to John Koogan's office, a small cinder block commercial space with scratched wooden floors and Persian carpets that rests high above the drop-in centre on Alberni Street. John Koogan loves to laugh, and ride his bike. But the practice of law has left him little time for himself lately.

Much of his time is taken by the long drive in from White Rock. This morning, he loaded up his late model, pewter-coloured BMW with his two battered chestnut brown litigation bags and his bicycle. His drive to downtown Vancouver is a long one. He arrives at court shortly before 10 a.m. in the morning which is a miracle given the traffic. He is greeted outside of the courthouse by Lee Anderson, who is also late for court.

"Hey, Koogan, are you going to the party tonight?"

"I fucking hate those retirement parties," he says.

"I hate those things too," responds Lee Anderson.

"Might drop by for one drink," he promises. Koogan smiles. "You know who else is going?"

His question goes unanswered as he drags his litigation suitcases out of the back of his car. They hit the ground at the same time.

"I hear Smith is sitting in 103 today. I just can't get a break lately," chirps Koogan.

Koogan is dressed in a dark navy suit with a crisp colourful tie he purchased in Paris. He is still "the working man's lawyer." Anderson admires him for still caring and finds him to be a unique blend between a vaudeville stunt man and a serious criminal lawyer.

He responds, "I will go if you do. I hear that Stirling might come and bring his new associate. You know what those things are like, after everyone has had a few drinks in them. You know, people start to get real, Koogan. Just one drink?" Anderson is now in full on bargaining mode.

Koogan makes his way to the front of the courthouse from the parking lot. The hallways are jammed with the accused and some bored kids on a school trip to see how justice is done. Kazan greets him in the lobby of the courthouse.

"Have you heard the news?"

"What news?" responds Koogan.

"Smith has arrived and is holding court in 103," Kazan says.

Koogan indicates, "When I woke up this morning, I kind of knew it was going to be one of those days."

Kazan looks at him like he is staring at a feeble man asked to swim the English Channel in a November storm.

"Unlucky bastard! I am just an unlucky bastard," Koogan mutters under his breath.

Kazan lets out a chuckle and makes Koogan smile, and both men enjoy a laugh. Koogan meets his client outside of the 103.

"Have you been here long? Have we been called yet?"

"No, I just got here, had to get someone to look after the kids," she says.

They push the door open, taking a second to bow to the presiding justice and stopping long enough to find a row of empty seats halfway down the centre of the courtroom. His client is shaking and appears confused by the others in the courtroom. Koogan is unparsed by the landscape and walks in casting a smile to the court staff who greet him back with a nod of their heads.

Koogan is well liked wherever he goes. He is famous for his generosity and his great sense of humour. When he was a young lawyer, some misunderstood his manic behaviour and dry sense of wit as insulting, but now he is greeted with smiles by everyone except Justice Smith. Koogan and his client sit down and he leans over to whisper something into his client's ear.

"Are you sure you want to plead today? It might be better next week. This judge is known to be a bit of a moron, and I don't think he is our best call."

His client shakes her head and assures him that she just wants to get things over with today, and she is okay with probation, as they had discussed. Koogan tells her that probation is not a given, and that this judge is a bit of a wild card. Again, the client tells him that she just wants to go home and that she feels sick.

"Let's just get this over with!"

Koogan is not easily intimidated. When he first appeared in court, he would never plead a client in front of someone he had not appeared before or trusted. Smith fell into both categories. Koogan understands that as much as his client wants to end this stress, there are no guarantees that she will be going home tonight to look after her children. He looks up and sees an elderly woman with schizophrenia being taken into custody in handcuffs. Her counsel, an out of town lawyer from Kelowna, looks troubled and surprised by the sentence just passed by Smith.

"Are you still hoping to enter a plea today?" asks the Crown.

"Well, perhaps I should just confirm things with my client," responds Koogan.

"Sure, we can hold your matter down then, until you have spoken with her."

Koogan puts his hand on his client's shoulder and whispers into her ear, "Let's go outside and make sure we want to plead today, you can see that the judge is not in a good mood."

As soon as Koogan has turned around, Smith growls from the bench, "Are you here to plead today, Mr. Koogan? I mean, is your client here to enter a plea?"

Before he can respond, his client has nodded her head and despite her headache and abdominal pain, she has stepped forward toward the gate that separates counsel from the body of the court.

"There are four counts on the information, what counts is your client prepared to enter pleas to, Mr. Koogan?"

The Crown then takes the initiative and with sensing the hesitation of his client, signals they are expecting pleas to Count One and Two on the information. The client begins to complain of being sick to her stomach. Koogan begins to also feel a tightness in his chest and a dryness in his throat. It all happens so fast, in a system that runs so slow. A small young Filipino girl has now pled guilty to assault and mischief for throwing a cell phone at her probation officer in a Safeway. The facts are read and the admissions are made, and the sentencing is placed into Smith's hands.

Koogan picks up on the annoyance transmitted by Smith. Sentencing is a craft, and Koogan knows all too well that rushing to judgment serves no one, and so he dutifully asks that sentencing be adjourned in preparation of a pre-sentence report. But Smith is not listening anymore, and wants to end the case right now, as his mind is made up.

"What are you submitting, Mr. Koogan?"

Despite his excellent sentencing submissions and stone cold reliance on undisputed case law, Judge Smith and his mood swings impose a sentence of sixty days in jail and two years' probation upon the rapidly deteriorating young girl whose soft speech has slid down to the point that neither Smith nor Koogan can hear her. She is pulled away from him toward the cells located in the damp and cold basement. A banging of the cell bars are overheard when the door leading away from the courtroom is opened.

"Nothing further, Mr. Koogan?" barks Smith.

"No," Koogan says and he begins to pack up his briefcase.

His anger is now on display for the entire courtroom. His suit has now become wrinkled, and he looks demoralized. He manages a soft revengeful smile when he leaves the courtroom. He runs into Lee outside of the courtroom. He is shaking his head, visibly upset about what he has just witnessed.

"Why don't you appeal him? That was ridiculous. Perhaps you can get one of the Crowns to agree to bail pending appeal?"

Koogan delivers a look of bewilderment. He knows the paperwork will not be able to be completed and heard before the sentence is served.

"He is not a judge!" Koogan shouts.

Anderson responds with a nervous laugh and both men walk through the maze of people that make up the courthouse triangle.

HYMAN KAZAN
18
BRITISHCOLUMBIA

THE PARTY FOR Judge Stephen Douglas is winding down and the empty wine bottles have begun to pile up. The hard core drinkers and the lonely remain. Koogan thinks he is drunk, having drunk enough wine to get through the evening. He is now following Marianne. He is mesmerized by her slender figure and tight black dress, and her shiny auburn hair. *God, she is beautiful. So young and vibrant, so innocent.* He moves through to the kitchen area of the home. He wants to touch her. He should leave her alone, but can't. She should not have shown up at this event in that kind of dress. She opens the French doors that lead out to the swimming pool area, steps out, and looks over her shoulder. She is now in the backyard, and they are alone. The air is cool and fresh, and a breeze comes down from the mountains.

"Koogan, come here," she says.

He is unsure as to where this is going, but offers no resistance to the unfolding of events. The edge of the swimming pool is bathed in a rich golden light offered up by the hanging decorative Chinese lanterns. There is a blood orange moon hanging in the sky. The sounds from the inside of the house are muffled and they feel far away.

"Kiss me hard, John," she purrs.

He takes her soft lips into his and bites the edges of her mouth. He tells her he wants her. The wine he has drunk causes him to take advantage of his luck, and then she begins to kiss him more and more, and then she pushes him into the small swimming pool changing house. She tastes and smells like a tropical fruit. The heat from her body sends an electric shock through his. He pushes her hard against the side of the cabanas wall so he can lift her up and place her legs around his waist. Suddenly, she takes a step back from their embrace. She is now scrambling to remove her skirt. His eyes focus on her deep brown eyes and hair as it falls into her face.

"Hold me up," she whispers into his ear.

And he attempts to gain his balance. She is so agile. She exhales and manages to tug at his cock as she pushes him into her. He staggers to keep himself inside of her, but because she is so light and he has such a grip on her hips, there is no danger of her falling. She is now biting his lips and moaning. He is now coming.

"Marianne! Marianne, Mare! Oh my God! This shouldn't have happened!"

Over her shoulder, he sees an outside light being switched on, his body shudders with each movement of her hips. The light casts a glow on both of their hot bodies, and makes their rhythm increase in intensity. She tries to hide herself in him, and tugs at his shirt while he tugs at her smooth well-trimmed buttocks.

"Fuck me! Fuck me!" she calls out.

He hears the sound of the sliding back door open, he is so close. The door is then closed. They both are now exhausted by their love making. Seconds later, the outside light is switched off. Marianne is now seated on the floor, looking up at him. She now regains her balance and begins to stand up, struggling to find her dress and torn underwear.

"Do you think they missed us?"

"Jesus. I don't think they care," he says. "I certainly didn't miss them."

"Did we just make a mistake, John?"

He is without thought of consequence and chooses to ignore the question.

"Are you still living in White Rock?"

"Yes," he responds.

"I thought you hated it and you were going to move to Whistler?" she asks.

"I know, I didn't see my life ending up this way. No one ever does."

"You didn't think you would be still practicing law or going to these retirement parties?"

"Both. I didn't think I would be spending time with those fools inside," he answers.

"You are not," she says, and a wide smile grows larger across her face.

He is starting to sober up now. The night air is damp and cool. He wants to tell her how much he loved being with her, but her back is turned to him, and she seems to be attempting to shake off that which just happened.

"I guess we should go back in there and face the music," she says.

"The music is offbeat there, and I want to tell you that I love you," he offers up.

"Don't feel you have to, John," she says.

This is all she has to say. He has given her his best, and now she is swaying back and forth and adjusting her dress, preparing to go back in and find another glass of wine.

"Fuck it."

Koogan pulls up his pants and finds his belt loops, stepping back to catch a view of the night sky, and thinks that it is much easier to leave a party that is winding up, than to return to a dead one. He follows her back to the sliding door from which they had made their escape. She pulls the door open and he steps back inside the hallway leading to the kitchen, stopping to splash some cold water on his face in the second level powder room.

Marianne has now disappeared from his view, but as fate would have it, he runs into the judge's wife who is en route to the bathroom too. Julia has a familiar face, one that is common to the area, sort of like the girl next door. When he smiles at her, she smiles back. He can't imagine why she is with the older judge. He can imagine her staring up at the ceiling from their four poster bed, wondering why she had made such a grave mistake. She has that look, it is as if she is drowning, knowing that all of the younger men in the room are feigning friendship in the hopes of landing the vacant judge's position.

He makes his way back to the comfort or lack therein of the kitchen, to be met with the large shadow of Judge Douglas, who asks him if he is enjoying the party. Koogan coughs and then begins to tell the story of a bicycle trip he had taken in Iceland. He is swift and tactful, breaking into the story in an attempt to divert any suspicion caused by his earlier absence. His language is that of denial and survival, or perhaps it is an attempt to find something in common with his host. The judge is having none of it. Refusing to pay any attention to Koogan is a skill he has developed over the past several years, and he is unable to focus on him now.

He sees Marianne rejoin the party, and her arrival back is a welcome sight. Her entrance strikes him as funny; her clothes look disheveled and torn. The judge is unimpressed by her return, and he is outwardly rejecting her now as being an unwelcome guest. The moment is completely absurd.

Kazan's face, when he sees the expression on Judge Douglas' face, gives him away immediately, as he is delighted by the obvious disgust of Douglas. He thinks that Marianne has transformed this dull event into a real pleasure to attend. Stupid retirement parties filled with bullshit praise offered by the less tolerated, and her little rendezvous with Koogan blasted the ever present judicial arrogance out of the water and filled the room with unexpected comedy.

When it comes down to it, it is harder to ignore the sucking up to power, than to turn away from the scene presented by Marianne. The more these morons attempted to act judicial, the more they exposed themselves to Kazan. But now he is pleased that a light has been cast upon those in the room who have been exposed by this ridiculous scene. He could choose to ignore it. He chooses instead to celebrate it, and the games that are going on for the majority of the evening.

A car engine is heard. The car's timing mechanism seems to have been broken. The sound of tires coming up the gravel driveway can be heard from inside the home. The sound of a passenger door being slammed soon follows. The click of high heels can be heard on the grey and green flagstone, getting louder with each step.

"Kazan!"

"I'm over here," he says.

"Jesus, Kazan, you were supposed to meet me at Bridges for drinks after work. I waited for hours, no call, nothing. What were you thinking?" Briar has made a grand entrance to a party she was not invited to.

"I forgot, I am so sorry. I just stopped for one drink and then . . ."

Her upset makes him feel ashamed. The perfect ending to his day and now his lack of respect for her is on display for everyone to see. She is still wearing her coat and flashes of a white starched blouse peeks out from the unbuttoned collar of the coat, her brown eyes and high cheekbones make her one of the most attractive women in the room. Her slender body looks rigid and youthful.

"I want to get out of here, let's go home," he says.

"But the party's just starting," says Douglas, who has suddenly appeared with a grin from ear to ear.

"Not for us," and with that, Briar climbs onto the edge of Kazan's chair with the Saab key fob in hand.

"I am thinking you could use a glass of wine," Douglas booms.

"What do you have?" asks Briar.

"I just opened a 1967 Villa Antinori Toscana," a grinning Douglas responds.

"What's the occasion?" she asks.

"Your arrival. It has been long overdue."

"I guess so. Kazan, are you alright to drive?"

Briar pretends to care about his response. She blushes and turns to Douglas.

"Me? OH, yeah," answers Kazan.

She extends her hand and takes hold of the stem of the wine glass that has been filled to the brim by Douglas, her grimace begins to evaporate from her face.

"Careful, the glass is quite full."

"It all depends on how you view it, I guess."

"I suppose it does," answers back Douglas.

HYMAN KAZAN

19

BRITISH COLUMBIA

A RUSH OF anger engulfs Kazan, and he is in a rage. He has finally taken a few hours to review all of the evidence that surrounds Simon Westfall's death. He has reviewed the hours of videotape from the Hotel Georgia and the witness statements from the hotel guests, staff and those sober enough to recall the Justice dinner. It is clear to him that Simon died as a result of a quantity of carfentanil provided by Justice Smith.

"Smith. Smith. Justice Craig Donald Smith!"

He is at a loss as to how to deal with breaking the news to Briar and instructing the police as to how and when to make their arrest. Will he just look like the jealous lover who has been rejected in favour of a respected member of the judiciary? Has Smith already concocted an iron clad defense with the aid of his judicial buddies? He stands at the crossroads of how to ensnare this blight on both his life and the judicial system. He spends long hours staring at the contents of the overstuffed brown banker's box that sits on the edge of his desk. He sees a packed courtroom in his daydreams, filled with a gossiping defense counsel and laughing cops. His anxiety is raised to an unbearable level as he is unsure if the image of the courtroom has himself in the prisoners' dock or Smith.

His cell phone and office phone trigger a fear that is foreign to him. He chooses to ignore the constant calls triggered by his inaction. Instead, the pressure increases by the day, and by the hour. He now shakes and is finding sleep impossible. When he is honest with himself, he knows his inaction is like a portal into the darkness, causing the pressure and anxiety to build and build. It begins to devour his soul, and he knows it.

Years later, Briar will wonder why he kept these emotional burdens to himself. It will seem like a nightmare that could have been dealt with by others including the police, but instead Kazan buried it away deep into his terror filled subconscious. She will be amazed on how much of the case was constructed by Kazan without the aid of the other lawyers in his office.

The rain is now falling hard on his windshield. The bankers box that houses the case against Smith rests on the passenger seat. Kazan does not know where he is driving to or why. He thinks to himself that he should drive over to Smith's residence with Briar and release himself from this tension through a well thought out confrontation with police present. He turns the knob that controls the heat in the car in an attempt to stop shaking. His body is rigid now and he feels the need for a drink to calm his nerves. He glances up to his rear view mirror and is blinded by the high beam lights of a car directly behind him. Then for a second, he thinks that it is a vehicle he recognizes as Smith's Mercedes. Suddenly, the threat passes him, and he realizes the car is being driven by an elderly Chinese woman. His mouth is dry and his heart is exploding as he grabs the wheel of his car and steadies himself against any further real or perceived threats. He reaches for his cell phone and dials the number for Marianne Cummings.

"Still interested in some part-time prosecution work?" he says.

"Sure, if you think your office will okay it."

But Kazan has already decided that he has already ruined one woman's life and now has chosen to potentially ruin others.

"Just a second. I am driving and need to pull off the road."

Kazan shifts the car down into third gear and looks for a safe place to turn off the highway. He is barely onto the gravel shoulder when he regrets making the phone call. When did he become so afraid of losing a case or taking on a corrupt judge? Kazan knows he should not disclose the entire case over the phone as it will only raise questions later, if the case is ever appealed or subject to judicial review.

"Trinity Rivers Residential School's headmaster is guilty of rape! Are you interested?"

"Rape? Sure, but what about the other lawyers in your office?"

"Regional director says there is money for outside help, are you in?"

"Sounds great, but when?"

"Next week. Are you in?"

"Sure, Kazan."

"But I need to tell you something."

"What?"

"Smith is the judge. And there might be a case out there against him, some day!"

A rush of adrenaline surges through Kazan's veins and the adrenal rush causes his head to spin. He then realizes that he has crossed the line, he has passed into the opposite lane into oncoming traffic with this disclosure. He realizes that she is almost as eager as he is to successfully prosecute Smith. It all happens so fast, this aching desire to disclose the results of the investigation into Westfall's death to someone far removed from it. Someone outside of his office.

"What have you got on Smith?" she asks.

"Video-tape, tox reports, witness statements," he sputters out the bare bones of the case against Smith. "He is going down!" he says. "I really think that we got him." He takes a moment to catch his breath, then asks the question that he knows the answer to. "Are you interested in bagging a judge?"

There is a long pause at the end of the line. He is unsure if he has gone too far. She assures him that he has not gone too far. He talks a bit more before hanging up and pulling back onto the highway.

Briar will be angry that she was not the first person he talked to about the case against Smith. It is hard to not speak to her about the case, but his mind is flooded with questions. What if she was a potential witness? What if Smith would call on her to offer up some type of alibi? He feels the strong need for a drink even more now. For the next couple of hours, he will drive around alone in the night in search of a quiet beachside bar. He decides to take refuge in the rainy night to gather up the right words to convince Briar of her lover's guilt. This causes him more and more tension and hurt: this putting off the suffering only adds to it.

For with what judgment ye judge, ye shall be judged and with what measure ye mete, it shall be measured to you again.

Matthew 7:1-3

SMITH STRUGGLES WITH the concept that he is responsible for Simon's death. He does feel that he is now vulnerable, should anyone discover that they were together that fateful night at the Hotel Georgia. He is now alone in his Point Grey condominium, sick to his stomach, thinking about how that night had gone down. The coke was spiked and he should have never removed it from the court exhibits. His mind races as he tries to understand why he survived and Simon did not. Did he have a weak heart? Did he take in more of the drug than him? He attempts to grab hold of something to solve the mystery. But there is nothing to grab hold of. He has to figure a way out of this mess! He has so much to lose.

Who can he confide in? Smith struggles to recall the night's events. He has no idea how to explain how this younger man died in his hotel room and how he had attempted to drop him off at the clinic in the hopes of covering his tracks. Reality and fiction can become blurred in a desperate second. Video cameras were everywhere; the hotel lobby, the Justice dinner, and even the parking garage at the hotel are now dangerous chess pieces on a board that is closing in on him. He will now do anything to take back his lack of discretion. Maybe he can explain that it was Simon who brought the drugs to his room? Then again, there is no easy explanation as to why he came to his room in the first place. His head pounds and he begins to shake when he attempts to conjure up some believable story that will make sense.

Smith now walks the flour white plaster hallways of his condo, looking like a cornered harbour rat in a rusty old tanker taking on dirty water. He has to find an unexpected volunteer to take the fall for him. This course of action had always worked for him in the past. He will now have to go to his much overused playbook in a feeble attempt to save his life and reputation.

He mutters to himself, "The secret is in the details, the particular! That which will be found or discoverable, and that which is left behind, that which can and will be overlooked."

He painstakingly goes over in minute detail, the tragic events of the night in his mind's eye. Searching for some little fact or detail that will spring his trap laddered fate, allowing the door to his freedom to swing open. Still muttering to himself, Smith reaches for his coffee cup on the coffee table in front of the couch where he is seated and takes a drink of the acidic cold coffee residue that is left in the cup from when Briar had unexpectedly dropped by. He only takes a small mouthful and spits it out, when it comes to him.

"The sugar packet!"

The damn evidence of the drug is still in the hotel room! He must get rid of this loose end. He feels the rush of both anxiety and adrenaline as he plots his next move. He scurries from the living room to his kitchen and quickly seeks out the beige kitchen landline. His mouth is dry and he is shaking as he dials the number. He hopes that Briar will understand why he is asking her to join him at the hotel. Another deep breath, and then much to his surprise, he hears a familiar male voice at the end of the line.

"Kazan! I was expecting Briar." He is lost for words as his chubby fingers fiddle with the phone. "This is Craig Smith. I wanted to speak about our situation." Smith is taken back by this change of events, but decides to press on with the cards fate has dealt him. "I was thinking we could meet for a drink to iron out things, you know, like we used to, back in the day!" Smith searches for some convincing argument to bring Kazan onto his side with the idea of a meeting. "One drink, Kazan, that is all I am asking." There is an urgency to his pleas.

There is a long pause on the other end of the line, and then Kazan responds, "Okay, one drink. Where do you want to meet?"

Smith lets out a gasp of air. "How about the Hotel Georgia? Downtown in about an hour? Does that work for you?"

Kazan glances at his watch and wonders what will this meeting between him and the man he loathes accomplish. It is not like he has anything to really say to Smith. Briar had made it all so clear that he is the forerunner in this mockery of a charade that has become their relationship.

"Please come, just for one drink. I feel so bad about sneaking around behind your back," Smith calmly pleads with Kazan. "Briar wants this to go as smoothly as possible, you know it does not have to be a battle between us? I promise just one drink," he pants.

Kazan rubs his forehead and stands alone for a minute, hearing the shower running in the other room. Kazan hates these moments where he is forced to decipher the puzzle of Briar's life without her knowledge or participation. He contemplates calling out to her that Smith is on the phone, and then decides to spare her the stress of it all.

"One drink then, in one hour," he responds.

Just as Kazan is hanging up on Smith, Briar is slipping out of the shower, her hair wrapped in an oversized white terry cloth towel, the steam still seeping out from the open glass shower door. He watches her find her way into her matching bathrobe that rests on the bathroom door.

"What is it, Kazan?" Briar asks.

Kazan walks toward her and squeezes her shoulder.

"Smith called. He wants to meet for a drink."

"I see," Briar closes her eyes. "The three of us or just you and him? I just think we should talk first." Briar reaches up and touches Kazan on the side of his face. "I told you he just wants peace. He is a good man, Kazan. You have misjudged him."

Kazan shakes his head. Briar struggles to fight off her fears as to how this might end, tears are now streaming down the side of her face, and she tries to compose herself, but she can't. She feels like she should have never let things get so out of hand. She wants to just disappear to the beach.

She wants to turn back the clock to the times when she and Kazan were so very happy.

"I will be back in a couple of hours, Briar. Don't worry, I will be civil."

Kazan turns away from her. She goes over to the balcony and watches him get into his car parked on the street and drive away. She is flushed with both anger and frustration about not hearing the words she hoped Kazan would have said. She knows perfectly well that this is a bad idea. She knows that while both men have worked for many years in the adjudication of the problems of others, both lacked judgment when it came to themselves.

HE STARES INTO his dark empty eyes. He is feeling the power of his uncontrollable rage. The muscles down his arm twitch with excitement. His compulsion is to punch him directly between the eyes. He is suddenly in a full and complete rage, blinded by his hatred and disgust for Smith. His heart is pounding, and his focus narrows to his fat double chin and neck. He can feel his jugular throb on the side of his neck in his hands. He is fully committed to the idea of snapping his neck. It would be so easy and so justified. It would rid the world and the justice system of a complete tyrant.

He hears that familiar voice deep inside his head say, "Maybe now you get it, for the penalty to fit the crime. To reap what you sow!"

He sits there in front of the Hotel Georgia, dreaming about how good it would feel to solve this problem in both his private and personal life. They both become merged into that dark line between his hatred for Smith and his desire to have him deal with the truth. The daunting question is, why does Smith want to see him? Why does Smith want to meet him at the same hotel where Simon gasped for his last breath? He knows that it is futile to reason with him. He knows that Briar will not trust his account of the meeting. He is now struggling with keeping his footing on the icy path leading to anger and torment. Kazan has played out this meeting so many times in his mind. He wonders whether or not he should follow up on this insane request to meet. He bristles at the thought of being a coward who fails to show up. He does not trust himself with being alone with Smith on unfamiliar ground.

Briar hopes that they can work out their differences, that the two men can reach some sort of agreement on how their lives can move forward, but she has no knowledge on Smith's role in Simon Westfall's death.

It is as if the brief beam of sunshine shining through his windshield is bringing on a twinge of reason, causing him to reject the idea of going into the hotel. If Smith wants a meeting, then they will have a meeting, but it will be on Kazan's terms, not his! Alone seated in his car, he is plunged into the quest to find a solution to his problems. With no safety net, or sense of how Briar will react to the fact that Smith was responsible for Simon's death, he feels the darkness of his own mine shaft of despair begin to draw him in. He knows it comes down to what particular fact or truth she will seize upon. He knows that he will have to marshal the evidence and facts, and present the truth to her. And he knows that he is running out of time.

He already understands that Smith will wrap himself up in the blanket of privilege and opportunity. What he does not know is how the roots of evil over time shoot through the stony ground of pomp and tradition. The wisdom afforded the judiciary might fool some, but it can also crumble under the forces of arrogance and his demonstrated lack of concern for justice.

After the passing of a few minutes, as he processes the stupidity of agreeing to meet, as the anger and need for revenge subside, he feels a sense of relief. It is common sense. It will be him, not Smith, who will decide when they will confront the truth.

HYMAN KAZAN

22

BRITISH COLUMBIA

DAYS BEFORE, WHEN they arrive home, Briar complains of a splitting headache, and she quickly goes to the medicine cabinet. Then she takes the only meds she can find: some valium that Kazan has left sitting near the sink. Her face is grey with disappointment. She quickly slips out of her dress and undergarments, and stands naked on the damp bathroom mat. She turns and speaks to him briefly. He had left the retirement party before her, before things got out of hand. It was obvious she had taken an alternative route home.

Her eyes are red rimmed and bloodshot. She has difficulty speaking clearly. He turns the water stained tap and pours some water for her to take the pills. By the time the glass is filled, Briar is asleep on their unmade bed. Briar is still naked, half drunk, and half asleep from the combination of the alcohol and the medication. An endless drizzle falls outside. He had driven himself home soon after she arrived at the retirement party. He had heard the sound of his own footsteps as they had traversed the crushed sea shell gravel road that led to their apartment. The sparkles and flicks of shell that were observable on her knees and cheeks, indicated that she had not been so successful. The wind gusted and blew all the plantings outside of their apartment and the waves were energized by a northern gale.

Kazan and Briar had come to Vancouver in search of a chance at renewal. Kazan wanted a simple change of scenery because it was warmer than anywhere else in Canada, at least that was what he had told his friends and acquaintances. Briar had come to British Columbia to feed her sense of adventure and romance. As it turned out, neither were entirely successful.

Their condominium resembles a green room from some low rent, off Broadway theatre. There are clothes and shoes everywhere. A dim light shines over their fireplace. The pallet knife painting that hangs over their fireplace hides deep colours of red and yellow. Kazan settles into the mission style oak chair overlooking the staircase leading to the wide verandah style balcony. From there, he can see Marianne has driven her late model Volkswagen over to their apartment. She is observed sliding out from the driver's side door before making her way to the front of the building. A rogue wind shakes her hair as she stands outside, keying in the code for the condominium. He stands inside the apartment, listening to the sound of the chimes ringing from the lobby, and thinking, *who the hell is ringing our apartment now?* His nervous habit causes him to draw his fingers through his hair, pushing it back toward the top of his head, revealing the salt dusted air that has been captured in it.

The ocean salt, it is everywhere, he ponders. This is a reminder to him, why he has come to the West Coast in the first place, his love of the ocean. He loves everything about the sea, its vastness, the way that it is so powerful and deep. They say that humans are 60% made up of water, so isn't it logical that we all would be drawn back to the very substance that is our life blood? The deep. Like him, the Pacific Ocean holds its secrets as it carves through both sand and rock to feed living creatures and nourish the nautical plant life that keeps the beach in check. The blood flowing through our veins is much the same, travelling through the miles of arteries and passing through our tissues to sustain our brain and heart. Water is life, uncontrollable and unpredictable.

Kazan continues to daydream. Most people never take time to listen to the sound of the ocean or their own heartbeat. He has decided from the beginning to be the type of person who grasps the moment, who understands gravity, whose spirit is not blocked. He takes a deep breath and feels oxygenated from the ocean air. The cold rain on his face awakens him from his surroundings. He closes the patio doors and hears the sound of the tide replaced by the sound of the security codes still chiming.

The early morning sun attempts to peek out from behind the dove grey clouds and gather in their living room. Marianne takes a step back and raises her head to allow her to see the top of the balcony window. Across the road, dark green breakers pound the beach. A few days ago, she had stopped by in the hopes of catching Kazan alone. Marianne had come to find him, to discuss one of the cases that she was working on with Koogan. She always found him to be able to distill a case down to its very essence, those important principles or information that would result in the case being successful or failing. He also had a calm demeanor. When the bullets were flying, Kazan became even more calm and cool, taking on a kind monk or spiritual leader type of quality. It was like chaos transformed him. It softened him.

Marianne opens the front door to the apartment building and dances her way into the lobby, jumping over the bend in the well-worn area carpet. Kazan greets her as the wind propels the glass door shut behind her. She is excited to see him and he is pleased to have her seek him out, that is always the way with her, to seek out Kazan in times of both personal or professional turmoil. She has been gripped by feelings of inadequacy from the start. She dislikes her appearance and thinks that her legal success comes from some unexplained cosmic luck or her ability to manage men, to whom she ambushes with her charm. It is her way of being equal with all genders, and now she is wanting Kazan to be her partner. And she despises Briar.

She finds a place to sit on the edge of a grey sectional placed in front of the fireplace in the lobby. When he arrived, she placed her arms around his neck and kissed his face. Now she remembers how strong he felt as she wrapped herself around him. He seems a much younger man than she had remembered, and she weaved her long fingers in his. The edge of her thumb traced the base of his hand, until their fingers were nestled together. She adores Kazan, and she admires his ability to speak calmly and honestly about any topic.

When they had first met, she had thought that they would have become lovers, but again that was long before she had met Briar. She had told herself again and again that eventually Kazan and Briar would flame out, and then she would be left holding on to him. She would then never again be forced to say goodbye. He also indulges this fantasy; he needs his desire for her in order to have some illusion of love or control.

Marianne kisses him again and holds on tightly. "Are you alone? Where the hell is Briar?"

"She is upstairs, trying to sleep off the retirement party. Can I help you with something?" Kazan says. "I am just on my way out, if you would like to grab a coffee with me? We can talk over things there, if you want."

Bean Brothers, a local coffee shop, is just around the corner from the apartment, and it will give them the privacy they both seek. A chance to shut out all the noise that comes between them, and provide a safe and welcome distance from Briar.

The apartment is dark when he finally returns. The shutters are shut except for those that are in the dining room. Briar is seated at the table, reading a case file he had forgotten to place in his briefcase. Crime scene photographs are splayed out on the dining room table.

"What kind of a man treats a woman like this?" she says, gazing down at the file in front of her. "He broke her nose while she was holding onto a baby."

Kazan just smiles and shakes his head. The common place of his work product escapes her. Briar walks over to the espresso maker and begins to make herself a double shot. She then opens the fridge door and peers into it. The fridge is empty except for some wilted lettuce and a half bottle of a lemony sauvignon blanc. Half bottles of salad dressings adorn the shelves, their size and shapes look like Christmas ornaments on an abandoned goodwill Tannenbaum.

"Have you had dinner? It looks like we have nothing here," she says.

"What do you feel like?" Kazan asks. "There is a new Ethiopian restaurant that just opened down on Laurel Street."

"The fuckin fridge is empty and you suggest that I eat with my hands?" barks Briar.

"I could make you a sandwich if you like? There is some old cheddar cheese in the crisper at the bottom of the fridge and some cucumbers hidden away at the back of the fridge."

His offer of pulling together a lunch style dinner falls short.

"I would like to go out," she says. "This place is closing in on me! I would like to go somewhere nice for a change. I thought perhaps we could go to Bouquet Garni on fourth. Eat some real food, and have a drink for a change."

"A drink, don't you think you had enough last night?" Kazan says.

"Maybe," she replies. "A change of scenery would do us both good. Unless you have other plans? I don't want to cramp your style," she grins with the sarcasm she has served up.

She then flops down on a chair in the living room. He takes out the quarter full bottle of sauvignon blanc and tips it to his mouth, taking a full gulp of the three day old wine before addressing her.

"When did it become so damn difficult, Briar?"

"Difficult," she quips.

"Yeah, so fucking hard to get along with you."

"What?" she says.

"Us, you know we were once so connected," Kazan replies.

"I think we better stop this," Briar warns.

"Do you even remember how we were? We couldn't take our hands off each other."

"What happened?" she says finally.

"Can you tell me what the hell happened?"

All he wants her to do is to stand up, admit that she has screwed up, look him in the eye, and shake it off, but no. He moves across the room and slowly sits down, looking out the window at the Pacific. His hand finds the lines on his forehead. He feels his arteries and the valves of his heart tighten.

"I am sorry, I didn't mean that. I mean, I miss us. It doesn't matter anymore."

"What? Please don't say that," Briar's voice is now shaky.

Briar reaches out for his hand and starts to cry.

"Oh, Briar. I have tried to deal with this the best that I could, but you know, I didn't want to believe this would happen." Kazan is now surprised by this bearing of his soul.

She just stands there silent and nods her head and begins to sob harder. He has to get out of there as soon as he can. He just can't deal with her anymore. He has to tell Briar he can no longer go on like this. It is killing him.

The beach facing their apartment is windswept and poked by driftwood, branches of tangled wood washed ashore by the wind and rain. He looks at the seagulls flying overhead, and allows his mind to wander. He walks down the beach, feeling alone, feeling the salty wind off the ocean. He looks out to the emptiness of the sea. There is something so meditative about the ocean, and he feels safe and calm. Briar is still inside the apartment, sure to be banging about.

His father had a similar relationship with Kazan's mom. Every Sunday afternoon, these types of arguments would happen. Midday, he would hear his mother's voice begin to get louder, as if they were gladiators attempting to prepare themselves for the fighting that would lead up to Sunday dinner. The arguments would go on for hours, and then it would become quiet. His father would leave their house. Staring out the living room window, he would drink a glass of scotch and tell the lost child Kazan that everything was going to be alright. Nothing was going to be alright, and the family was slowly disintegrating. Finally, the arguments went silent and his father was gone.

Kazan does not want to return to the apartment yet. He wants to stay in the calmness of the outdoors, teetering on the edge of things. He feels suffocated by his situation. He walks further and further down the beach. On the edge of his neighbourhood, he runs into some unemployed actors who have rented places while they look for work in North Hollywood. Briar is friends with most of them that year, and so Kazan, while not knowing their names, is familiar with their faces. He smiles at them, hoping to mask his unhappiness and avoid any unnecessary conversation. The wind begins to pick up and dark clouds drift over the mountains.

It suddenly occurs to him that like his own father, he has chosen to simply walk off, rather than deal with things at home. The lonely beach and dark skies paint out a scene that resembles his own emotional turmoil. He takes a few more steps and then turns around to make his way back to the apartment. He hums the words to a song whose title escapes him as he traverses the shoreline home. *Funny how some tunes just stick in your head,* he thinks. Perhaps the notes confirm to him that he has finally acknowledged that he is trapped in a relationship that just does not work anymore. Then he hears her angry voice over the roar of the tide and the cries of the seagulls.

"Are you coming back?" Briar's voice echoes along the strand.

The sand below his feet has begun to shift, and he steps on a piece of driftwood, causing his ankle to roll. He turns his face away from the wind and waves back to Briar who is perched on their balcony overlooking the beach. An electric shock runs through the tendons of his ankle, and he feels a sharp pain.

She looks so alone and windblown as she stands against the grey cedar clapboard of the apartment. She wears one of his cotton dress shirts with a fine blue stripe and a pair of Birkenstocks, holding together the top of the shirt with her other hand.

"Kazan, are you coming back?"

What is he to do? He has nowhere to go and nowhere to return to. *I guess we can try to get back to us,* he thinks to himself. A flash of silver aluminum appears in the ebony plum skies overhead, a jet marked for the SeaTac airport. *They are the lucky ones,* he thinks, *at least they know whether they are coming or going.* Briar smiles and looks down at him and then walks back into the apartment, shutting the French doors behind her.

HYMAN KAZAN

23

BRITISH COLUMBIA

THE FIRST TIME Kazan ever saw Briar, she was wearing a tailored Italian dark suit and was drinking a glass of wine while attempting to look interested in a one-sided conversation with a software technician named Paul Quezada. He had placed himself strategically at the bar in the hopes of seducing some local girl with his dry wit, and Kazan, who was watching this foolish game from a small table overlooking the harbour, couldn't help himself from seeing how it was all to play out.

He was caught by how beautiful she was, and how her hair danced upon her shoulders from the sea breeze that crept into the restaurant every time a patron opened the door beside the overcrowded patio. He walked right over to her and stood between her and Paul. He found himself falling in love with her right then and there; he fell in love with the idea of rescuing her from everything but himself.

In the beginning, he craved her constantly; he kept losing himself in her kind face and tanned body. Her past, and even her former husband, offered no resistance. Briar liked to wear soft detailed French underwear and buttery soft boots. Her appearance energized him, and caused him to fantasize about the public places they would make hard aggressive love. Once over a third glass of wine, he had admitted to her how much he ached for her orgasm. She blushed and told him that she too fantasized about making love on his desk during office hours, while other lawyers walked up and down the hallways. She recalled the time when she was near orgasm when there was a loud pounding on his office door, alerting him to a waiting pretrial judge.

He just could not get enough of her. But as time wore on, he noticed that Briar's passion appeared to burn less bright each time they made love. She appeared distant, or preoccupied with something or someone. Her eagerness was replaced with excuses, or her eyes remained closed when he became entangled in her. It was like she travelled through space and time to be with someone else. And then the love making became more mechanical or nonexistent. They became tolerant roommates rather than lovers. This slamming the door on their passion made him feel old and mortal, and scared him about their fragile future. He remained beside her each and every night, despite the fact that he felt alone. He too imagined a life filled with romantic nights and yearned for the lover she had once been.

His thoughts races through his past relationships, and then to Marianne and some of the other younger women he has worked with or had cases against. When one of those women showed the least bit of interest in him, he felt foolish for even entertaining the thought of turning his back on Briar. The women he has shown any interest in end up confused by his advances, and after a couple of glasses of wine, they ask him what he really wants out of life or with them. He hates the paradox between his success and unhappiness.

And yes, he does not know the answer to this question. He still remains with Briar. He has been with her for the past two years. He can't believe where the time has gone. He knows that breaking up with her will result in long sessions of sobbing and uncontrolled rage. He knows that time is running out on what they mean to each other. His life is evaporating right before his eyes and so is hers.

Once, while waiting for a late-night flight to the island, he ran into one of Briar's old conquests in the airport bar. His name was Jensen Bennett, and he was a smooth thin caricature of a man, with a talkative side. He approached Kazan at the end of the bar.

He said to Kazan, "Briar is so fuckin destructive, you know she will end up killing you!" And then he shook his head and kind of chuckled.

A year into their relationship, he overheard Briar talking on the phone with someone late one night. It was only after she put the phone down that he learned that Jensen had died under mysterious circumstances. Many of Jensen's friends blamed Briar for both their break up and his early death. Kazan just wants to survive.

*   *   *

The sweet aroma of freshly ground Kona coffee floats across the bedroom as sunlight pours in from the outside window. The window to their bedroom has been left open overnight and a cool sea breeze blows into the room, causing the sheer white curtains to dance. He has come home late from the previous night and is now in search of a couple of Tylenol and some cold water. He over indulged the night before and is now paying for it. His stomach is not ready for coffee, but he feels that a strong cup of it might combat his earlier stupidity.

Kazan watches Briar push down on the French press. She cradles the glass carafe so as to not let it drop on the bedroom floor. She looks disconnected and exhausted. Her bare feet slide across the dark hardwood in the bedroom. The edge of the soft cotton shirt she is wearing catches the remaining slivers of sunlight in their room. He wants to take her up in his arms and pull her onto the bed, but her body language speaks of a desire to not be touched. On the side table beside the bed, she places a large Dutch blue ceramic mug of steaming hot coffee.

"Kazan."

"Huh."

"I thought you might need some coffee."

"Yeah, it smells fantastic," he says.

She smiles but looks down at the floor, choosing to avoid any chance of eye contact. She turns the mug so that the handle of the mug is now facing him. He places his left hand around the top of the mug and grabs the handle with his right hand.

"I have some oxy," she says.

"I think just a couple of Tylenol will do," he says.

"I wished you wouldn't come home like this, Kazan."

"Like what?" he says.

"Like you don't give a shit whether you live or die."

"Don't be so dramatic for Christ's sake," he says.

"You give me little option when I wait for you all night and then you show up like this."

He feels ashamed. He hates feeling like death and hates it when she holds it against him, like she has no part in his voluntary suicide attempt. He thinks about something that Detective Chmura once said to him, "All suicides are murders."

"I get it, you are unhappy. But for fuck's sake, so am I." Briar challenges.

Kazan is dumbfounded. He hates it when she suddenly turns on him. Briar can enter into a rage at any second.

"You know, I know about you and . . . ?" Briar attempts to project her guilt upon him. "Fuck it, doesn't matter anymore, it just doesn't matter," she snaps.

"You always do that, you know, act like you don't care," Kazan replies.

"I am trying to talk to you, can you? Are you able to have a serious conversation about this?"

"Who is trying now?" he answers.

She grabs his coffee mug that had been returned to the bedside table, and with one overhead motion, she sends the mug and its contents crashing against the headboard of the bed, spilling hot coffee across the room. He wants to escape. He hates these moments of unbridled hatred.

"Jesus, Briar. I am trying my best here." It is a lie. He has no intention of admitting his unhappiness to her in her frenzied state. He will just wait for the mushroom cloud of rage to dissipate. "Well, we've been over this too many damn times. If you don't love me anymore, why do you stay?" Kazan is now raising his voice in response to the deteriorating moment.

Briar grabs his arm and pushes him back.

"Damn it, Briar," he says. "Stop hitting me before someone gets really hurt." Kazan is getting more and more agitated.

"Do you like it?" she yells to him.

"Just stop it, Briar."

He is starting to feel the room spin and the medication he had taken for his lack of judgment is beginning to wear off. He pulls himself from the bed, and stands there naked before her. She begins to unbutton the shirt she is wearing. He touches her hair. She lets out a soft sigh.

"You are still so damn beautiful."

He kisses her neck and then feels the edges of her lips in his. She smells like lavender and the sea. The sun shines through the large window in the bedroom and catches the end of the bed and bounces off his watch on the nightstand. A rainbow of colours fill the room. She slips off the shirt she is wearing and with tears in her eyes, bends down and kisses him harder on the mouth. He feels his body rise up to greet her, then without hesitation, she flees, holding herself as she turns and walks out of the room. He gets up from the edge of the bed and finds his pants on the chair in the corner of the room. He slips on the shirt that she had been wearing seconds before, and goes outside, leaving the French balcony doors open behind him.

She turns on the shower full and it can be heard throughout the apartment. That's what she does when she wants to cry and block him out. Kazan hears the shower roar and then looks down at the tide as it begins to roll in. The sun begins to fade and dark rain clouds begin to form over the coastal mountains. Vancouver is like their relationship, unpredictable and yet filled with either promise of more light or more dread, with rainy days that will go on forever. The wind catches the balcony door and slams it shut. He reaches for the handle to the door and opens it, about the same time the shower water stops.

"Are you still here?" Briar shouts from the bathroom.

The anxiety and hurt fill his chest.

"Don't worry," he says.

"You are never really here, Kazan!" she says.

He looks back toward the bathroom door and sees her standing in the door frame, dripping wet, wrapped in a single white terry cloth towel and saying, "I can't keep doing this, Kazan."

"I know, I know, neither can I," he says.

He stands there for a second and wants to take her up in his arms again and promise her that things will be different, but he knows they are not going to change. He has no answer to this rift between progress and unhappiness.

"I have to go out, we can talk about this later," he says.

"I am not sure if I will be here when you get back," she says, and with that, he tosses on his dark blue suit jacket over his white shirt and leaves the condominium, hesitating for one second outside of their door before leaving the building.

IT IS AFTER 2 a.m. when he finally makes it back to the apartment. He switches on the light in the ensuite and watches Briar gently sleeping; she appears to be so much at peace, lying motionless in a tangled mess of sheets. The window in the room is partially open and the crisp night sea air fills the room. Her small and well-toned body is partially visible as it escapes from the pewter-coloured bedclothes. Her breathing is deep and rhythmic. He walks over to the window and takes a glance up to catch a final glimpse of the translucent silver dollar waxing crescent moon. The ocean breeze fans the curtains as he stands there in the glow of the night. It is all so peaceful. He loves these moments of pure peace and calm. He loves her, especially when she is free of any tension or anger. He wants these images to be captured forever.

He steps away from the window and switches off the bathroom light. He then tugs at his shirt and removes it by pulling it over his head rather than taking the time to unbutton it. His shirt catches his wrists, and he pulls at his belt and removes his trousers. He sits on the edge of the bed, attempting to ease his naked body below the sheets without causing her to awaken. She moves slightly in response to the shift in weight upon their mattress.

"I missed you," she says in a quiet and half asleep voice.

"Briar, it is late, go back to sleep."

"I want you," she says.

It is like he is being directed by her subconscious, and he is unsure of her expectations.

"It's late and we both need our sleep. Go back to sleep, Briar."

It is not like him to turn her down, but he does not feel like dragging the razor across his wrist later in the morning for having abandoned her, only to have returned to her bed in search of sex. He attempts to fall asleep, but is unable to do so. He gets up from the bed and makes his way to the extra room that is across from the kitchen. He pulls the high back office chair away from his desk and sits down. He thinks about working, but has no energy left to open the stack of files that are piled up on the corner of his desk. He is confused about his reasons for returning to her. He has to sort out what his next move is going to be. He has to find a place within himself where he can find peace and meaning.

His life with Briar does not resemble anything he could have dreamed. He did not want to return to the apartment, and yet he had done that as he still loves her despite her cruelty and unpredictable personality. Just once he wants to know exactly what to do. He knows that their relationship is deteriorating quickly as are his chances of finding happiness. Again, he is confronted with the paradox of emotional happiness versus a rational decision about their future. Clear thinking has taken a backseat to his unbridled love of her. He sits at his desk pondering what to do. He reaches for the bottom drawer of his desk and removes a half bottle of Glenlivet as if it were some long lost key to finding some rest. He tips the bottle to his lips and takes a long deep gulp of the amber liquid in the hopes of taking the final edges off his conundrum.

After some time, he makes his way back to the bedroom. She has returned to a state of stillness. What is he going to do? Perhaps it is the scotch, or the realization that their relationship has become toxic. Her brown hair is now fanned out on the thick feather pillow; it resembles a dark storm raging off in the distance. It is at this point that he decides his return tonight was another foolish mistake. His mind is made up. He is leaving. He closes his eyes and quickly falls asleep from exhaustion.

*   *   *

Months have passed since Kazan left and Briar wakes up around noon; the combination of having little sleep and missing him causes her to oversleep. She listens to the crystal raindrops against the bedroom window while curled up in the soft blankets that cover her bed.

It is now late November, and the wind has brought cool damp air to the lower mainland. She still walks along the beach despite the change in temperatures. She has felt his loss more with each passing day, and often stands by the shore, staring out across the bay toward the city. She will stand there alone on the beach and close her eyes and reach for his absent hand. Sometimes, in her loneliness, she will feel the presence of her late father who had passed away that past summer. His voice and spirit appeared to guide her through most of her difficult times. The sand from the beach is mixed with sea air and the wind, and it kisses sea salt upon her lips. Her hair is tangled by the wind and her eyes are filled with the signs of loneliness. It is like the years before she had met him. Her pain was real and relentless.

Briar looks over the sand dunes and elephant grass toward the western horizon and feels that she sees Kazan walking out of the mist created by the damp cool sea air. She tries to gather the strength that is required to carry on. It causes her to never look into the eyes of others, so as to not disclose her sadness. *Death,* she thinks, *steals away those moments that you try to etch into your memory but are so hurtful to summon to mind.* She cannot come to grips with how sad she feels. She misses her father and Kazan.

During these quiet times of self-reflection, she cries and casts her mind back to when Kazan had first stepped into her life. This only causes her greater pain, and makes her shout into the wind, challenging God, and questioning why she is being punished. These emotional blows cause her to lash out in order to seek some sort of emotional equilibrium. In an attempt to regain some emotional strength, she will cast her memory back to the summers they had spent together along the St. Lawrence in Charlevoix. They stayed at Le Manoir Richelieu, a large stately hotel with a castle-like appearance that felt like a mystical stone cottage in many ways, largely because of Kazan growing up in a nearby village. They would wander the long dark hallways and marvel at the huge century old stone fireplaces and rainbow streaked windows that were dotted along the side of the hotel that faced the powerful St. Lawrence.

Each room was grand in scale and appointments, largely from another period of time, that captured the spirit of pre-Confederation Quebec and the romance of the region. She thinks about the forest green cliffs and carpeted golf course fairway lawns that led up to the water's edge, where schools of believers would crocodile their way toward open water.

At night, they would dine out on rich fruit basted roast duck, and countless glasses of smooth velvety red wine before retiring to a fabulous room overlooking the sea. The windows were still the type that could be fully opened to capture the sweet night air, and she would demand that after making love, he would get up from the bed and quickly open the window to allow the fresh oxygen generated by their surroundings to be ushered into their room. It was a magical place, far from the business of the city, or the obligations that had unwittingly tracked their way into their lives.

That is what she longs for now, a place of pure escape. Anything that will allow her to feel happy again. Her body is filled with weariness and grief, and she wants the return of spontaneous laughter and white hot passion. She misses being lost in the convertible fire engine red sports car that once resembled their life together, being driven at a breakneck speed along a narrow winding ocean highway.

AS THE GREY autumn clouds hang outside of her condominium, she reaches into a pocket of her navy-coloured cardigan in search of a single wooden match and lights a fire in the hopes of warming herself. She fumbles with the worn knobs on the old tuner that sits balancing on the stack of luggage in the corner of the room. She is in search of some music to help her avoid any further self-imposed disintegration. The sound of the security system and front door buzzer pierces the silence of the room.

"Briar, are you there?"

"Yes, who is this?"

"It's me, Marianne. Can I come in?"

"Ah, okay. Can you just give me a couple of minutes? I will buzz you into the lobby."

She goes to the bedroom and removes her sweater and tugs on a soft faded pair of jeans before wiping her face with some water. She pulls at the side of her pants as she straightens herself in preparation for Marianne's arrival.

She comes in holding a bottle of scotch, and funny enough, it is the brand that Kazan was so familiar with.

"I thought you might need a drink," she murmurs.

"Sure," replies Briar.

Marianne has a long slender athletic body tucked into a pair of college aged, faded blue jeans, and walks like she is going up on stage. She resembles a racehorse trotting up to the starting gate, pulling at its bit just as it is loaded into its position before the start of a race.

"I always loved your apartment," she says. "Should you find it all too much to stay, promise me that you will give me first dibs on this place. Can I sit? I just finished coming from court. Everyone is asking about what happened, Briar."

Briar appears a bit taken back by this attempt at friendly conversation.

"Take a seat, make yourself comfortable," she says. "I'll get us some ice."

Briar goes into the kitchen and returns with two heavy glass tumblers filled halfway with crescent shaped crystal clear ice cubes. She talks, and Briar attempts to listen, and thinks how strange this would have appeared to Kazan. She keeps looking around, wondering if someone else will be entering the room. Her chestnut hair is pulled back in a ponytail, and she pulls it in and out of the rubber band that holds it in place as she talks. She appears nervous for no apparent reason.

Marianne has also suffered losses, and Kazan meant so much to her as a young lawyer in town. Like so many other young lawyers, she had started out in something akin to a concrete sweatshop in Toronto, and had soon become fatigued by the lure of Bay Street. *Vancouver is going to be different,* she had thought. While the work was going to be the same, there were the snowcapped mountains and rolling tides to provide refuge from the madness, even if it was only going to be on weekends. *If I meet the right person, all the better,* she had thought.

Briar is surprised by her attendance at their apartment. Marianne is not the type of woman to be comforting female colleagues in her spare time, unless it is part of a court imposed community service order. She is more of the type to swoop in and attempt to steal a loved one while the spouse is away attending to a sick relative. She must think there is something in it for her, to drop by the condominium. Briar is running out of things to say, and the scotch has done little to take the edge off her visit.

"I am so sorry, Briar. I just don't know where to start or what to say," she offers up. "I just feel so bad about what happened."

"Why? It is not like you are to blame," Briar nervously responds.

"Really? What a hurtful thing to say, Briar!"

She watches as Briar takes a long drink of her scotch. Marianne is looking at her in a funny way. There is a glint of happiness in her eyes, almost a celebration of the hurt that Briar is feeling. She adjusts her shirt and her tanned chest peeks out, and Briar is caught by the beauty of her youth. *How uncomfortable are things going to get?* thinks Briar. Marianne grabs the clear three quarter full bottle of scotch and pours herself another drink. Briar laughs and finally discloses to her that she is quite surprised by her visit.

"Well, I know you were in love with him, don't try to deny. It doesn't matter anymore, he is gone. We are both alone now," Briar speaks with the bravado supplied by the liquor.

"Well, that is not true, Briar. You see, both Kazan and I knew you were fucking Smith."

"Fucking Smith? Jesus, what the fuck are you doing? Coming over here and bringing up Judge Smith at a time like this? What is your game plan here? Why did you come here?"

"Well, you are free now, Briar, to love or fuck anyone you like." She pushes her chair back and grabs a cigarette from her tanned leather bag. "Do you want one?" Her wrist curls and extends as she produces the small package of French cigarettes, a throwback to her early college days.

"I thought you quit?" Briar responds, shaking her head.

"I just need something to help me relax, Briar. It wouldn't hurt if you found something to get your mind off things too." Marianne is speaking with some authority now.

Her hand shakes as she places the cigarette into the corner of her mouth, skillfully avoiding smudging her dark-coloured lipstick. The smoke dangles from her mouth, and makes Briar think of how Kazan would have been attracted to her and it makes her relationship with her that much more awkward and confusing. She hates the smell of smoke, but does not want to fight further with her.

Her mind wanders to her relationship with Smith. Briar stands up and looks out toward the ocean. She begins to daydream about the time she met up with him in his office at the courthouse. Briar evaporates with her daydream of Smith. For a brief second, she can feel the surge of emotions run through her as they face each other at the corner of his desk. Smith was something new, and offered the illusion of power and money she deserved. After all, she deserved to feel inherently superior through his interest in her.

"Come closer, Briar," Smith said.

"Is this better?" she asked.

Briar felt this surrender to Smith filled the persisting moral gap that had existed between her and Kazan. The emotional toll she had been powerless to stop now screamed out and caused her to conclude she deserved to feel worse. She was more than accepting of this deluded version of herself worth perpetuated by Smith. He wrapped his thin bony arms around the small of her back and lifted her off the ground, bringing her close to his hips, and percolating pelvic girdle. His eyes sparkled with mischief.

"I am not sure if this is a good idea."

"I know it isn't," she sighed.

"I just want to feel you close, let me feel the way . . . should I stop?"

"No," Briar said.

Self-worth was contextual and she felt she had already gone too far. She smiled at him, and there was a glow of light around them as if this was how it was meant to be. She felt his arousal and the desire he had for her. His mouth tasted like bitter chocolate and coffee. Her hand shook a bit when she grabbed the back of his court shirt. She drew him closer as he started kissing her.

"I have dreamed of this moment for days," he said.

And then, she grabbed a tuft of his hair and pulled him down onto the edge of the desk. She laughed as he fumbled with his belt. She started to pull back, but his grip on her only became tighter. They looked into each other's eyes. She kissed him again and again as the intensity between them grew with each kiss. Then suddenly, there was a loud bang and a pounding on the outside of the door that led to his office.

A female voice chirped, "Hey, is Briar there? Hyman Kazan is looking for the two of you."

"Damn it," he said, adjusting his pants. "Kazan always shows up when he is least expected!"

She smiled and the light in her eyes grew brighter as he pulled himself away from her.

"I need him to be where I am, when I am," said Briar.

"I guess we better see what he wants," said Smith.

He met them in the small office reserved for pretrials between opposing counsel.

"Jesus, Briar!"

Kazan was insulted more by the playing field than the participants, but wanted to show his displeasure at this recent encounter.

"We are all adults here," he began. "It goes like this, you two can be together, if we are not together, but for Christ's sake, Briar, you can't live with me and sleep with that asshole." His face was now red as he attempted to equalize his emotions.

It all seemed to be happening too fast: the deterioration of her relationship with Kazan and this new found misadventure with Judge Smith. *Well*, she thought, *if Kazan was there for me, then I would certainly not be here with Smith.* But it was not true. The loneliness and lack of excitement and risk had vanished from her relationship, and that had caused this sudden bout of sexual awareness and passion which was now burying any hope she once had in her love with Kazan. It was a mistake, and when she closes her eyes, all she can see is the hurt and darkness that surrounds Kazan. Her body is in a state of emotional suspension, anaesthetized, cold, and empty. She needed something or someone to make her feel superior. The passion was temporary. Smith was nothing and meant nothing. Nothing is all she has now.

Her daydream continues with images of Kazan as he reached for the door knob, and pulled the door open to reveal two poorly dressed junior counsel who have been ushered in to discuss their proposed guilty plea arrangement with Smith. They appeared like teenaged voyeurs who had been caught by a familiar neighbour. There was enough shame to go around. Briar was now fading from an excess of adrenaline and she knew it. Seconds before, there was a erotic kiss which reminded her of Kazan and her insatiable hunger for his maleness. She tried to speak, to find the words to say, "I am so sorry, Kazan! I still want you," but instead she became silent and drew back into herself with a ghost-like quality that captured the vacancy of the room.

She opens her eyes, and waits. Marianne is asking her if she is okay.

She says to her, "I am so sorry, I just can't do this right now."

She looks at her and sees the fear and pain. Briar is still seated and she is now standing over her, looking down at her, taking in the moment like shards of someone else's dream, a bit at a time. This was the way it began, the stealing of time from Briar, wanting to be with Kazan, repeatedly showing up at their apartment without invitation, reservation, or conscience. Kazan wanted Marianne too. Her constant presence caused their bodies to be inflamed beyond any physical limitations. Marianne's face hides the strain of the loss too, her womb empty and her relationship with Briar mysteriously causes both women to feel disconnected by their shared loss. Kazan left this world deeply in love.

Months later, looking back on it, Briar will think that her visit was a sign that she was worried about the secrets she had shared with Kazan would bubble up to the surface with him gone. If only she had been able to stop and think about this scene, things might not have turned out like they had. Later still, she will tell a Vancouver detective that she was in shock at the time, unaware of what was really happening, that her visit was like spending the day in a waiting room or a cold damp spider infested concrete morgue whose walls were closing in.

IT IS EARLY Sunday morning when Briar is finally able to extricate herself from the apartment, having showered and dressed herself in something that did not remind her of him. Her hair is still wet when she makes it out into the pouring rain outside of their building. The taxi driver is waiting for her at the end of the lane, but she pretends that it is an old friend who has come to rescue her from her darkness, so that any neighbours who might catch a glimpse of her will be unaware of her loneliness.

To the southwest, where the new developments dot the landscape, the towering buildings with amber kitchen lights begin their assault upon the quietness of the harbour. From her vantage point, she can see a rusted old tanker moored up to a steel yard across the bay, its huge rusted anchor and chains imprison the boat on the North Shore. Smaller vessels shake and tremble when their engines are engaged, and she cannot help thinking to herself, how much the place has changed since their arrival.

She thinks about how much she misses him. She cannot come to terms with the time that has been lost, how those things that matter the most are those that evaporate like rain after a summer storm. The wind moves through her hair; the sea air is damp and cold, the light struggles against the dark heavy clouds that hang overhead. She thinks she hears or feels the presence of someone behind her. She stands motionless, and feels his spirit draping itself over her. His scent dances upon the wind. He is there.

"Kazan," she says.

It feels like he has wrapped his arms around her. She is afraid to open her eyes and catch the cool clear light and moments of the ordinary days that have escaped them, so afraid she keeps her eyes tightly closed, she wants to not lose the moment with his spirit loving her, both of them safe and comfortable, breathing in the freshness of the day.

"Briar, are you okay?"

"What? Okay?" she says while gently opening her eyes.

"It was like you were somewhere else," he says.

When she turns around and looks at him, she is shocked by his age and appearance, just as she had been when they had held each other in the mirror that was in his upstairs bedroom in his downtown condo. Smith takes her up into his arms. The wind sweeps the presence of Kazan away, and replaces it with Smith. She wonders why she has taken up with him. He is no substitute for her passion for Kazan.

She does not care about his station in life. She couldn't care less about the respect others show him, or his lack of respect or position in the unhinged BC judicial system, she only cares that he takes her somewhere else.

"Let's go downtown," he says. "We can find some dinner and maybe a bottle of that wine you like. Looks like you need a mood changer."

Smith has long greasy thinning auburn hair, and likes to wear suits absent the tie for every occasion. He is ten years her senior, and constantly attempts to keep up with her fashion sense and desire to look around age forty. He speaks with authority when he is trying to impress her, so their conversations are more like lecture series, than the sharing of thoughts, one would expect between a couple.

"I heard they are releasing a Rothschild that is rated a 97," he coughs and he clears his throat. "My people say it is an excellent vintage, lots of fruit and a tobacco-like finish. We should pick up a bottle," he says.

"You sound like one of those wine snobs you detest."

Smith laughs, and takes hold of Briar's hand. "Maybe I am," he says.

"You can sound like such an asshole sometimes, really," Briar states.

They walk toward his parked car. The gravel shifts under their feet as they make their way to his vehicle. The trees around the parking lot are lush and green, filled with birds. This is quite unusual given the time of year. Briar keeps looking at the broken and twisted branches to see some type of aviary sign from heaven. The misshaped branches offer the best shelter for both her and the birds from the early day drizzle. She wants to have a sign from Kazan, like the way in which a sudden gust of wind would appear when she stopped by some ancient stone church and on impulse go inside and light a candle for him. But it is unlikely that Kazan will make himself known to her while she is in the company of this over exaggerated politician. Still, she and her world need him.

"Are you here? Hello, Briar?"

"What?"

"You look like you are still somewhere else or with somebody else."

"I am just kind of sad."

She attempts a smile, her mouth is dry and she feels the early start of a sore throat.

"Maybe a hot cup of coffee will help," he says.

He looks like he has no idea of what she has been thinking. He resembles those municipal politicians that arrive at your door seeking your support to augment their salaries without you having a clue of what they stand for or want. They look like anything other than a couple.

"Yeah. Coffee might help," she says.

They drive through Kerrisdale looking for a convenient place to park, so they can walk to an open air bistro. She stands on the curb, watching him attempt to parallel park his car without striking a white platinum-coloured Mercedes convertible occupied by a twentysomething hipster.

In that quiet space that lies between your thoughts and your heart, she holds close to her memories of Kazan. She feels his presence as if they are holding each other for a long time, and when one of them tires or draws back, the other will hold on tighter and tighter, kissing and drawing the other in. Briar keeps thinking about the last time they were on this street, how they walked against the wind, holding each other's hand tightly, and how she kissed him just prior to traversing the door of a crowded bistro.

"I want you," she said.

The thud of the car door breaks her spell and the wind tousles her hair. A flock of Canada Geese flies overhead, casting shadows on the grey sunlit roadway.

To Kazan, who is seated in his car outside of her office, the sky mirrored the traffic on the highway, row upon row of constant movement and change. He is drumming his fingers on the hard plastic black dash as he watches for her to exit from a building on West Boulevard. Even though the car is parked, he keeps his feet placed firmly on the brake, and his hand on the steering wheel. He wonders how pathetic his appearance is. His head pounds from the consumption of wine from the previous evening. *Maybe I have bitten off more than I can chew,* he thinks. His head pounds. He thinks he has caught a glimpse of Briar's legs splayed across the passenger seat of his car. What a fucking headache, he rubs his forehead in an feeble attempt to stop the pain. He has rehearsed explaining the why and why nots behind their relationship, until it became obvious that the words escaped him. But, how was it possible that he had made such a terrible miscalculation?

HYMAN KAZAN

27

BRITISH COLUMBIA

IT IS A dark and cloudless night, and Marianne's thin gymnast body is well camouflaged in her black turtleneck and Lululemon yoga pants. She has been lost in a melody that pierces the quiet of the night. She needs something to soothe her spirit and help her avoid the overwhelming feelings of self-laceration. Her tongue traces the edges of her lips continuously as her heart beats with the rhythm of obsession. Taking another sip of an already cold coffee, She convinces herself that Kazan will make her happy and content. She likes the feeling of waiting, the anticipation of a climax of emotions. Nothing and nobody can divert her from pulling the razor across her exposed artery. Her desire knows no bounds.

While she was born in Huntsville, a small village that rests in Northern Ontario (if it is known at all, it's for its proximity to Muskoka), like Briar, she studied at the University of Western Ontario in London. There she had worked and graduated, and if the truth be known, she was one of the few female students who worked nights while completing her degree. It was at Western that she begun to develop her close attachment to Modigliani style artists, single malt scotch, and cigarettes. She was neither bound by cultural norms or sexual stereotypes, and found the deformed bodies splashed about the drum tight canvases fed her colourful world view, and provided her with an escape from the local conventions and expectations of the time. She gazed at those captured in colour portraits and became more and more admiring of the chaos behind their lives. It punctured her veins and caused rivers of adrenalin to flow directly into her heart.

Now in Vancouver, she is still surrounded by young women who drink hard liquor and chain smoke while bathed in their struggling feminist ideals. At night, she traverses Hemmingway's concise descriptions of love while drinking cold glasses of pinot grigio. She wanders through such issues as self-identification with the ease of a figure skater on a frozen pond. She has to escape her past. She only needs a supportive partner to guide her.

When Peter left her for her younger friend, she made a deal with herself to never surrender to the draw of a causal relationship again. She wanted something more. She did not know what had caused him to be so callous, or what she had done to earn such cruelty. She hated him for being the great escape artist. He had promised her gourmet meals, but had fed her only bread and water to keep their struggling relationship alive. The crumbs had left her hungry for more. She now seeks an equalization for her emotional loss.

Peter had taken all the abuse he could handle, having attempted to deal with her explosive temper. She left broken dishes and hearts everywhere. When he thought about it, Marianne had brought nothing to their relationship, everything had been drawn out of her previous romantic partners and encounters. What amazed him most was the moment of silence that would invade their time together. They would be seated together at home or at a restaurant with the sound of wind outside or the click of the furnace coming on, or the sound of downtown traffic in the middle of the night, low beam headlights pushing through the milky fog of night. The quiet haunted him, and caused him to lie restless for hours in bed.

When their relationship ended, Peter went into a state of complete loss. He joined a local running club, and with the rhythm of his strides and the music blaring, he was able to escape his grief. He was told by his sweaty newfound companions that he was better off without her, but there was nothing he could do to fill the void left by her absence. Marianne refused to answer any of his calls or emails, so he was left with feelings of abandonment. It has been about six months, and she still will not return any of his calls. It is like they never existed, or that she evaporated like smoke.

With the passage of time, he stopped running with the other men. He just wants to feel the wind in his face and not be bothered with their constant prying into his personal life, or desire for his friendship. He regrets the way things ended with her, but realizes that like most things in his life, he can't control it. He grows thinner each day, and sees himself grow harder and weathered in his complexion. He becomes angrier with each pounding step.

He attempts to hide himself in his work, like others who take to gambling or drinking. He writes feverishly, attempting to find some self-preservation in his writing, a form of nourishment for his soul, he thinks. The pain disappears when he scribbles out his thoughts. That is the love of writing, the way he is able to control the characters who dance across the page, as they live up to his expectations or wants, or they are simply erased from the page. His use of language, semicolons, and descriptions frees him. He writes alternative versions of his failed life, partial truths that make him able to look at himself in the true light of his failings. It is a failsafe relationship, this thing with the words upon a page and himself. Still, he finds conflict in his writing, the prose tugs at his loneliness and feelings of loss, and reminds him about the things he has given up. His words haunt him and stare back at him from the page, reminding him of his insecurities and relationships fraught with fraud.

Sometimes, he will show up in the middle of the night, and park outside her house for days. All he wants to do is to see her one more time. He dreams that she will suddenly come back to him, that she will forget about his shortcomings, and swim across the swamp of stupidity he has created due to his lack of emotional maturity.

Then suddenly, she is there. Magically, she appears in a black turtleneck and a pair of faded jeans. He swallows the last bit of wine he had poured into a white styrofoam cup and pulls down the sun visor as to provide cover for his embarrassment. She pulls closed the front door and walks across the dew soaked lawn. He sinks further into the driver's seat, filled with tension, sweat poured across his forehead. He tugs at the immoveable sun visor and by then she is already across the street, making her way down past his parked car. He fumbles for his keys and starts the engine of the car. Slipping the clutch, the car turns over like a wave from the curb, and he begins to follow her. He is careful to drop back to a safe distance, so he can continue undetected.

HYMAN KAZAN

28

BRITISH COLUMBIA

THERE IS A magical time between the offerings of a late Pacific afternoon, and the early evening sunset, when the light in its amber glow softens all things. Kazan gazes out from his quieted subconscious, seeking some meaning to his life. He is a middle-aged man weaving in and out of traffic. Briar is a much younger woman, full of energy and passion. It is the fall, and the northwest wind scatters the forest green leaves upon the damp pavement. This is a time of change and transformation. In his mind's eye, he drives past a dented sedan pulling out from the curb, and catches an unexpected glimpse of Marianne further down the block. Glancing ahead, he focuses on some school aged children debarking from an dark yellow VSB school bus. He can hear them laughing and calling out to one another, the smell of pine trees, the seagulls flying overhead. He ponders the edges of his daydream.

Staring blankly at the folded coffee ringed Vancouver Sun newspaper on the arm of his chair, he catches sight of the date, November 3rd. He wonders where the year has gone, and looks up to see Briar, dressed only in a bra and a pair of white faded jeans, enter into their living room. She twists her hair back from her neck, then glances upon the thin silver watch on her wrist. She is already planning her day and she has no time for him.

He daydreams of Marianne turning on to their street, her carefully sculpted shoulders wrapped in a dark cashmere turtleneck. Her car shudders to a stop, allowing a group of students to walk in front of her against the yellow light, and he watches her disappear into a restaurant with blue tables and a terrace out front. He drives slowly past her, and wonders why he has become a chauffeur to everyone else's relationship, always driving them to another relationship while never reaching his own destination. And then it comes to him, the date, the day. Today is the day when he is to meet with Smith for a drink to discuss his, or better put, their relationship with Briar. His mind wanders back to his thoughts about her. What he remembers is inverted through a strange prism. It is like looking at a undeveloped negative being brought to life in a dark room. The restaurant is pushed up against a stone sun bleached wall, the walls cracked and pounded by traffic and time, but the rows of tables cascade with vivid blues and whites, the umbrellas shimmer in the moonlight and candle lights. The thing that causes his heart to skip is the glimpse of her knee length sand-coloured dress under the strings of twinkling lights over the tables. She is talking with an awkward young waiter who is attempting to seat two older women near the curb. The cobblestones still have a clear coated slickness to them from the afternoon rain. Whatever she is saying to him invites a large smile upon his face. Kazan imagines for a second that he is a waiter working at the same restaurant.

Then Briar appears through the large archway that leads to the entrance of the cafe. She appears taller than her younger counterpart, and her hair looks damp as if she has just stepped out of the shower or have been caught in the rain. He recognizes them both instantly. It is as if fate has brought them both there at exactly the same time. Her face is tanned and looks relaxed. Briar is laughing and then she suddenly stops. Kazan, who has been waiting for a table, stands beside them both, smiling at this chance meeting, before gesturing to both women.

Something snaps him back into reality. He sees the wind catch the hem of Briar's dress, how it resembles an embassy flag on a cold November day. She struggles against the wind as if she is looking for a way out of a cage that has trapped the moment. She backs away from the cafe tables, and is walking back down toward Smith's car again. With a glance toward Kazan's vehicle, he feels puzzled why she has not seen him sliding down into the driver's seat. He only has dreamed of this moment so many times. The translucent sky, the cars turning the corner between yesterday and tomorrow.

He closes his eyes, recording the scene one last time before feeling the coldness of the steering wheel in his hands and the loneliness of the passage of time. Why do we daydream? The grasping of the mist of what we so desire, the illusion of being taken up and away from all that has escaped us. Kazan wants to know why, he wants to know and feel the difference between want and desire.

When Briar appears there on the streets of his memory, she looks much younger than when they had met. Her face is full of enthusiasm and light, she wears bracelets on both of her wrists, her hair is pulled back in a ponytail. She is a picture of hope and kindness, but there is another side to this illusion. Sometimes, Briar cannot contain her frustration with everyday events. The parking of a car, the loud sound from a neighbour's apartment, could all but send her into a blind rage.

She wants to escape, and Kazan also feels the urge to disappear, sitting in his arm chair in the living room overlooking the street, staring at the comings and goings of the street. He feels so lost recently, feels like a faceless version of the grey flannel man. He is trying to not feel sorry for himself, but he can feel the draw of the darker side of daydreaming. His depression has built up with the passing of each hour, only to accelerate by the consumption of alcohol. The waiting for her drives him crazy, and this thing with Smith . . .

When she does come home, she is usually wet from all the sex with Smith, her hair still damp from her clean up shower, the tension that she feels from being discovered disheveled and empty. She has gone missing, not from him, but from much more.

"Where did you go? Who were you with?" he wants to say, but he never does.

He holds the words in the back of his throat, and swallows hard, not letting her see the pain that has invaded their relationship. But she will look into his eyes and see the hurt. The touch of his face and the warmness of her mouth surround him, and he laughs at his good fortune at finding her. When they are alone in the apartment, he will quickly pour her a glass of wine.

He says, "Maybe it will help you relax."

It is like he is a nurse preparing her for surgery. He offers the anesthetic, but the wounds will be opened by others. He is in love with what they have been, rather than what they will become. She laughs and takes hold of his hand and leads him to her bed. He watches her lift the arm of the turntable and watches the lines of her fingertips balance the ebony disc. The music comes out smokey and familiar. *I am too old for this,* he thinks. The sheets are a battleship grey and hold a softness that is welcoming to his rigid body. The mattress is crowned by a leather headboard that has a saddle like appearance to it. To make love with her is like tapping into a cosmic religious force—she is like a falling star that has climbed back into the sky in the hopes of tasting life again.

He closes the bathroom door, washes his face, runs his fingers through his hair, and then leaves the bathroom. The rarely used apartment stairs smell of pine scented cleaning agents. She emerges behind him in the dark, carrying a half-drunk bottle of champagne. The sunlight pours in through the small rectangular windows that adorn each fire door. It is like a student dorm or hospital hallway, splashes of light casting shadows down the corridors. It reminds him of the bright sun that has greeted him after leaving a darkened pub midafternoon after the hours he spent following her in his car.

Drawn back up to their wind-swept terrace, she is that young girl again in a soft pair of jeans, talking on her cell phone. She is thin with an athletic body and dark unruly hair. She has one leg swung over the arm of a wooden Adirondack chair and is holding her cell phone up against the side of her chin, away from her face in a nonchalant manner, laughing and tilting her head back in a way that is meant to look carefree. And Kazan, who keeps walking toward her, can feel the ocean breeze caught between the building and the roof line.

"I thought you didn't like heights?" she hears Kazan say.

"Just afraid of falling," she replies.

HYMAN KAZAN

29

BRITISH COLUMBIA

TO SAY ONE thing and then do the exact opposite is the straw that breaks the moment. The next time he sees her, she will be sipping on her cafe au lait like this illusory chance encounter never happened. A dark roast that produces a cloud of steam rising up from a large styrofoam cup. The snowy cloud froth from the steaming hot beverage will sting her upper lip and cause her to glance over his shoulder toward the busy street. They will discuss her relationship to Smith, but will do so in cautious tones like advancing toward a predator who has ventured down from the savannah to a local watering hole.

He meets up with Briar again that week at a local wine bistro just off of Kitsilano beach. They have trouble keeping their hands off each other, perhaps sparked by the visit from Marianne. Briar tugs at his raincoat, forcing him into the backseat of a waiting cab, where she kisses him long and hard, leading him back to their apartment and upturned bedroom, where they make love and both lay exhausted on the bed, watching the stars through their rooftop skylight.

Briar recalls his first meeting with her father, and how he loved to tell stories about her childhood on their family farm. He was a large man with a deep voice and callous hands from working outside. He had grown up in Northern Ontario and his father had been a horseman. This caused him to be both a strong and disciplined character who attempted to correct or corral the shortcomings he saw in others. Her parents had married in Collingwood. Years later, her mother would say that they ate toasted tomato sandwiches and drank lemonade on their wedding day.

"Your father always put the farm first," she would say.

There was a black and white photo of them holding each other outside of the screen door at the front of their farmhouse. Briar often thought their happiest times came early in their relationship, prior to the death of her brother in the fire. She did not talk often about the fire, but it raged through her subconscious, destroying her self-confidence, and shattering their family as quickly as it had destroyed the August dried kiln that had been their home. Nobody other than Kazan knew. Ten years later, her mother had moved out, and her father stayed on the charred ground of what had been the family home, until his untimely death years later. Briar notices that the telling of her family history is getting more and more difficult. It now comes out only on the rarest of occasions.

Early in her adult life, Briar married a slender athletic doctor before surrendering herself to Kazan. She said he was a good man who was also fighting his family's expectations and demons. She married far too young. He was a surgeon, who was never there, she said. It was impossible, he would be there for a second, and then the next moment, the phone would ring and he would be gone. They would be sitting down for dinner in a French restaurant, and suddenly he would be called away to put back together an impaired driver or his passenger, or rescue some aging athlete whose ACL was ripped from his kneecap. And that would send the evening into a shouting match. He would start to sweat and curse her for her lack of understanding about his job. She would beg him to stay, and he would have to leave. Unlike Kazan, he was the most risk averse and self-conscious person she had ever met.

She had gone to Quebec immediately after the end of their marriage, where she had met up with Kazan. He said it was fate, she said she loved his sense of adventure.

She says, "I do not know where you would be without me."

He asks, "When?"

"Right now, that is, if we weren't in BC," she says. "It should have ended somewhere else."

He apologizes like always. He tells her how his young mother died when he was seven, that cancer claimed her life and changed him forever. He clutches the silver St. Christopher medallion that a long gone aunt had retrieved from a basilica in Rome to mark her passing and to shield him from some similar fate. This aunt felt her sister's spirit on the back of Kazan's neck beneath his overly starched collar as she fumbled with the clasp, and she did not quite understand what that meant.

Home soon became a one way ticket to Montreal and a temporary residence with his estranged uncle. His father told him that it was better this way, a new country, a new beginning, and a chance to make the family proud and forget about the hardships found in motherless countries. Home was a place to hide, a place to go when you had nowhere else to go. A place where only black and white photographs would capture his absent brother and sister. They remained home, home with his father, while Kazan and his uncle stood around the airport like a constable and his juvenile prisoner, waiting for transport. His uncle now became his father, a shady and misunderstood character who did not welcome this new role. He had gone into the development business, and made a lot of money renting out retail and small business spaces in strip plazas in the sixties. Everything he knew about his father now became the stories he would hear being told by his uncle and his semi famous friends.

"This is why you can never leave me," Briar says, as if it is some sentence he will never be able to serve.

He tries to remember if he went to the cemetery when his mother died, but all he can remember were those long drives to the limestone hospital for treatments or medications that were supposed to remove the pain. He dreams of her often, but can never recall how or when she became ill. What he does remember is the way she smelled, the mix of florals and spice, and the way she would fill the crevices of a room, and how her lips were always garnished with a deep garnet-coloured red lipstick, and how she would reach out for her boys' hands when she went off to the local market. She liked to wear a soft linen jacket with a sleeveless blouse underneath that trapped her fragrance, only releasing it when she took each of the children tightly in her arms.

"My mother," he says. "She was like you in many ways. She liked to dance and drink wine and read books." Briar smiles. "She also avoided housework," he says. "She was very organized but loathed giving the appearance of a housewife, or what was worse than that, a housekeeper. She disliked law school. It was a breeding ground for those soulless capitalist and those twenty or thirtysomethings who had totally fucked up every other aspect of their lives. She thought I was some kind of a new rebel, a lawyer who cared about the people. The type who if asked, would pull you out of some dark thorny pitfall."

He gets up from their bed and stands there naked and gazes out at the ocean through their open window. She rolls over and sees him standing there. He is so good-looking that it feels embarrassing to stare at him, but that is how it was, when it was new.

HYMAN KAZAN

30

BRITISH COLUMBIA

A MONTH OR so later, Kazan purchases a fractional ownership in a crumbling old Victorian house that rests near Jericho Beach. Marianne, who has been in an apartment in Yaletown, moves into a condominium across the hall from Briar's place, since she plans on moving out to be with Smith. Briar would have liked to have rented the apartment out, but couldn't bring herself to organize a move, or have Kazan agree to a sale of their unit. They are caught in between.

Briar plays loud music when she is alone at the condo. Living across the hall, Marianne can hear it over her television. Briar adjusts the volume to keep up with her wine consumption. Marianne sometimes pounds on the door, pleading for her to take it down a notch. She will scream that she is trying to sleep. Sometimes, Briar arrives at Kazan's door, hoping to stay the night. He argues with her, but gives into her request for a one night lodging, in the hopes of holding on to her. When he is alone, sleep becomes something beyond his grasp.

He is reading a novel, ironically it is a book about the perils of insomnia. She does not understand his love of fiction, especially when it deals with problems that he battles with. She complains that he relates too much to the dark characters with depressed moods that hide in the chapters he pours over nightly, and he smiles knowingly to himself when she comments on it. She keeps walking around his place in his work shirts, often with nothing else on. He doesn't complain, but dislikes the way it reminds him of his work day. She stands there at the window, drinking coffee, and he becomes wrapped up in her shape, her mouth, her eyes, and their history.

Briar loves this hold she has on him. She can feel the strength in his chest and hips as he moves from one room to another. She feels overwhelmed at the sight of his tanned naked body, or the way he sits propped up in bed with one cupped hand resting at the back of his neck after sex, with the blankets raging all around him, and that beautiful collar bone sloping down from his soften beard and wonderful neckline, that lead to his soft wet mouth that had been full of her. She is in love with his physical sex in a way she never was when she was younger. Now it is full of excitement and passion and she adores it but she also finds it so much harder when he is away from her. In the middle of the night, when she finds her feet stepping on a slightly damped towel, the coldness strikes her, her face and breasts still flush from the thought of time spent tangled up in bed. She takes a second to look at her dilated pupils in the soft glow of the bathroom light, and starts to caution herself about wanting him so much.

She is eager to feel him inside her again, so struck by the sheer force of their love making. She comes to the realization that she is hopelessly in love with every aspect of their time together, whether it is living in the moment or planning for their future together. These nights she sleeps in unwashed bedclothes so as to capture the smell of him one more time. It makes passage of time bearable and becomes the closest thing to the reality she longs for.

In late November, Barry Pickard from the court office calls Briar in a panic regarding the Trinity Rivers case. Jury selection is due to start in a few days and no one has heard from Kazan.

"He is getting squeezed by everyone: the cops, the judiciary and victimized witnesses," he says. "To have committed to do this trial, and then to just disappear is crazy."

Briar stands at their bedroom window, wearing just a pair of jeans and holding the phone between her shoulder and ear. She hangs up the phone, stumbling over an ill-conceived explanation as to Kazan's whereabouts. She can see the boats travelling across the bay, the air is cool and the sky is bubbled with the morning rain. Kazan sits on the edge of their bed, wearing a pair of black jeans and a white T-shirt.

"I should not have gone to Juneau to see Cookie," he says.

Tim Cook was a longtime friend, who had gone into the hotel business with his friend and lover, Eliza.

"I should have stayed here and prepared for the Trinity case. I just assumed that Marianne was all in, but she can't be trusted with anything this big. What will I do now?"

"How was Alaska?"

"Cold and rainy, just like Vancouver, just with less traffic," he says.

"You know everyone is looking for you?"

"Yeah, I figured as much."

"I see that Pickard has been calling." She laughs. "How is C?" She is about to say Catherine but catches herself, or leaves it like a foul ball for him to deal with or ignore.

She wonders if they spent much time together while he was away. Catherine was a mysterious woman from his past, and Briar was jealous of her. She had taken up residence in Homer, Alaska, after a falling out with a film producer. *There is enough distrust in the room to go around,* she thinks.

"Tim is fine." He coughs and bends down in search of some shoes to wear. "Sometimes I just miss talking with someone who has absolutely no interest in the law or the stupid people here below the 49th. Sometimes hard choices come back to haunt us," he offers up. "The bullshit sometimes just gets to me."

"No kidding," responds Briar.

"Briar, what am I going to do? I am so fucked."

It seems almost comical to her that he is now asking for her help.

"You could move in with Marianne or ask Koogan and Stirling to help dig you out of this mess."

"I did not mean that."

"You know the thing about moving in with Marianne!" She catches herself as she is heavily steeped in sarcasm. It is impossible to retrieve the punchline that she has just delivered.

She starts to pace the living room, which appears out of place, as she is in no danger here, but she still feels a heavy pressure suddenly crushing her shoulders. Kazan can see the rock pile forming, but is at a loss as to how to deal with this situation. He has dumped all the chemicals together and now is awaiting the explosion, but he still fails to understand how this situation has developed so quickly and easily.

"I know!" Briar offers. "You could talk to Craig."

"Who?" he sputters with an awkward response. He cannot believe her! "You are not suggesting, talking to the fucking trial judge, are you?" Kazan snaps.

"Just off the record, you know, like the old days. I could put it together, Kazan," Briar states. "I know, Kazan, this is the last thing you would consider, but just think, you could rid yourself of this case, and you would not have to see Smith again. You must admit, this could be brilliant? The conflict, the judicial meddling, the scandal!"

"Are you fuckin crazy?" he shouts. He cannot believe what she is suggesting. "Don't you see, this could amount to obstruction or tampering, or, or, fuck it. He is already responsible for one death." Before he can catch himself, he has disclosed the fact that he knows for a fact that it was Smith who killed Simon Westfall.

"Well then, you might as well just go before the jury and make this case up as you go along, just like when you took on that case, Johnson wasn't it, the name? You know. Do you know who is acting for the defense?"

"I am not sure. I think it's Ted Marsh. Oh, no, wait a minute, there's someone at the door."

Briar presses the number for the building's intercom, and walks out onto the balcony to get a glimpse of the front door.

"Hey, is Hy hiding up there with you? Or are you alone?"

Kazan is struck by the sound of Smith's irritating voice.

"Hang on, I will meet you in the lobby. Just come in and make yourself comfortable," she says, taken by surprise by Smith's unannounced visit.

She looks at Kazan and says, "Well, you better decide what you are going to do, you can't guess who is waiting downstairs?"

A crooked smile comes to her face, as she is aware he has overheard his voice on the intercom. The two destructive forces in her life are now within shouting distance! She quickly pulls on a sweater and makes it out the front door to make her way down to the lobby. He struggles to find his way into the kitchen. He finds the half bag of coffee beans left in the freezer that a client had given him from Costa Rica. He places the small bent silver espresso pot on the stove and switches the gas on to simmer. The coffee smells of dark chocolate and hazelnut. He suddenly fears he has made it too strong and that it will taste bad. With the palm of his left hand, he pushes a letter size space in the steamy kitchen window, and sees that Briar is nowhere near outside of the lobby. The afternoon sun is overcome by dark Pacific clouds and he thinks of going downstairs to look for her when the phone rings again.

"I have to see you," the voice says. A female voice is now adding to the comedy of the moment.

"Who is this?"

"Kazan, it's Marianne."

"What? Where are you?"

Crazy, how things play out sometimes? He thinks to himself. There is a hesitation in her voice and yet he can sense a hunger too.

"I want you," she speaks with an urgency that is foreign to him. "I need to talk to you about the Trinity trial."

"Excuse me?"

Briar appears in the doorway, she reaches in and grabs the car keys from the small redwood roll top desk just inside the front of the apartment door, and then she is gone again. Kazan feels like he is standing on a thin layer of spring ice in the middle of the lake, and that with rising temperatures, he is about to fall through. Nowhere to go but to the bottom. He is speechless.

"I need to talk to you. Jesus, I have not heard from you in days. Where are you? When can I see you?"

"What?" Kazan says.

"I am in the car three cars down from your front entrance," she replies.

Kazan can just imagine her sitting behind the wheel of her icy silver Volkswagen with her white blouse open at the neck, hair tousled, sipping coffee while watching Briar exit out the lobby door. He recalls that they once sat in the back of her car with her, sipping a glass of wine, trying to avoid the awkward urge of attempting to make love in the car. He had just finished his wine when the glow from her cell phone interrupted the moment between them.

"What the hell," Kazan raises his voice in response to her location.

"Please, try to understand. Can you just come down?"

"Why should I?" he asks.

"Jesus, Kazan, we are in real trouble here." She is now raising her voice and is pleading with him.

"We are in real trouble here. What do you mean? I am the one trying to figure how to put together the case against Trinity. My world is imploding, don't you get it?"

Kazan feels the stress of their situation which is now starting to pile on.

"I don't really know. But have you heard that Smith is our trial judge? He is out to really screw with you, Kazan, things are out of control!"

"I know, I know, you probably passed him on your way here!" he answers back. "I don't really care anymore. People are going to do what they will, and I am really at the end of my rope," Kazan adds. "You know, I just don't really care anymore. I just don't care!"

"I have been told, Kazan, that we better watch our backs. He is out to get us this time. It is really us versus the system. I know you still give a shit about us, them, and everyone in between, especially Simon Westfall! You said Briar and Smith will do anything to make you look bad. You said that they are just waiting for the right moment. The clock is ticking. I just saw them together, Kazan!"

"I don't care. I don't need this! You don't want to be a part of this." He is now attempting to save Marianne from this bizarre circus that has become his life.

"Please, Kazan, let's do this!"

"It is too late," he answers back.

"What? It is never too late, you taught me that a long, long time ago, Kazan."

"I just want to get the fuck out of here, alive. That's all I want now." Kazan is now raising his voice and speaking with both a desperation and passion unknown to her.

"I want the same things as you do, Kazan. Not a few bread crumbs, I am starving for a real relationship. I did not know that working with you would turn into this." Marianne is now pleading for him to come down to her car. She is now unravelling. "I did not know I was going to fall for you," she adds.

At that exact second, he becomes struck by the clarity of his situation. He feels part of something beyond their relationship. Their banter has made him feel used and ashamed. He knows Briar was using him and for some reason, he just accepted it. Marianne and her attraction to him adds to his confusion,

"Wake up, Kazan! We are wasting time here. We have to get a game plan together. We have to prepare this case and expose Smith! We do not have any other options. You fucking get that, don't you? Get your ass down here before it is too late!"

She is waiting for him to say something. Kazan walks into the living room and sits down.

"The wound just got infected," he babbles. "It doesn't matter anymore what that arrogant bastard thinks, what Briar does, or how it is reported later. It really does not matter. It never did," he mumbles to himself, attempting to find a way out of the chaos.

"When did it start to not matter, Kazan? You said it all mattered. You never did the job for the money, you never gave a shit about the justice system like this. And besides, you were fed up with Smith being with Briar. Now is the time to clean up this mess."

She has summed up the problems, but has not offered any solutions, he thinks to himself.

"What happened, Kazan? What the fuck happened?" her voice now breaks as she speaks.

"Nothing happened, I just don't need this anymore. Do you?" Kazan says again, in a feeble attempt to convince himself and her of his decision to go no further.

"It is over, what part of this is unclear to you? Briar and you, Smith, it all does not matter. You did that." She is now arguing a case with facts that are not fully known to her.

"What are you saying?"

"A few mixed drinks and a few confused fools, and now you want everyone to leave the fucking playground. It does not work like that, Kazan. That's not what life is about. Love and justice mean something."

For some unknown reason, he starts to laugh. And she realizes that he has wandered into a psychological corn maze, a Rorschach, a broken Rubik's cube, and he has now surfaced, gasping for air. He now is convinced about what he has to do. The noise suddenly falls into a melody.

"I love you!"

He responds quickly, "I know you do. I love you too. I am just ground down by all the bullshit."

A lie, but he wants to say something that will cause her to understand his darkness and provide her with a way out. He is tired of lying. Instead, he has pushed her away.

"Good luck, Kazan," she says, hanging up the phone.

She has tried her best to pull him from the burning fire, but now she feels a strange sense of relief as she drives away without looking back.

HYMAN KAZAN

31

BRITISH COLUMBIA

"SHE IS JUST not worth it," the good-looking, tall young bartender at Bridges calls out as Kazan sits in the darkened room in the midafternoon, looking out over Burrard inlet. He cannot bring himself to make it into the office yet or face Briar. She looked so misplaced when she left the apartment. Her face was drained of all colour and hope. Kazan had seen this far too often, how anxiety would take away the light from behind her eyes. It was like grey stone clouds blocking out the sun.

Their end unit apartment has become like that too, it has become this dark and grey cold cave that he no longer feels comfortable in. The rooms are smaller than he remembers, like their bedroom with its dull grey paint, the rooms begin to close in. The paint colours have faded from the cool designer upscale retreat that the builder had shown them. Now it is full of papers and books and a fireplace that does not work. It is a narrow room that squeezes out any oxygen in the place. He had stopped breathing there, and it caused him to pack up his things and find a landing place near Kitts. There, he would smoke, drink, and cradle his hidden Beretta handgun while seated on a butterscotch-coloured Queen Anne armchair that had followed him from Quebec.

Kazan had a good life, a life filled with opportunity and adventure, a better life than this. He had come to the West Coast filled with exotic dreams and aspirations, not the kind of cold dark cage he now finds himself in. The apartment is now a collection of her things, paintings she likes, French cookware they never use, Italian coffee makers, the kind of stuff that creeps into your life and expands to paradoxically create a void rather than to make a home. He recalls one such discussion.

"Wow, this is really good coffee," she said.

"Thanks."

"Did you make it? I really like when you take the time to make us coffee in the morning."

"Yeah."

"Did you use the coffee from Costa Rica? Where did you say he got it from? Did you use my coffee maker?"

An everyday pedestrian conversation about nothing, he thinks to himself. In the moments that follow, he closes his eyes and thinks about the long winding drive north from there to Whistler. He can see the rushing cold water and hawk filled cotton candy cloudy skies. He looks up from the rim of his coffee cup and sees her standing there.

"I don't know anymore, and does it really matter?"

He gazes upon her, the silence lasts for eternity. He has no idea where this is going.

"Okay, I thought I was in love with Smith. For a long time, you just weren't there for me . . . It was a mistake, a waste of time. I am sorry if it hurt you."

Her confession and apology puzzle him.

"Apparently, it took you a very long time to come to the realization of how much of an asshole that guy really is?" he responds.

"What?" she chirps. "He was so charming at first, you know, like you were."

"Smith is, and always has been, an arrogant son of a bitch," Kazan barks.

"Why do you say that?" she asks.

"Briar, everybody knows that. He has screwed over everyone he meets. He does not care who he hurts. Everyone is roadkill or collateral damage to him."

"That makes me feel sick," she says.

"Oh, don't feel you are special," Kazan offers up. "He makes me feel sick all the time."

"That is different. Anyway, it doesn't matter. I hate him now, just about as much as you do. You have to understand, it was a stupid mistake and it was not about you. I do not know why I even try to make you understand." Her words fall like snowflakes, each one covering the statement made before, but all of them melting into a frozen blanket of regret. "He came into my life at a time when I was so lonely for you. It was a scintilla of sunlight in a very dark and depressing time, and he touched something in me, a dormant belief that there might be an escape from the darkness and suffering that you were embracing."

It is funny, he thinks, *that she assumes by talking about Smith, she can erase my disgust for the two of them.* Humiliation is the misplaced, unwrapped gift under the leaning Christmas tree in the corner, propped up each year of their relationship. The whole thing fatigued him. He pleads with her to stop this nonsense.

His mouth is now full of Scotch whiskey. She puts her clear silver grey laptop down, and smiles at him. He wants to touch her face and erase the argument they just had, to rinse away the sand from the steps that once led to their passion, and so he swallows and walks toward her and places the palm of his hand softly against the side of her clavicle and touches the back of her head, drawing her toward him. She opens her mouth to find his, and begins to unbutton his shirt. He tugs at the remaining buttons and removes his shirt and she places her hand upon his chest and kisses him harder. She likes to feel the hardness of his chest, and runs her hands down his thighs, and touches his penis as her kissing grows stronger and then lies on top of him, and only then controlling when and how much he would be inside of her. His response to her is instant. He has never known a woman like this, she is vulnerable but in control.

"Should we go to the bedroom?"

"Maybe just draw the blinds. I like it here on the steps," she says, and with that, she begins to remove her jeans.

His face is now buried in her hair and he can smell its mint and floral scent.

"I love you, Kazan."

Their clothes fall like November leaves on the stairs leading to the bedroom. The hallway is dark and a glass picture frame catches the dark and wavy reflection of their naked bodies in motion.

"Time is a funny thing. When you try to hold on to it, it slips through your fingers like beach sand," she says.

Her cell phone chimes. He is filled with anxiety as he watches her physical presence disappear. The world turns and time does not stop.

"What did you say about time?"

He begins to pace the cage and feels his chest tighten. His daydream once again is shattered.

"Briar? Is Kazan there? It is Krystal McDermid at the courthouse," the voice breaks up on the speakerphone as the answering service catches the errant call. "Are you there? Briar, are you there? Please pick up. Please call the trial coordinator's office immediately."

The harmonics of the call ending signals an end to the call. The telephone call ends the moment and so much more. Kazan glances at the picture frame that held the moments before, caught their likeness, only to see that their naked bodies are now unrecognizable to him. They are void of any electricity.

"Briar, let it go," Kazan says, and then she begins to run with the phone in her hand, looking for some paper.

And he is left there, seated on the edge of the steps, head in hands, naked with the hallway light casting a shadow on him alone. His skin is now cool to the touch, and he feels like a discarded extra in her life. He imagines her warm body and erect nipples bouncing against his chest. The moment has ended.

"I love you, Briar!" he calls out.

From the bedroom comes the voice of Briar as she has given in to the lure of the cell phone, the sound of her voice is now muffled and incomplete.

LYING IN A cool dark bedroom, they can hear the rain and wind scratching at their blinded windows, and Marianne and Koogan are arguing about how to handle Kazan and Briar. She reaches for him, and he turns away toward the bedroom wall.

"What is wrong now?"

He is distant and unresponsive.

"Nothing," he says.

Koogan holds her in the darkness, only to be revisited again and again by Kazan and the gossip surrounding Kazan and Briar. She is now whispering in the dark, breathing in the quietness of the room, while his eyes adjust to the room and he is able to focus on her as she looks at him.

"Why do lawyers end up like that? My God, I hope that we don't end up like that."

"We are not like that! If anything, we can learn from their mistakes. Think about it, they just got what they deserved. Each other."

"John, I just do not get it. They started out so happy and so in love with each other."

"People grow apart. Or they grow into something they were not at the beginning of their relationship. There is always a price to be paid in this profession."

"What do you mean?"

"Well, look at Kazan. Every day, he meets with some victim and starts his day with a description about what was the worst thing to ever happen to them."

Koogan suddenly feels like he has stepped over the line. He is not sure if he has insulted Marianne, but it is changing the mood in the room.

"The law can eat away at you," he says, not knowing why he says it. "I sometimes feel like it is eating away at me." Marianne stares at him. "Why do we let it?"

"What are you trying to say?"

"I don't know." He places his hand on her shoulder. "I remember Kazan telling me about one of his cases early on. It involved a husband and wife, where the wife was tragically killed on a back of a motorcycle. She was split in two by a transport driver who had celebrated the birth of his first daughter at lunch. A liquid lunch. Anyway, despite the shrinks and psychologists telling him to try and move on and to forget about the horror of that day, Kazan told me about the need to have the husband go back again and again, over and over, and describe the event in minute detail in preparation for trial. Years of that, has to go somewhere."

She nods, closing her eyes briefly, breathing deeply. "Yes."

He is tired of just fucking. He wants his own bed, and some peace and quiet, away from the law and tension of trials, and far away from any talk about Kazan and Briar. She is eager to have more of him, as it helps her escape from her surroundings and brings about a release of tension.

"I need to go home for a while," he says. "Just for a bit, you know . . . I am sorry, I am just not in the mood . . . I just need a little bit of a break, nothing personal, you know."

"Just go if you have to, I am alright with it," she says.

He decides to not say anything more, the damage has been done. She has moved to the edge of the bed and is now talking to herself. Intimacy has been exchanged for isolation.

"I was in love with him before Briar, you know. I just never told him and both of them have despised me ever since. I know it is not right, and I still have to work with him, because you see, if we were really meant to be together, I would have been there for him."

"Marianne, why tell me this now?" Koogan asks.

"What do you mean?"

"Please, I do not want to hear any more about Kazan and Briar! It is like a wound that never heals, all you do is pick at the blood soaked scab and reopen the wound again and again."

The loss of blood and feelings outside of this open sore is killing me, thinks Koogan. He struggles with the shift in the mood. She is now starting to well up and he knows the tears are soon to fall.

"Can you please just come back to bed and stay for a little longer?" she asks. There is an urgency in her voice.

"I really think I should go. Maybe I could come back later," Koogan replies.

"Promise me, you will come back later then. Promise me. I just can't stand to be alone right now with everything that is happening." Her voice cracks as she speaks.

"Okay, I will come back later tonight if you want."

He wants to run, to feel the ocean breeze on his face. He feels like he is suffocating from being with her, but loves her still the same. He wants the tension in his chest to be replaced by huge amounts of clean oxygen, and he wants to float away on a sea of tranquility. He turns and takes a final look at her as he pulls the door shut behind him, and then realizes that she is seeking the same escape as him, except her escape is through him being present.

The shadow of Justice Smith! Koogan's thoughts turn to Justice Smith. His mind wanderers back to their first meeting. Cold empty eyes, his bulging waistline, his heavily starched court shirt untucked, Smith stares at Koogan, who is crouched behind a scratched wooden platform. There is a bent and broken Criminal Code open on the sideboard beside the desk, one of those that is years out of date, and he is balancing on one foot behind a wooden Diaz, making his submissions to a non-receptive Smith. His hands show his age, but they are slender, unlike Smith's hands which are fat and soft.

Smith, who has vacant eyes, suffers from early hair loss. He combs what he has left down to avoid a cadaver-like appearance. He is a Saint Mike's graduate, an old Toronto boys club filled with both clandestine homosexuals and hostile homophobes, who now wield power throughout Ontario and the province of British Columbia.

"Are you going to be much longer?" Smith says. "This is the third request to move the case along."

"Yes, Your Honor. I am getting to the end of my submissions."

"Yes, I feel like we have already been over this."

The emotionally stunted Smith has no patience or empathy. His time is his only concern. Speed is the enemy of attention. He cares not for counsel or the accused. Koogan stiffens and begins to highlight the weaknesses in the prosecution's case. Smith interrupts him once again and thanks him for his submissions. In short, he is telling him that he has already made up his mind and is not listening.

"Thank you, those are my submissions," concludes Koogan.

He lets out a heavy sigh so as to release him from any further torment. *Such a son of a bitch, how that bastard ever got appointed, and how he doesn't give a shit anymore about the justice system, the accused, the victims, he just wants to load up his pockets with as much cash as possible and avoid being centered out by the court of appeal. It is just so obvious that he does not care,* Koogan thinks to himself. Unfortunately, an innocent man goes to jail or a guilty man is let go on a technicality. This has been going on for a decade now. This fat little man had done so much to reduce the respect for the administration of justice. The whole scene disgusts him.

Smith's eyes are now focused on the public school sized clock at the back of the courtroom. He is dreaming of the night, and how he intends to spend it with Briar. He appears like a sinister Catholic Bishop with his cardinal red sash and obnoxious facial expressions. The silence lasts forever. Koogan is afraid to break it, Smith is an unpredictable powder keg, and has been known to explode without warning, especially when challenged. Smith's eyes glance up periodically from the sea of papers on his desk. His hands are always clenched as if he were a boxer entering the ring. He clears his throat and attempts to adopt a professor-like tone.

"Counsel, you have presented a challenging defense which I have considered along with all of the evidence, and I . . ." He pauses in search of a word.

Koogan prepares himself for the need to control his anger and disgust for him, and feels the sweat run down between his shoulder blades beneath his tightly stretched court shirt. He finds all of Smith's comments legally and factually flawed, and they tend to bring out the uncontrollable hostility he feels toward him.

"I have applied all of the applicable legal precedents to your situation, and have considered your client's evidence very closely, counsel."

Now his vacant eyes show a lost and empty appearance, as if he knows those seated in the courtroom know he is about to release yet another example of his lack of intellectual integrity. He looks like a grade six student at a spelling bee who is forced to spell a word that he swears comes from an ancient dialect or some language foreign to him, or is only found in the lexicon of the aerospace industry by a small percentage of Russian scientists. The silence continues. Koogan is unsure if he should say something to break the ice he is standing on. Finally, Smith falls out of his trance, clears his throat, and attempts to take on a more serious tone. He begins to parrot the usual.

"Well, in any case, the burden of proof is on the Crown and stays with the Crown until the conclusion of the case. Then and only then, should the court find that the Crown has proved its case beyond a reasonable doubt, and the accused will be found guilty. In this case, I do not find that the case has been proved beyond a reasonable doubt. I need not review all of the evidence, given the comprehensive submissions of counsel."

The air is so full of bullshit that the clerk staff can barely contain themselves. Another example of intellectual dishonesty courtesy of Judge Smith and everyone in the room is aware of it.

"As you know, justice must not only be done, it must appear to be done." The phrase dribbles out of his mouth like a waterfall. "I'm fully aware of the evidence marshalled against the accused and the vast resources used to conduct this trial. My own salary has been limited due to the hours spent hearing this case. Are you ready to move to sentencing, counsel?"

"I'm sorry, but did you not just acquit my client?"

"You know, counsel is correct! I am sorry, Mr. Koogan. It has been a long day of evidence."

He is really sweating now! thinks Koogan, *that stupid bastard was never really listening to any of the witnesses. That prick never really listens to anyone. His gerbil-like eyes and large drooling mouth is incapable of focusing on anything other than himself.*

"Please release the accused. If there is nothing more, he is free to go," Smith chortles.

Smith finally moves from his perch and looks up from the papers scattered across his desk. He suddenly stands up and extends his hands across the desk.

"I want to thank counsel for their excellent presentation of the evidence and the manner in which this case was conducted."

Koogan watches his heels turn and he begins to disappear behind the wooden wall that separates the presiding justice from the rest of the public. Within seconds, he is out of his sweat stained judicial robes and into his car, punching the accelerator and leaving the parking lot in a cloud of dust. Oz has left the building!

HYMAN KAZAN

33

BRITISH COLUMBIA

KAZAN RECALLS THE day he and Briar first discussed the idea of moving to the West Coast. They were to venture there together or separately, but it was time to escape the cold winters of Quebec and Ontario.

"Kazan," she said. "You know I love it here, but we both know we could be much happier out west. We should look at just packing it up and going west."

"I hate Calgary," he replied.

"No, no. I think we should move to Vancouver. Maybe Kitsilano Beach or the North Shore. Or White Rock."

"BC?"

"Yeah, BC. The weather is warmer, and Christ, you know the winters are only getting colder here. Quebec has no future for us. We need to get to Vancouver. We need a change of scenery! Everything is there," said Briar.

She had worked out the scene many times in her head: walks along the beach, nighttime skiing, and if Kazan played his cards right, maybe even a judicial appointment.

"We should go to BC and have the life we planned."

"You mean the life you planned."

"What? Kazan, don't you want to be happy?"

"Briar, it is entirely different living somewhere than just being on vacation. I have a feeling that you are just getting bored with me. I am sure that you will find things you do not like about Vancouver once you live there."

"Oh God, you should listen to yourself! It is like you have given up on happiness," said Briar, looking at the mirror just above the fireplace, studying the lines around her eyes while putting on a pair of chestnut brown glasses. "Well, I can tell you that I certainly have not given up on happiness. If there is a chance to breathe in clean air and walk a sandy beach or ski a mountain top, it would be a shame to pass it up."

He bent over to raise the window which would stick, so even with his strong arms, it involved some effort. As the cool winter air began to flow into the cabin, they were standing together, breathing deeply in the cold of the night, and Briar asked him if he had any dreams about their future together. He raised his eyebrows, and glanced around the room before leaning back on the mantle of the fireplace and smiling.

"Well, since you asked the question . . ." he started. "The whole purpose of moving would be to run to something rather than run away from something, don't you think?"

Briar cut him off immediately. "I know it is not easy to just pick up and move. But if not now, then when?"

He chuckled to himself. "Then I guess it is now, as we are drawing so very close to my best before date."

This made perfect sense to me at that time, he thinks. Her arguments were bolstered by how damn beautiful she was. He had thought Vancouver would be his own salvation island, and like the early penal island of St. Joseph, it was going to become his own institution of isolation, like those in French Guyana. His dreams and reality seemed so far apart. At the time of their conversation about moving, they were on a weekend getaway to the Laurentians. His mind held fast to the image of an Upper Canada old wood cabin and a roaring fireplace that had transfixed his dreams. After a half bottle of red wine, he nodded in the affirmative and booked their flights to the land of overpriced real estate, mountain views and seaside walks. He was all in. He signed on and boarded the plane to the West Coast willingly, yet blinded by what might have been and dismissive of what actually had been.

His heart sank when he had to make the trip alone. Finding her in Vancouver started the process wherein his heart began to cave in on itself, and the demands of his job in Vancouver began the slow and constant process of whittling away all of his and her dreams. Living in Vancouver at first, steps from the ocean, invigorated him. He would dance down a set of old grey wooden steps and spend the entire day listening to the roar of the ocean and the whisper of the driftwood and stones being bathed in the tide, letting the truth of his situation come to his own acceptance. Within these special moments, he knew that for all of his hopes and dreams, he could not change to fit into her life. He had to deal with what he had become, accept that his dreams were evaporating. He needed to search for the truth in his work and himself.

Years later, it is Smith who is blinded by his own distorted reality in how he sees Briar. While stopped at a stale red light, Smith daydreams about Briar and his impromptu plan of romance. Smith lets go of the stranglehold he has on the hard plastic D ring steering wheel of his late model Mercedes. He had maneuvered himself through the bumper-to-bumper traffic to find himself outside of Briar and Kazan's condominium. He glances down at his thick silver self-winding watch and notices the sweeping second hand appears to have the same nervous twitch that now inhabits his own body. *You are one hell of a judge*, he thinks to himself. Kazan will be stuck in Courtroom 103 for hours, while he has dispensed with his overscheduled trial in record time. Briar will be waiting for him to greet her at the front door of the condo. He can hardly wait to hold her.

Out of nowhere, Smith thinks he hears, "Hurry up, we have the place to ourselves. Kazan must be stuck in court."

He now feels the weight of the moment resting upon his tired shoulders. *If I had an ounce of self-respect*, he thinks, *I would drive by Briar's place.* Instead, he feels a tightness in his chest as he reaches for the door handle to his car, and pulling it toward him, he dances his way out the vehicle and into her waiting arms. She smells like alcohol and flowers, and he feels his libido rise to the occasion as he draws her closer. Soon they will be in the bedroom making love, with a careful eye on the time and the falling darkness of the autumn night.

"Bye, Briar."

And the weathered wooden door to her residence will close behind him. *That is the fucking end,* he will think. But it never is. He loves being with her as much as he likes punishing Kazan. His dream passes as he punches the accelerator and drives past Briar's darkened condo. The end of the road will be twisted and curved and full of potholes that will tug at their lives in ways they could never have imagined.

Kazan soon learns of their rendezvous which causes him to feel invisible. *I am nothing to her! A fucking failure!* His dreams evaporate with the knowledge that the woman he once loved is apparently devoted to a man he despises. He wonders to himself: *it doesn't make any sense. Was this the inevitable outcome of their coupling? Why did fate produce such a tragic result?* What could he have done to avoid this humiliation and emotional crash? If only he had the courage to let his pent up anger out and confront him, to expose the prick. To have him removed from the bench.

Emotionally drained and half drunk, Kazan arrives back to their apartment and finds it empty. He turns on a hallway light and dials Marianne's number. He is so used to coming home to a dark empty place, so used to being an indentured fool, that he listens helplessly for her to answer his call.

"Funny, I was just thinking about you," she says. Her voice is soft and welcoming. He is surprised by the intimacy of her tone.

"What were you thinking about?"

"I just thought we should talk about the Trinity case and everything, catch up, you know. We need to get together to work things out."

"What things? We have two women who can barely talk about being abused and a judge who does not give a shit about victims and who hates us."

"What a great chance at redemption or revenge then," she repeats softly. "The two outcasts are now closing in, finding a way to find some justice."

"Stop it!" he laughs. "Marianne, are you free for dinner?" The words come out so easily.

"Well, sure. What about Briar?"

"The hell with Briar! I am alone here and I could really use company right about now."

"Only you and me," she says with a loving kindness that is foreign to him. "There is so much to learn, so much that has to be worked out. Gee, Kazan, I would love to grab some dinner with you." She welcomes the opportunity to be alone with him.

"Great, I will come by your place in about forty minutes. Just need a quick shower to wash away this day," Kazan replies.

"Okay, I will meet you downstairs in about forty minutes. Just buzz me or text me when you get here."

"Great, see you soon then."

He laughs and hangs up the phone, surprised at how happy he is to be not staying in the apartment alone. He stands there in the shadowy glow of the hall light for a minute; he wants to run as fast as he can from the apartment. He begins to unbutton his dress shirt and drop his pants as he walks toward the en suite in their bedroom. He is eager to feel the warm shower and feel cleansed from his relationship with Briar. Eager to escape the unhappiness of the moment, he thinks about how the secret is to not be the one who is left behind.

In the shower, he lets the hot water cascade down upon the back of his tense muscles in his cramped wiry neck. He fumbles with the coconut butter shampoo, breathing in the deep smell of summer. His tense muscles begin to relax, and the soap bubbles cover his thick thighs. He thinks about Marianne and daydreams about her joining him in the steamy shower. In the fog of the shower, he dreams of her being right there behind him, rubbing his back as the shower water increases in temperature. He feels his heart swell and he is lost in a daydream as the water begins to lose its heat. He wants to caress her. He wants to give his heart to her. He wants her to lift him out of his depressed state, smile and hold his hand until the darkness vanishes from his loveless soul. He wants to breathe again and regain hope for tomorrow. Caged for far too long, he wants to give flight to all those special moments that make up a life.

"Oh, Marianne."

And at that moment, he hears the bathroom door open. *Damn it, she has returned to the cage.*

HYMAN KAZAN

34

BRITISH COLUMBIA

"BRIAR, WHERE HAVE you been?" A question posed with no anticipation of a response.

He gathers himself and steps from his shower, and the door of the bathroom is left wide open to reveal a sky that is silver grey above the snowcapped mountains framed by their bedroom window. With a plush white towel slung causally over his sculptured shoulder, he drips small droplets of clear bubbles of water on the grey barn board-coloured hardwood living room floor as he steps from the steamy fog created in the bathroom. The softness and warmth of the shower is replaced by the icy coldness of the condominium.

November is exceptionally wet this year, with cold damp days and windy nights. The trees that line the boulevards are stripped of all vegetation and light, twisted and broken branches lie scattered about the wide boulevards and car lined streets. When it rains, there is a feeling of sadness that is everywhere. Grim and cold winds blow in off the Pacific and empty the beaches. Cold snaps crush the huddled flowers who have survived October, only to be stamped out, eliminating any fond memory of the sweet summer. Kazan struggles to get himself out of bed each and every day, and will often spend hours just lying in bed, dreaming of sunlight and his joyful summer walks along the beach. The birds in the neighbourhood darken the noon hour sky, and naked branches shake in the gales that sometimes shake the lonely depressive fluid emotions that overwhelm him.

Briar does not comfort him during these dark days. Instead, she will linger outside of their apartment, drinking coffee or chatting on the phone with Smith. She begins to worry about how infectious his sadness has become, but she attempts to hide her concern from him. She does not want to reveal to him that she is consumed with the planning of the next chapter of her life and her desire to end their relationship. She pretends that it is only a rough patch in their stony and weed infested patchwork of a relationship that will be traversed quickly if they hold on to their once treasured history.

Sometimes, he will come home with his arms full of sunny yellow tulips or colourful market fresh wildflowers. Or he will stop off on his way home and pick up come cherrystone fresh oysters from Granville Island that he prepares for her with a clean cold glass of a lemony sauvignon blanc. Briar loves seafood and loves the smell of fresh flowers in every room.

"The flowers are calling cards, reminders of their past and predictors of the future," she would say.

He loves to see her happy.

Remembrance Day sets the somber mood for the month, and it comes and goes. Kazan works many long hours preparing for his endless string of provincial court trials. Briar stays at home during this time, finding salvation in an Okanagan bottle of wine and some artisan candles she has purchased downtown for when he will finally arrive home. She always prepares the stage for the night's performance, whether it is to be a romantic comedy or a heartfelt tragedy.

By 10 p.m. Kazan will arrive home, exhausted and lonely. The streets are quiet by then and he can navigate the West Coast traffic with little difficulty. The lobby of their place is then often occupied by young gay men. Young boys who work as waiters in the east end make their way out to their older lover's place for a night of frolicking. Their clothes are always neat and their ironed shirts are heavily starched as they parade in and out of the building. It is like they are showing up at a fine restaurant in search of something from a well familiar menu that will fill their expectations and reduce their loneliness. Briar will sometimes apologize for being so tired or for being out earlier in the evening when he arrives home. She is feeling the strain of his absence, and finds it more and more difficult to come to terms with his growing unhappiness. *Would another woman put up with his emotional and intellectual absence?* she ponders. Numb by the over consumption of alcohol, she will greet him swaying in her manicured bare feet, wearing a mid-length cotton dress, gathering comments and luring views from the neighbours whom she hates or completely ignores. Briar wonders whether she is mourning a dead relationship or setting the stage for her next one. A combination of regret and hope.

Sometimes, the gay boys engage her fantasies. They gather at the front door and offer a glass of wine from a bottle they have taken from their employer's secret cellar, often a bottle of champagne. Briar will laugh and extend her hand, already with a fine crystal champagne flute in it. She will bend down and tilt her head as if she is being knighted or congratulated for surviving another battle. She is gently kissed on her forehead, more like comforting a mourner than greeting a lover. It is not difficult to understand why she welcomes them. There are many young men of questionable sexual orientation in their neighbourhood, peddling circles around her, their taut young bodies within arm's length. Scooped up in the moment of each other's company. A dreamscape so foreign to her. They gather around her neighbourhood, going from house to house, in search of a never-ending party. Briar finds herself caught up in the merriment of strangers. She wants to be fearless again, free to laugh, cry, and dance. Not this waiting or longing for something that may never happen. She wants to be part of something, rather than just a distant observer.

A few short days before, she takes the LRT from downtown after a shopping excursion on Robson Street during the early afternoon hours. Kazan had been unreachable by phone and Smith was nowhere to be found. Koogan had sent her a copy of the menu for a new restaurant on the outer edge of Stanley Park. There was no mention of who might attend for their late lunch meeting. Her thoughts wander as she sits on the high-speed train and looks at the blank stares that feel like they encircle her. Flashes of light and colour race past her window as the rattling of the tracks is interrupted by the rush of air as the door to the car opens and closes at every stop. Briar reads the messages on her cell phone, reads them and rereads them as the train speeds past the next couple of stops, only to find herself lost in the passage of time and space.

She can see how she has widened the gap between her and Kazan. The passengers outside of the car huddle in an attempt to escape the singing rain as grey water bounces off the side of the train's window. She never imagined how lonely it would feel to be surrounded by so many rain soaked disheveled strangers. The sky is dark and grey with thick towering cotton candy clouds that block out all forms of light. Briar touches the rounded edges of her time softened leather bag. *Nothing,* she thinks, *is as it seems.* Some bad luck, some poor choices, some missteps, have cast her in this performance that borders on the absurd. She can feel the curtain dropping.

"BRIAR! WHERE THE hell have you been?"

Koogan gets up from a small table in the back of the glass enclosed restaurant hidden away on the edges of Stanley Park. He kisses her gently on the side of her face and pours her a glass of a dark familiar red wine.

*   *   *

Koogan is noticeably surprised when Briar tells him about her plans to leave Kazan and return to Quebec. They are huddled together in a friendly exchange when she unfolds the map of her unhappiness. Briar stares at him blankly as she awaits his response.

"You have to make a decision," Koogan says.

He is dressed in a dark blue suit and still has his tie cinched up to his five o'clock shadow throat, asking the many questions that race through his head.

"What are you going to do? Are you selling the condo? Why now? Do you think he will stay?"

Choosing to not answer his questions, she responds with: "I have been downsizing since we moved into the place. I guess I will just take a few odds and ends and have the rest shipped."

"Sounds expensive. I don't think I could ever go back east."

"I cannot imagine staying," she sighs.

"I'm sorry, Briar," Koogan responds. "I really had no idea of what was going on with the two of you. Work and time always gets in the way of those things that are the most important."

Briar pushes her hair back behind her ears and licks the bottom of her lip. She speaks confidently about the future with brief punctuated moments of hesitation.

"Sometimes, you just have to change to remain the same, you know, to get back to the way you used to be. I always felt like you, of all people, would understand that. You know, the need to get going," she says.

"You have me figured out. I just lack the courage to make a change," offers Koogan. "Still, why are you doing this now?" Koogan asks.

"He has already moved on. He wants me to move on too, pack up all our memories and turn the page on the few unwritten pages left in the stories of our lives," she says, attempting to put some poetic spin on her dilemma.

"Can you really let go?" he asks. He regrets asking the question as soon as it leaves him.

"I have to," she replies. "Or it will take me to depths of somewhere I cannot survive." Her eyes glisten with each answer she gives on how she feels trapped by her despair.

Koogan takes a measured sip from his glass of wine, and rubs the side of his head. His mind is contemplating his own thoughts of regret and guilt. The pause and silence alert Briar to his silent obvious reflection upon his own situation.

"We are different, John. Don't compare yourself to me," she whispers. "Because you can always let go of the things that pull us to the bottom."

"I have to find a way to survive. I do not know if I can, Briar."

"Well, you know in your heart, it is the leftovers, the crumbs of life, that cause us to stumble. They make us look over our shoulder, they cause us to feel regret, and they give us feelings of anxiety as to who might walk into or leave the room. To have a clean slate, John, sometimes we have to check out, so we can check in. We all go through this stuff together too often, John." She then takes a long swallow from her glass and looks up over the rim of the glass. "I am so sorry to have vented to you."

"I'm sorry too," he replies.

"Well, it is true that we go through this stuff together, too often, sometimes you just need to speak to someone who knows what to expect," she responds. "Remember, how I would phone Fridays when you were driving home from court. You would always call me when you were stuck in traffic or when you were forced to wait for someone?" She takes another long sip of her wine. "Jesus, John, we should have just fucked, then we would not be speaking to each other! Then we would hardly know what to say to each other anymore. Just please forget what I just said. Please, I am just so fucked up right now. Let's pretend that this conversation never happened."

"It is like walking down a dark alley. You hope you know where you are going, but you never really do, until you reach the street at the end of the alley or see a familiar street light, or wake up from an anxiety induced dream," says Koogan.

Briar runs her fingers again through her hair. *I have to go,* she thinks. *I have to get out of this conversation and out this place.* But before she gets up to go, coincidence deals an amusing and unexpected card.

"Hey! That's Casey Franklin. What the hell is he doing here?"

He is a judge known to both Kazan and Koogan. He wonders why they have wandered into the same restaurant as they had.

"I can't believe my luck. How can this be happening? Jesus, I need a break. That settles it, I am moving away from here, before this place destroys me. This place is like an ant hill, you just kick over one hill, and they start crawling around the place from another!" Briar exclaims.

"This is a sign, Briar!" Koogan adds. "You have to admit it. The road signs are all saying that your exit is coming up. You just have to just keep the car between the lines, or you will end up in the ditch or involved in a rollover," he quips.

They both laugh. It is a strange set of events, too unlikely to have ever occurred. No mercy for the weak of heart or those void of a sense of humour. Briar rises to her feet and pushes herself away from the table. Being discovered there with Koogan is a cosmic reminder of how things have gone terribly wrong. The likelihood of this happening is astronomical. How do you stay in the game, when the odds are stacked against you? Briar always felt confident that she knew when the right time was to leave the party, and it is becoming obvious that she has over played this losing hand. The glacier is within striking distance of the hull, and the time before impact is closing. Walking out the front door, she turns back to flash her mysterious smile in the direction of Franklin. Briar laughs to herself, and can now swear that it is his turn to feel uncomfortable.

HYMAN KAZAN

36

BRITISH COLUMBIA

KAZAN SEES MARIANNE walking outside of their apartment. The wind blows through her cinnamon hair, tossing it up toward her upturned collar. She is huddled down into her tan trench coat in a feeble attempt to stay warm and dry. It is a damp, raw day, and the temperatures are dropping. Watching her from the fifth floor of the condo makes him feel restless. He wants to run down to her and gather her up into his arms and give her some sense of shelter from the cold northern wind. Instead, he steps out of the reluctant elevator just in time to brush up against her shoulder. Her coat is now wet and cold, and turns up at every rain soaked corner.

"Hey, you," she says as a sad smile grows upon her face. "I just thought I would drop in and see if Briar was here."

"You just missed her," he replies.

Both of them stand there feeling relieved by their good fortune. She takes off her wrinkled coat and shakes the crystal clear raindrops from it. She is shivering as she enters the elevator. He attempts to hide the fact that he is staring at her. By the time their eyes meet, they are both feeling the warmth generated between them. He feels a strong uncontrollable impulse to ever so gently push her rain curled hair back from her forehead. She takes one step back, feeling a bit awkward by his attraction to her.

"It is so good to see you. I am going to stop there, before I say something stupid," he says.

"Too late, if that is your goal."

Her laugh is muffled by the sound of the wind when she opens the front door. She feels a bit of shame, being there with Kazan, and it feeling so familiar and comfortable. *I hate being judged by all those who have little or no knowledge or a true grasp of any of the facts,* she thinks. Her mind goes to the judicial system. She wonders why it is stacked full with entitled pricks from Southern Ontario, the bastard son of a banker here, or career politician there, who have come to BC via Toronto or Thunder Bay or elsewhere. They build their struggling careers on back slapping and political payback. None of these privileges are acknowledged by any of them, who often just consider themselves more intelligent or deserving than their bitter counterparts like her or Kazan.

Kazan takes her upstairs to the chaos of their apartment. He digs out a very expensive bottle of wine and takes down two glasses from the kitchen cupboard.

"I am having one, will you join me?"

"I guess, I can't have you drinking alone," Marianne says and finds a seat near the fogged window overlooking the edges of the parking lot.

She watches Kazan give the glasses a ceremonial wipe using a crisp white linen table napkin, as she watches him then gently unearth the cork from the bottle and pour the glasses half full of a deep purple wine and hold it up to the very little bit of daylight that filters into the room. He nods approvingly as he takes a small sip of the wine, and then gently places a glass into her small soft hand.

"What brings you over here?" he says. "I have been meaning to call you."

"I needed to talk to you about this upcoming trial. Smith has been a real son of a bitch and I am thinking of getting us off the record before this gets too out of hand. Maybe we can talk Stirling or Koogan into picking up this case for us. I used to care about these things, but God damn it, I know with this trial, it will never be a fair one. I just can't take it anymore. I need to feel we have a puncher's chance. I am not just going down to the amusement of Smith on this one. The victims of Trinity Rivers deserve a chance, don't they?"

She has sputtered out all of her concerns without stopping to take a breath.

"I get it," he replies. He studies the concern and anxiety that is splashed across her face. "Where I am standing, it looks like you want me to give you a reason to stay."

"I just can't."

"What would you say if I told you we will not lose this case, that it is a tap in? That all we have to do is rid ourselves of Smith!"

"I would say you have finally lost your mind, or you have something on Smith."

"I can't go into it right now, but sure as Bill Bennett was a Social Credit or Jimmy Pattison sold signs, we will not lose this case."

He then shines a crooked smile that lights up the room and his eyes twinkle with a phosphorus light and mischief that she has never before witnessed. She laughs at this new found gift of hope that he has left unwrapped in a riddle at her feet.

Later that day, they end up at Kafka's Coffee, a popular twentysomething occupied coffee shop down the street. Her latte comes as soon as they are seated, and he is surprised by the size of the cup of steaming hot coffee in contrast to her own diminutive size. Coffee houses like this dot the north and western shore, becoming the new speakeasy for those who seek shelter from the rain while refusing to overspend on a mounting bar bill or an honest conversation.

He is staring at the wedges and curves of the sand-coloured sandwiches lined up in a fogged glass cabinet near the cash register. They are large sized crusts of bread jammed full of soft milky cheese and fire roasted root vegetables. There is a mouth-watering array of freshly made panini sandwiches, reminding him of both Manhattan and San Francisco.

Just as he is imagining the crunch of the fresh bread between his teeth and the silky creamy cheese in the back of his throat, he hears Stirling call out, "Kazan! Kazan!"

Coincidence and circumstance have found him.

"I heard you are going to trial, is that true?" he says, shaking his head.

Kazan stands up and nods in the affirmative ever so slowly.

"Really? Do you think you can win this one? Do you think you can even get a fair shake, with the Briar thing and all?"

"I don't know, but I am running out of options," Kazan answers back.

Stirling finds it difficult to contain his excitement as he thinks about the potential fireworks that could erupt between the two men.

"I have never heard you say that," Stirling responds.

"Well, it is hard to admit when you know that you are pissing against a very strong wind," Kazan jokes.

He seems unphased by the anticipated tension created by the thought of appearing before Smith on such a media-fueled circus of a trial.

"And what about your co-counsel, what does she think?"

"Oh, well you will have to ask her yourself."

Marianne glances a hesitant grin in the direction of Stirling, laughs, and responds, "We have nothing to lose! Prepare for the worst, and hope for the best."

"Spoken like a true follower! Only Kazan would go running wildly into a fire with a gas can. But you should think about your future, you know, give some thought about the case that will follow, after this one, the case that you will be remembered for."

"This is that case!" she responds and then further adds, "I am not sure there will be another case."

"What? There is always another case, Marianne! Even when we don't want one, there is always another case."

"Not for me. I am tired of this meat grinder. I want to live a real life, an honest life, a life without everyone else's problems. Where my thoughts and problems are my own!"

"Damn it, Marianne, we all want that," Stirling says.

He has ignited a response from her.

"I am serious!" And as she says this, she realizes that gravity and reason are in short supply. "But you know something, Stirling? You must make it stop or it will pull you into the grave with it when you least expect it. Fate is a very unwelcome friend."

Stirling is taken back by this emotional philosophy lesson he has just received and says, "You are starting to sound like him," as he points to Kazan.

She laughs, pushes him away, and just takes a second to think about all that she has just said. Maybe she disclosed too much.

Kazan can sense that she is totally emotionally invested in their case beyond his expectations. The scenario is so familiar to him: another woman he has pulled into a bloody fight with him and others, with little hope of winning. Kazan rises to his feet and pulls on his coat, and then with a dancer's grace, orders a glass of expensive scotch from a young bespeckled waiter.

"Isn't it a bit early?" Marianne says, gripping her half-drunk coffee.

"On the contrary, it might be a little too late," he scoffs.

HYMAN KAZAN

37

BRITISH COLUMBIA

KAZAN HAS A few short weeks to prepare for the Trinity trial. He needs a place to think and isolate himself, so he decides to go out to the island location of Tofino. The village of Tofino is full of places to escape. The smudged headline of the much read travel section of Vancouver Sun says so. Late November brings out the dark nimbus storm clouds and tower high waves and crazy blond hair surfers in search of their next high energy adrenaline rush. Young men and women from both Toronto and Vancouver fall upon bohemia to ingest the fresh cool Pacific air and escape their suburban cages. Something about the wild Pacific coast, Kazan thinks, where the roar of the ocean and the force of the wind can melt away all of one's tortured anxieties.

He takes a sweeping second to close his tired eyes and focus on the distance between perception and memory, and then to open his eyes and stare outside at the blueberry stained storm clouds that are forming. The blast of a rogue wind out of the southwest causes the beach to swirl, spinning grains of sand and time against those who have chosen to walk the strand. Movement is everywhere, shuffling the deck of his reality. It could be that he is just captured in the moment, a bit stoned on the scotch and the morphine prescribed for his back pain. His head and heart are full of conflict and paradox.

It could be that he is just trying to escape his life back on the mainland, the scotch and the leftover morphine he discovered in their suite had orchestrated his feelings of floating upon the tops of the waves. A flock of dove grey seagulls cry overhead. He wanders into a half empty seaside bistro in search of a buffer from the sound of the wind and his loneliness.

A couple of scruffy hipsters are seated by the fireplace. The twentysomething woman has blond hair and aqua-coloured eyes framed by sienna eyebrows. Kazan is caught by her physical beauty. Her dumbfounded male friend looks like an over toasted piece of rye bread. Their faces are lit up from the orange glow from the fireplace. Kazan cannot help himself from eavesdropping on their animated conversation.

"When are you going to tell her?" she asks. "She is going to find out one way or another. There always comes a reckoning!"

It is like she is drawing a line in the ever-shifting sand of their relationship. He squirms in his redwood stained hoop back chair, looking for a way out of this loosely fashioned snare she has set for him. Kazan has seen this beginning of a sense of an ending in his own fractured life. He smiles at his male counterpart from across the room, as if to provide some assurance as to the thickness of the ice he has unknowingly ventured upon. *It is foolish,* he thinks; *he has already slipped from the cliff with no easy landing in sight.*

And now the background music has been turned down and so as to create the illusion of privacy, he excuses himself from his chair and stumbles in search of the washroom. He is a bit unsteady on his feet, a combination of the alcohol and the lack of movement. He hopes that when he returns, they will be gone, and that he has escaped from any further drama that was about to unfold. When he returns, he flips through the assortment of discarded papers that he has removed from the case file. The meat of the case against the accused, a few statements, a police narrative or a synopsis outlining the fiction of what was the spine of the case he would have to tackle. A waitress flashes him a smile. She stands in front of the vacant table beside him, moving the empty glasses around the table like toppled chess pieces in search of the right juxtaposition for one of the younger staff to remove them. She picks up the crooning flowers from the small blue vase on the table and draws them up to her face and smells them. Then she brushes her hair back and carefully wraps them in a white towel to be hidden away until her shift is over. The lights are now being dimmed for the later crowd. She is like a performer in a play that no one will see. She moves around her stage with both grace and a mechanical movement. The bartender appears from behind the bar and saddles up to her.

"They are finally gone. Jesus, I thought that they were going to fight here all night long," he sighs.

"No, she just wanted something he couldn't give her," she responds.

"I am sure that no man could keep a woman like her happy?"

"It is not about happiness. It is about honesty."

"In their case, both were undoubtedly absent!"

Kazan looks down at his mound of drink circled papers and thinks to himself that his life had taken a similar path. That point when you reach the inevitable bend, the blind spot on the road, you sense that you know the right way to turn, but in truth, it is a 50/50 chance you will miss the turn. The rough road ahead sign is rarely posted. The road is washed out due to floods, no such sign ever contemplated. He did not recall any fear of the unknown, he did not have the self confidence that everything would be alright, despite the repeated incantations of positive thoughts and phrases. He knows the cost of failure all too well. The paradox of life, it was the best of times, it was the worst of times, they all awaited his decision. He knows all too well, that success is not a continuum, that it is voluntary. He catches himself in the moment, and then folds the vanilla-coloured drink bill in a couple of twenty dollar bills and places it under a thick water glass. Payment for the privilege of being reminded of his failures rather than criticized.

He walks away from his scattered thoughts and the bar is empty and lonely. *I want to get a life,* he thinks, as if the key to the cage is somewhere within arm's reach. He feels empty and alone. Outside, it is a typical damp cold day. The temperature drops as the rain moves in over the mountains. His coat is stylish but not nearly warm enough. He starts walking west bound in search of his car, and by the time he has reached his driver's door, his teeth are chattering and his body aches from the cold damp air. He arrives back at the ferry terminal just in time.

Hours pass until he finds his way back to their condominium. He has not been there in days, and the first thing he sees as he enters the shadowy hallway to their unit is the amber flashing light on the top of their cheap plastic telephone. He fumbles with the phone, standing dripping in the living room, and feels the rush of the warmth from the room. His throat is dry and irritated. The room is in disarray, papers and a collection of wine and drinking glasses are spread across every smooth surface. The shutters are wide open and catch the dim glow of the street lights and nearby late afternoon traffic.

Her lack of consideration is obvious, she is too self-involved to take time to clean up their residence. She has not left a note or a message, explaining where she might be. *What the hell happened to caring about each other*, he thinks. The phone just keeps flashing as he staggers through each message left on their answering service. *Why the fuck have I returned?* He shuffles from room to room, cleaning up and turning the lights on, and walks over to the phone and presses the icon for his messages. He searches his memory for the code that will take him to the menu option to retrieve his messages. Briar found it so incredible that he would often struggle with this bargain store twenty dollar answering service.

"It is damn annoying," he would say.

The whole process of scrolling through menus and inputting codes made him regret throwing out his old Panasonic answering machine. It worked good, just press rewind and then play. The bedroom is warm and the bed is disturbed. He imagines her lying there with the softness of cotton sheets draped over her midriff. Maybe he is losing his mind. Maybe she left him and only took a brief second to leave him a message on the blasted answering machine.

Why does she do this to me? To have this control over my every waking thought and emotion. He imagines his hands around her hips as he draws her closer to his electrified cock. Once inside her, he will melt into her and she will fold all around him, causing many thoughts of complaining or leaving to vanish. Briar controls him, makes him feel and acts like no other woman before. She presses the electrical nerves that run down his spine, she reaches into his abandoned childhood and manipulates his imagination and is worshipped by him.

"I ache for you," she would say. "Quickly remove your pants," as she tugs at his belt. "I want you now."

He would get so excited with her, he would abandon whatever plan of seduction he had conjured up and replace it with his feeble attempt to keep pace with her insatiable sex drive. *I should have never returned!* Cut and run, how can you escape the cage that you have carefully constructed for yourself? This question haunts him. How can he forgive her for her transgressions and unfaithfulness? Angry, he wonders why his life has taken such a turn. Like the tide of the Pacific below him, wave after wave, the constant pounding was eroding the essence of that which kept him whole. *Fuck the messages!*

He finds his thickest sweater and grabs his weathered briefcase. He reaches for a pad of yellow legal paper and begins to write out a note for Briar, but then throws the crumpled up paper into the dented grey waste paper basket, and locks the front door as he pulls the door shut behind him. Outside, the rain and wind have picked up. *More rain, will it ever stop?* He tilts his head back and feels the rush of cold water on his forehead. He looks up at the sky in search of the source of the cold air and darkness that has plagued him. On days like this, he reminds himself of the joy of living on the West Coast, far from the cold snow of Eastern Canada. He longes for the crackle of dry wood on a well stoked fire. He drives down Cordova street to a small late night bar where he finds her.

HYMAN KAZAN

38

BRITISHCOLUMBIA

SCOTCH OPENS THE lines of an array of curious conversations. It makes Briar softer and more open, as if she no longer has to pretend to play a role she is ill-equipped to perform. The more she drinks, the less he knows about her. She becomes more and more mysterious with each glass consumed. Sitting in a Queen Anne chair across from Briar and Koogan, Kazan spins out his trial tactics. It is like handing out coupons for a new restaurant to a series of bored and contented patrons. Koogan resembles a patient going in for a root canal and Briar can't wait to refill her glass from the scotch bottle. She feeds lines to Koogan between muttered obscenities and half-baked television scenarios. She drops case names and judges, and keeps pouring herself another drink. He watches her, but says nothing. Looking out the window, she senses that he wants to provide something to the titled conversation.

So, she stops mid-sentence, cracks a smile and asks him an open-ended question, "What will you do to get out of this mess?"

He cocks his head, looks at her, and wonders if they are thinking of the same predicament.

"Where is the way out, Briar?" Kazan asks.

"I know that you need to nail down a solution quickly as the boat is taking on water! Especially with your poor swimming skills," she chortles.

He looks confused and yet carefree and consumed with his incredibly daunting task. Still, she senses a confidence and humility about him. Perhaps it was the alcohol she had consumed, but she finds his self-confidence to be very interesting. He is a master litigator, there is no doubt about his skill level, but this situation is very different. She wants him to show her the cards he is thinking of playing, to include her in the game. She wants to understand how he can determine the outcome, rather than the fluid situation that is always surrounding him.

"I think advocacy is a bit like chess. You choose your next move in anticipation of your opponent's weaknesses, anticipated inclinations and moves. It would be fatal to just react to the circumstances, rather than to take some form of control over them. Trial work is spontaneous and explosive. Sometimes, you just simply hold on as the ice breaks underfoot. Other times, you roar into the wind. The secret is to play the odds."

Who is he trying to convince or win over now? she thinks. She is attentive and eager to be part of the scenario. She is concerned that the game is rigged or that the puzzle is missing a few key pieces.

"We need to know when to attack and encircle, and more importantly, when to retreat," Kazan says.

"Retreat! There is nowhere to go. This is not an option. It is an act of desperation without merit." The thought of giving up makes Koogan sick.

Kazan brings his right hand up to his face and holds his chin, before addressing the standing Koogan and Briar.

"What choice do I have? I never even wanted this one." He looks so lost and challenged by their lack of support for him. "Every damn time," he continues, placing his hand on her shoulder. "I allowed myself to get caught up in all the bullshit, I ended up wearing it."

"I think you can't help yourself," Koogan chimes in. "You like the rush from trying to run down the stairway of a building on fire. It is in your DNA."

It is 8:30 in the evening, but it feels like an exhausted midnight. The rain has turned to sleet, and they have chased the scotch with two bottles of red wine. Briar gets up and disappears into the lobby of the hotel. Koogan staggers out into the darkness amidst the forest of tables that hold overturned chairs. When Briar returns later to the apartment, she is greeted by his soft lips and fingers running down the side of her neck.

"Just us now, Briar, just us!"

"I am caught in the kaleidoscope," Briar says and laughs, swaying as she stands in front of him.

Her clothes are tumbling like autumn leaves from her body. There is a small crack of moonlight now shining in from the balcony. Briar and Kazan hold each other in the shuttering darkness. They are quiet, but her eyes grow wide as he holds her tightly. She sees that he is drunk and that he wants to escape with her. His anger and anxiety have now been discarded, and he becomes tender and confident. He grows more and more firm and hard as she grows softer in his hands. His lips seek out her breasts as his hands caress her.

"I need to tell you something."

"What? Oh sure, anything," he says.

"I am going to leave for a while after this trial."

The room becomes silent. She hears his breathing change. It is as if someone else is in the room. Kazan lets go of Briar. He becomes pale and appears breathless and excited.

"Briar," Kazan calls out, and attempts to catch her before she has left the room.

There are tears in his eyes as large as raindrops. Looking back, she sees the pain he has attempted to hide from her for so very long.

"What just happened?" Kazan asks.

"I am okay."

"What do you mean?" he asks her, but his question goes unanswered.

She makes her way into the other room and finds a chair and sits down. There is a small amount of blood falling from the corner of his mouth. The blood looks crimson with an orange hue and runs down his chin. Briar gets up and grabs a towel and places it against his face.

"Do you need me to get something or take you somewhere?"

Kazan grabs the edge of the towel and cleans his face. This is the first time she has seen his blood, the evidence of his ill health. He does not know what to say, or how to explain the sickness he is suffering from. *Another complication. Another problem to be explained or ignored,* she thinks to herself.

"Are you sure you are ok?" Briar asks.

"I think so, it is nothing," he replies in a tone that suggests he is not telling her the complete story. Kazan's complexion tells another story.

"I am worried about you, you really don't look that well," Briar says. "You kind of look like you have been run over . . . Maybe we should call someone!"

"It is nothing, I just have been at it . . . going at it a bit hard lately. I guess . . . maybe I should just slow down and catch my breath. I was feeling okay and then all of a sudden it's like one more fucking thing to worry about," he sighs.

"You have to get a grip on things, or all this bullshit is going to kill you. And I just can't take it anymore," she answers back.

The moment has passed and he always returns to her. His breathing becomes a bit laboured. She can be suffocating at times. Briar thinks about the sight of his blood, and the sacrifices that they have made in search of a better life—the life that seems to be evaporating from the room. The towel is now soaked with a tan like crimson in his shaking hand. She offers up one more attempt to drive him to Lions Gate Hospital. He rejects her like she is a used car salesperson in search of commission.

"I will be fine!" he says with a slight slur to his words. "I have to meet with Marianne and prepare."

"Suit yourself," is her only response.

Looking back, it all appeared so unreal and cruel at the time.

"I am sure you and Smith understand what it is like to have to prepare a case, in the hopes of serving someone other than yourself," he cracks.

He is holding on to the counter, attempting to steady himself.

"Jesus, Kazan, why do you have to bring up this shit now!"

And with that, he lets go of the end of the counter and falls into a chair in the living room. At first, Briar is relieved that the worst might be over. It is such a typical ending to a familiar fight. Then she kneels down beside him as he appears slumped in the chair. She dials 911 and asks for an ambulance, while never letting go of his hand. Briar watches him as she waits for the ambulance to arrive. He looks pale and unresponsive. He appears lethargic and in a dream like state or trance. She knows immediately that something is really wrong. Just before the EMC staff arrive, Kazan opens his eyes and trembles.

"Just try and relax, they are on their way," Briar says while holding his head and brushing his hair back from his forehead.

Briar holds his head against her chest while he attempts to regain his balance.

"You are going to Lions Gate. Just close your eyes and relax!" she orders.

Briar and a young ambulance attendant named Todd help him lie down on the dented and scratched aluminum gurney that takes him to the waiting ambulance. The other residents of their building gawk from their balconies as he is loaded into the van. They have never seen him look so vulnerable, as he always has the appearance of strength and vitality.

The waiting area of the emergency department is over crowded with kids screaming, wives with scowls on their faces and old men shuffling about. Masked Chinese immigrants look like bandits walking among the wounded. Wheelchairs and babies are tucked into the corners. The television sets blare out the breaking news broadcast by CNN. The only ones given priority are those suffering from heart attacks or a failed chemical suicide. Briar demands that Kazan be seen ahead of those with fever or the elderly in search of conversation. The hallways are also jam-packed. The fog and rain of the day has caused many accidents that night, so young RCMP officers scurry about like ants on a piece of rotten fruit. Cases of impaired driving and those that had fish tailed into hydro poles dominate the landscape.

It is hours before a young intern approaches Kazan who is lying in the hallway with an ice pack pressed against his face. He mutters that he is fine, and that Briar has simply overreacted to a minor health problem, but he looks like a boxer who has been knocked out on his feet. He struggles to regain his balance and attempts to prop himself up on the edge of the stretcher in the hallway. His athletic body now looks exhausted and weak as it dangles over the edge of the starched white cover sheet.

"Let's get out of here!" he says.

But Briar demands that he gets a scan or an x-ray or something before being let go. It is like she lacks any confidence that he will make it back to a taxi without falling down. She paces the hallway with her machine made coffee, waiting for someone to acknowledge them further. Dr. Kelly Martin, a third year intern finally sees Kazan. He wears a pair of light blue scrubs and scuffed dirty ivory New Balance running shoes. His hair is chestnut brown and the band of his underwear peeks out of the top of his gaping blue cotton pants. He looks to be about twenty-seven years of age. This is not what Briar expected or feels is needed to calm her fears about Kazan's lack of a solid diagnosis. *This is a boy who should still be an undergrad,* she thinks as she struggles to see him as a doctor fully qualified or one to have hospital privileges. Confusion is what his face advertises. A hipster doctor who has been called in at the last moment to usher around the sick before a real physician will arrive from the city.

"How are you feeling?" he asks.

"Just great, how about you?" Kazan quips.

Briar barks at his nonchalant manor. "He is sick and he was oozing blood," she offers.

"I see."

He removes his stethoscope and places it under Kazan's shirt and listens to his heart. He rubs his forehead and looks back at the two of them.

"You think you are okay to go home?"

The question baffles Briar as she knows exactly what his answer will be.

"I am fine, just need to get a bit of rest."

"Jesus, Kazan!" she pleads. "We are here now. Tell him what the hell is going on. I mean, explain the trial and the pressure you are under."

"Please, Briar," he replies. "Let's just go home. I will be better tomorrow, just need a bit of rest."

Still, a couple of hours are spent there while they monitor his heart and watch him for signs of a stroke. The doctor urges him to get some rest and book an appointment with his family doctor, and a follow up visit to see a cardiologist or neurologist to determine what has caused this recent episode of medical distress. They leave the hospital with his medical prognosis remaining a mystery.

It is cold when they reach the taxi that has been called to take them home. The temperature has dropped and ice is beginning to form on the roads and parking lots. The coastal mountains are now dressed in snow caps. Kazan is awakened by the rush of cold air and jokes about their hospital visit. He holds her hand tightly and talks about the age of his attending physician.

"He kept saying, are you okay, are you okay?"

He keeps looking at Briar in the side mirror of the car. She sees how he is focused on her.

"I love you. You really had me worried this time," Briar says as the car turns into the driveway of their complex.

It is early morning now and Briar fumbles with the keys to their unit. Kazan is overheated by the drive and quickly removes his shirt and goes straight to the living room couch to fall asleep. He still has the clear blue plastic hospital bracelet on his wrist and is naked under a soft cotton quilt left out on the coffee table from the night before. Rain mixes with ice pellets outside the balcony window. She stands there, looking at him as he sleeps. She is over tired, but still feels the adrenaline from the way the evening unfolded.

In this moment, she is struck by how fragile he looks, and recalls her own father's attendance at the Emergency department in a hospital back in Ontario. It was a brief stay. He had driven himself to the hospital, only to die a short few days later of congestive heart failure. She recalls the width of his hospital bracelet between her first and second fingers, and the rough edge of where it had been fastened. The sight of Kazan's bracelet brings a flood of these memories back for her. To Briar, the hospital is viewed as the door you cross when all hope is gone. It is not remembered by her as a healing place; rather it is a place where death comes calling. A dirty and dark place where germs and uncaring medical staff usher in your final demise. She hates the place, and the brutal way in which those that are most vulnerable are left to die alone. She promises herself, and Kazan, that she will move heaven and earth to not allow them to suffer the destruction that is masked by the BC medical community.

Outside, the stars struggle against the wind and clouds. She steps into the bathroom to look into the mirror and sees the emotional scars that have bubbled to the surface from the worry and anxiety created by the night. *Breathing,* she thinks, *is the sign that can't be faked. It reveals when you are calm, when you are in distress, and when life has escaped your grasp.* She takes in the air from the open window in their bedroom deep into her lungs. She recalls the last night they slept together, and how Kazan had a calmness to his breathing patterns, a sign of an absence of worry that she now longed for. Briar focuses on that wonderful memory as she finally falls gently asleep.

"THEY ARE FUCKED. Trinity Rivers is a complete cluster—enough work for five lawyers! Marianne is way, way over her head! And Kazan is killing himself!" Briar is raising her voice to a perplexed Koogan.

The situation is not lost on him.

"Maybe he has found some evidence that will crack the case wide open," Koogan responds with a tight grin across his flushed face.

"Not likely," Briar responds.

"You don't know Kazan," Koogan barks.

"I know he is very tired and just got out of the hospital. He looks like he going to drop at any moment."

"Can we talk about something else?"

Koogan puts his late model BMW station wagon in third gear. The car jerks and then accelerates up a rain soaked Burnaby Mountain toward Simon Fraser University. The car lurches and slides with the quick acceleration all the way up Gaglardi Way. The rain on the roadway causes the car to hydroplane as it rounds the bend before coming to the lights that shine red just before the campus. The worn windshield wipers pull and bounce across the front window, making an annoying sound as the window becomes more and more streaked. An expensive car with cheap

Canadian Tire wipers, none of it made any sense, but everything seemed that way at that time.

"You will love the view from up here. It will remind you of Norway or Switzerland."

"I somehow doubt that," says Briar. "You are always selling me on Burnaby. When are you finally going to sell your condo and move back into the city?"

"When the market settles down. Damn Asians are driving up the prices, and plus, I like it up here. It can be raining down where you are and sunny up here."

"More likely to be raining up here," says Briar.

It is so awkward to be spending time with Koogan while Kazan is healing back at home, she thinks.

"Do you think maybe, just maybe, you could give Kazan a hand this time?"

He swallows and looks into the streaked rear view mirror, allowing silence to pass for his answer. All this time, he considered himself a friend of Kazan's but never even spoke to an adjournment for him. Once upon a time, he and Kazan were close friends, but everything was different now. No matter their past history, there was now some unspoken misunderstanding that plagued their relationship, and the time spent with Briar, just enhanced it.

Kazan makes it up off the couch in time to call up Marianne at the courthouse. It has been months since his last serious trial. He is feeling the ring rust.

"It is good to talk to you today, Marianne. I guess we need to start putting together the case against Trinity Rivers."

"Are you okay? The courthouse said you had a stroke or a heart attack," she says.

"They wish it was so," he replies. "I just had a bad reaction to some day old sushi, nothing serious. Now, when are we going to get things together for this trial?"

She does not know whether she should take him seriously or just brush it off as gallows humour. She asks him if next Wednesday works for him. They could meet at their office and review all of the statements and put together a war room. He hangs up the phone having agreed to meet with her and start the wheels rolling on their case. He has just hung up the phone when Briar returns home.

"Is there any of that Saxon cheese left over from last night?" Briar says.

"Yes, it is in the bottom drawer beside the prosecco."

She grabs the neck of the dark green bottle and tugs at the embedded cork. The cork comes flying out with a pop, and she places the bottom of the bottle against her lower lip. She takes a slow and sensual sip of the bubbly Italian aperitif. She breaks off a small piece of cheese and twists it into the corner of her mouth. The mixture of the crisp apples contained in the prosecco and the smoothness of the cheese dance in her mouth.

"Mmmm I love that. It is so good in your mouth." She lets the smoothness of the cheese and wine melt in the back of her throat.

"Briar! You just got home. Maybe you should take it easy for a day?" Kazan raises his voice.

"If you are not up to it, Kazan, I bet you Marianne would be."

The thing is, Marianne lacks the same energy as Briar. *It is strange to have this venom filled dialogue with her now,* he thinks, *moments after just speaking with Marianne. It is like some strange twisted Samuel Beckett play with the disoriented audience being asked to determine the outcome of the play.*

"Briar, you are one of a kind. I love you."

He is tired but still amused at her energy and desire to engage him in an argument. A whispered silence follows.

A week later, Briar will recall that night to be a very romantic evening that led to significant love making and promises of a new future. There was no lack of willpower on the part of Kazan when it came to changing things; every compromise that could be made was made, and done so in the name of progress. But there was the lingering sting of the upcoming trial. Later, he will be so embarrassed about the way he had become ill and was taken to the hospital, that he will forget how sick he had really become. He will forget about the blood and the weight loss and how unstable he was that evening, and she will forget how worried she was that he may not be able to return home.

The living room of their home now becomes a second office with scattered papers and cracked books and tapes strewn everywhere. After several glasses of scotch, the room sways and he will seek out Briar for an eager interruption from his problems. Stumbling around, she will approach him while he works in her half buttoned shirt. He will stop whatever he is reading immediately and stand up and reach in under her shirt and remove her bra and then slide his soft fingers over her cupped breasts. Her body will warm to his touch, and she can feel the electricity generating between them. She will allow her body to become light and drift from the corner of the room in front of the French doors that lead to their balcony. She becomes the art that is displayed in the room. Translucent like a diamond caught in the sun, she will turn and float into his arms. He will then kiss and caress and probe her while he makes promises of giving her more of his time. This will result in her unfolding, a softness dampens her thighs and mouth. She will softly kiss his mouth while holding tightly onto his wrists. He will tell her that once the trial is over, they will be free of all stress and pain, and for those few seconds, she allows herself to be free and filled with the radiance of his desire. The bond between them is so strong, so all encompassing, it spreads an energy like a late bone dry summer forest fire on the island. She is often drunk with emotion at these times, craving to be rescued from all her fears and dashed dreams. The room smells of fresh cut flowers and salty sea breezes. She lifts up the tulips on the stone faced fireplace mantle, and stares into his eyes.

"Do you love me, Kazan? Do you want me as much as I want you?"

She understands his vulnerability, and this causes her to persist in her playful questioning.

"I do, sweet Briar, I do," he will say. "But I must work. I must figure this damn mess out."

"Oh, come with me, let's make love," she will say.

"Jesus, Briar, can we just . . . will you just . . . and then . . . God." He lets out a deep sigh and makes his way to the bedroom.

It is like he is auditioning for the rest of his life. She will have already removed her clothing and climbed under their striped sheets, waiting patiently for him to climb in beside her. It is then that his cell phone begins to ring.

"Just answer it," she says.

He attempts to ignore the ringing. It rings four times while he walks toward it. And then it finally stops and flashes as a message is being recorded. It is an interruption in a hyphenated day and she just wants to walk along the sea wall with his hand in hers. He rises to his feet from his chair. Outside, grey cold clouds are forming and the wind begins to howl. The drizzly rain starts to fall and continues to fall, fat puddles begin to pool outside their balcony door. It is one of those days when you just want to light a fire, pour a glass of wine, and curl up under a soft throw blanket. This is winter weather. She holds herself and jumps up and down as she pulls on a heavy charcoal-coloured sweater. Kazan follows her lead and grabs a sweater from the back of the chair in the bedroom and throws it on as he begins to fumble with his cell phone. He always forgets to put things away: books, phones and sweaters all end up in the corner of the room. It is mid-morning now and the rain has finally stopped. He stretches and releases some of the tension in his back and places the phone on the top of his dresser. He wants to walk on the beach and simply throw it as far as he can into the deepest end of the ocean. Briar gets to her feet and gathers up her night clothes and skips into the bathroom.

"You can't just ignore all the calls, Kazan," she calls out from the bathroom.

"I know," he barks. "Likely a robo call from Eastern Canada. You know, I had four of those damn calls yesterday. But you know, I will check for messages later."

"What are these, Kazan?" she asks while holding a pill bottle she found in their bathroom. A few white tablets are cradled in her palm. "What are you doing," she says. "Are you trying to kill yourself or me? I know you have been under a lot of stress lately, but why are you taking these?"

She is always so dramatic and her sense of timing cannot have been worse. Moments after discovering his pills in the bathroom, she begins to spin out of control.

"I knew you were on something. You just have not been yourself lately."

Later when she has settled down a bit, she attacks him with this, her eyes filled with both sadness and regret.

"I think you enjoy dragging the razor across your wrists!! I am not going to just stand here and watch you disintegrate. I want out!"

"I am sorry," Kazan answers back.

". . . just can't sit and watch you kill yourself and me."

"Hold on, Briar, it is not like that. I just have a lot on my plate right now."

Something comes over him and he is filled with a gut wrenching nausea and pain, accompanied by a sharp twitch in his side. *What am I going to do now that she is thinking of abandoning me?* He can tell from her voice that she is at the end of her rope. He begins to pace the floor.

"We just can't run from this one, Briar," he whispers. "You know this is the last case for me."

Briar is standing in the doorway of their bedroom. She is now fully dressed and is wearing a raincoat and appears very nervous. She motions for him to retrieve her shoes from beside the bed. He bends down and retrieves them for her.

"Why do you always do that thing?"

"What?"

"You know, you drop your voice and kind of mumble when you want things to slow down, or you want a jury to listen."

"I'm not."

"Yes you are, and it is about time you were honest, Kazan."

"Honest! Honest!! What the fuck do you know about being honest, Briar?"

"Don't get nasty with me. I do not have to take this from you."

"No, you don't."

She turns away and starts to walk towards the door.

"Hold on, hold on. Can you just give me a minute?"

He wants to find something that will put everything back to the way things once were, but he is afraid to engage her rage.

"Please don't go, Briar, just give me a minute."

"Okay," she says while standing steps from the front door.

"I just need a bit of time to sort out this mess."

"You have had months, Kazan. You should have not agreed to do this," she says.

"What? I thought it was something that would help our situation."

"Don't give me that, Kazan. This is all about you."

And then she turns around and walks out of their apartment. He stands there in the silence of the room for a few seconds, and then walks back to the living room and pours himself a drink. He thinks to himself, *what could I have said to have changed things?* He wants to find the words to make her understand the stress he is under. He wants her to jump back into their bed and pull the covers up. He wants a steaming hot cup of cappuccino and the sound of her reading aloud from the morning newspaper. He wishes she had never left him, and especially not now. He grows angry with himself. He should have found the words and promises that would have stopped her cold from walking out that door. He pours himself another scotch and leans up against the kitchen counter. Looking at the isle of papers spread across the living room, he sees the painting that he had bought in a small gallery in Quebec City hanging on the west wall of the room. He listens to the gathering silence of the room. The sun is now breaking through the stone-coloured clouds and reflecting off a mirror, causing a rainbow to form across the floor in front of him, an illustration that hope and colour are still somewhere in his world. He wants to call her on his cell phone. *Don't do it, don't go running back to something you cannot fix,* he thinks.

Later, when he finds the courage to leave their apartment, he will find the faint scent of her perfume on his cold damp jacket. It will remind him of her, and his mind will be flooded with the memories of their walks on the beach. Once seated in the car, he feels the cold emptiness of a small space. Streaks of raindrops across the windshield remind him of the sadness of her leaving. The windshield wipers wince as they cut across the glass. He feels a shudder as the wind begins to pick up. Oh, how he wants to find her beside him in this moment in the car, talking about what they would do later that day. He is losing Briar and it is beginning to set in.

Later that night, when the winds grow calm, and all the broken and tired leaves and branches have piled near the water's edge, he will see the unfolding of the colours and emotions caught by that French Canadian painting that hangs by itself in their darkened condo.

THERE ARE THOSE who feel that Hymen Kazan was never the same person after that night. That something deep inside of him died. Briar saw the changes. She had watched him throw himself into the preparation for a trial before, but nothing like this. He shows no signs of fatigue. In fact, he appears to grow stronger and exceed expectations. He is sharp and calculated and speaks with a newly founded confidence. He walks more upright, and with every step, he is fluid and responsive to every situation, so that his well-planned attacks are sudden and surprise his opposition. Whatever has brought upon these changes, he is more than ready to try any case.

Months before he is to go to trial, he is saddled with another very difficult case filled with pitfalls. On that day, there is an energy that floods the rooms at the courthouse. It is a cold December day, and the waiting room for counsel is packed. Lawyers gather in soft leather chairs, drinking dishwater warm coffee and talking too much, energized from adrenaline and nerves. The light sneaks in through the ground level basement windows and falls upon the well-worn carpet that hides the scratched wooden floor in the lawyers' lounge.

His case file is the size of a New York phone book, and reading it is like jogging through a minefield. Mistake after mistake, statement after statement, the brief is chock full of problems. Each problem brings a subset of problems and evidentiary challenges. There are constitutional breaches bobbing in the waters of the details, gasping for air. Not one piece of the investigation offers any solace or confirmation of any hint of professionalism. No shred of light, no sign of hope. Time is running out.

Kazan sees his emotionally and physically scarred Vietnamese victim as neglected. She has suffered multiple knife wounds inflicted by a mentally ill companion. He had thought of her as useless to him after an unacceptable courtship. This was not going to play out well before a court stacked of fat lazy jurists who don't give a rat's ass about her suffering. That was justice, the kind that played out in Southeast Asia in 1969, and now in Vancouver. It would be a fight between competing interests. A wrestling match between the new morality, and the old boys club.

This reminds Kazan of the unfairness of the judicial system, a cold brutal deceitful snare. This fuels the bitterness and rage within him, and gives him no interest in the money sucking merciless judges who oversaw the process. The bold printer typed face on the pages and pages of disclosure fly by him as he struggles to keep his red rimmed eyes open and take in all that is on the page. The effect of fighting through the blurred faced type is amusing to him, as he mines it for the one evidentiary nugget that will spring the truth from the abattoir. The words become like notes or poetry, producing images that are scattered across the page, lifting his spirits and tainting his idealized view of what the law should stand for.

Marianne stares out the sun streaked window and contemplates the whereabouts of Kazan. She has signed on for a great adventure. As second chair on the Trinity case, she yearns to fight the good fight. She fumbles with her copy of the disclosure disc as it is placed into the side of her laptop. She watches the glow of her computer light up the room. She begins to read the text to herself and listens to the quickening pace of her voice fueled by excitement and fear. She is surprised by how heartbreaking she finds the case to be. She started out wanting to defend all those that had been victimized by the ruling class. The one percent soon became the ninety-nine percent as her disgust and distrust of the system grew with each case. She wants the betrayals in both her private and professional life to evaporate like steam from her coffee cup. She manages to place each fact of the case, and each emotion, into a compartment in her mind, all of them sealed up with her images of what she thought she wanted in her life.

Kazan is the one person she has placed her faith in. He represents the good, the uncompromising, the one person not to be bought or sold. Fame and fortune are not the sole ingredients of a good life. Instead, he places people ahead of such interests. He is the leader of a revival, and she is his disciple. Together, they will be unstoppable, unfazed by corruption or self interest. She dreams of a life with him, and she is elated with thoughts of lust and happiness which would be embarrassing to admit or be spoken of. Women who are attracted to such men are always left waiting or wanting more.

There is an incredible amount of work to be done. Kazan's portion of the work appears insurmountable in her mind. She wants to try to share some of the burden of the work, but Kazan keeps the bulk of the witnesses to himself. This causes her concern for his health to grow, as he has clearly taken on too much. She thinks she can hear the tapping of an oil deprived engine as he discusses the case with her. She thinks that at any moment the motor that drives him will overheat, causing him to veer into oncoming traffic, killing them both.

When she finally raises it with him, he thanks her for her concern, but tells her that she need not worry because he is fully up to the task.

"You cannot take all this on at your age and with all the stress you are under. Something is bound to give." She blushes as she calls into question his well-being.

"Do I sense a lack of confidence, my dear?" he chirps, thinking that perhaps there could be a mutiny that he needs to address.

Demons, fucking demons. As trial counsel, you are forced to deal with your own shortcomings and demons. Those things that you hide away, or those subconscious fears that bubble up in the night. Kazan has witnessed all the ways in which people can be cruel. He too has fallen short of what others expected of him. A twinge would bite its way into his own circuit board, causing shame or disgust. Guilty . . . guilty . . . sins of various types, crimes against lovers, friends, and opponents, attacking his thoughts at the most inopportune time. Fucking bastards, we all arrive at the point where we judge others, including ourselves.

When he is at home, late in the evening, Kazan would catch Briar's eyes, and he could see the fear in them. Like a paratrooper waiting to jump over enemy lines, he sees the tension in her face. She holds tension and anxiety close to her wounded heart. He has seen how it altered their relationship and formed deep lines around her eyes and mouth. It causes her to pull back from him, to hide away when things got too crazy. Now he gives her a cool nod of confidence that does nothing to suppress the pain in her chest. In a pleading manner, he asks her if she is okay.

"Please just try and relax and think about what we will do when this case is done," he would say.

For a brief second, his attempt to protect her just makes it worse. Briar grows more and more anxious as the fear inside her grows.

Marianne can sense the constant shift in Kazan's confidence, and his lack of preparation makes everyone worry. They take a break after the preliminary hearing. Briar and Marianne are now locked together in this weird unfolding of events. They team up together in the early morning hours in the apartment, going over witness statements and evidence that will be marshalled at trial. Kazan pushes himself away from the dining table and goes on long unannounced walks to consider things, leaving the two women seated together, bleary eyed and yawning. When he is out of the room, both women would wonder about the other. His scent and presence catches both women in the most unlikely of trysts.

"Maybe he is turned on by the stress?" Briar says to Marianne. "Maybe he gets off on the feeling of the nose dive just before it is too late to pull up. That would explain why he has not just walked away."

"Don't worry, it will all work out," Kazan would say, and he would smile at both women.

"Worry we have in abundance, Kazan! You need a fucking plan!" Briar says. "You simply can't fly over the Indian Ocean miles from land and eject, thinking that you will land somewhere soft. You have to have a plan!"

Marianne would confide in Koogan about the lack of direction or planning in their preparation.

"There are two problems," she would say. "The first is that we are simply running out of time. Everyone agrees that it will take at least another six months before we are even close to conducting a trial. The other difficulty is that many of our witnesses are uncooperative or simply cannot be found."

Marianne, who has always believed in Kazan, feels that he simply refuses to accept that the odds against them are crushing, and that he will never stop and sit down and discuss these problems further.

"Let's grab a glass of wine," Kazan will say.

Briar would excuse herself from these moments when she finds Marianne lingering beside Kazan late into the evening, quizzing him on what matters to him, and why he is still with Briar. Briar would show up at the dining room and attempt to reveal the hour by informing them she was going to bed.

"Hey, Briar, do not worry, we are just about done here."

She would just keep walking toward the bedroom, stopping only to look back at him and give him that long suffering look. That winter's night at home with the wind howling outside, she looks at him and feels so alone that she feels as abandoned as she has ever felt, but keeps her comments to herself.

In his Thurlow Street office, he gazes out over what he can see of English Bay in the hopes of finding some answers. All around him are photographs of desolate windy beaches. He catches a glimpse of his appearance in the glass that covers the photos. His face is white and illuminated like a harvest moon, pale with the lack of colour or warmth. The office is cold and dark and outside the sky is grey. The snow on the curbs is slushy and black. There are lights visible from Grouse Mountain where young professionals are cutting paths in the snow. Their dark figures are cast upon the white blank slate. Kazan calls home, hoping to find Briar waiting for him. Instead, the answering machine comes on and reminds him of the sacrifices of working so hard and late.

Briar appears to him now like an early Colville or Modigliani painting. She is lit from behind with her long face showing hurt and loneliness. After all, he has placed her on the wall of his office, in that corner, only to be called upon when he needs to be cheered up or reminded of life outside of work. How did it come to this? Why was he alone? What was he thinking? He rubs his left wrist with the edge of his thumb of his right hand, as if it holds a razor. He feels the flat portion of his wrist and the thick purple veins that run down from his heart. His mind goes blank. He is bleeding inside. His life looks empty and ugly. He realizes in this moment how he longs for her embrace, causing him to imagine her softness and warmth all around him.

My dearest love, Briar thinks and sees him walking down a deserted beach toward her, but somehow he appears overdressed for the weather. His eyes look distant and void of emotion. It is as if Kazan has checked out of his body. She rushes toward him, her wedding gown caught by the sea breeze.

"You came," she says.

They draw each other closer, holding hands and walking toward the ocean.

"You look so beautiful," he says.

But it is an apparition. A dream left unfulfilled. Looking down at her fingers, she is clutching her birthstone that hangs from a rose-coloured gold chain, she awakens alone in bed. She lies there for a moment, holding on to the emotions so as to not disturb the best part of her day. She will stay another day until the dream becomes real.

41

HYMAN KAZAN
BRITISH COLUMBIA

IT IS INCREDIBLE how Koogan can track Kazan down. He calls out when he sees his name attached to the court list outside of a quiet Courtroom number 3 in the foyer of the courthouse. He feels a responsibility to call out to him when he sees his name up on the worn peanut-coloured cork board beside the names of the judges assigned to particular courts. For a long time, they had little in common. It was a connection based upon their mutual distrust of others.

"Hy," he says, "I see you are going to appear before our friend Smith."

"I did not think you could appear in front of him, given, mmm, you know, Briar and everything. Isn't it a bit ironic that he could decide your case involving Trinity?"

"Yeah, for one who prides himself on being a prick, he has become rather good at it," replies Kazan. "When am I scheduled to show up?"

"It says you are in number 2 on Wednesday at 10 a.m."

"Fuck! You know how much I like to appear before him mid-week. Can things get any worse?"

"I supposed they can," Koogan replies. "You know, I could lend a hand if you need it."

"Jesus, Koogan, that is awfully kind, but I got Marianne working her ass off right now on our case. Perhaps you can take on the appeal? When that lazy prick screws me on some obscure points of law he read in the Law Times over breakfast."

"Then you are safe, Kazan. Smith does not read any law."

"I see," Kazan laughs. "Why don't you meet me at the club for a drink and we can talk strategy?"

"What time?"

"I don't know, let's say around 9 p.m. That will give you time to hang up on your other friends and make your way there."

"Sure, Kazan. That will be fine." Then with the slipperiness of a defense lawyer, he ends the conversation with a common question: "Maybe I could bring a friend?"

"You have friends?"

"Just one."

"Why the fuck not."

Kazan stops and picks up Marianne to work on their case. They make their way toward Crescent Beach out toward Surrey and the US border.

"It doesn't feel like Vancouver out here," Marianne says.

They are still blocks away from a small grey cedar shake beach house that will serve as their official war room. The houses here are large glass structures designed to capture as much of the view as possible. The cliffs or hills overlooking towns like White Rock grew as wealth and architectural innovation stretched out toward the US border. Rows and rows of huge houses and privileged estates dot the landscape. They occupy street names that reflect the influences of the birds that once ruled the area. Seagull, Waxwing, Sparrow. As a young man, Kazan had always seen the cold uncaring faces of businessmen who had overdeveloped the lower mainland and had moved out there to escape the plight of the unbridled growth in Vancouver.

"Money and no plan for growth or infrastructure," he said. "Real estate speculation and Pacific Rim money."

By the time he could have afforded a home, there were none to be purchased for under 1.6 million.

Marianne looks bored and begins to tire from the long drive out there. She is not the type of person to be impressed by large houses or expensive cars.

"I think they are trying too hard," she says. "You know, trying to impress all those who care about how their neighbours are doing. I don't give a rat's ass," she smiles. "I admire you, Kazan. You never got sucked into this game."

They stop the car and get out. It is raining and her coat and hair become damp as she steps from the car. She bounces with energy and smells like fresh flowers and spice. She is wearing a sand-coloured trench coat with a cream-coloured belt.

"You should have been a writer, Kazan, instead of ending up in law. And then you met Briar."

The rain mixing with the sea air is fresh and enticing.

"Breathe deep. Doesn't it smell so good? Nothing like a fresh sea breeze to cleanse the soul eh?"

He is not sure where this is going. Now he is feeling a bit uncomfortable for bringing her all the way out here with little plan on how they are going to prepare. He walks up the bleached grey wood stairs toward the black oak door. There is a brown coarse front door mat below the door. It comes back to him that there is a small wooden compartment under the mat that contains the copper-coloured key to the front door. He thinks for a moment that perhaps he should not have invited her out there.

"Let's put on a fire," she says. "A glass of wine to get us in the mood?"

"I am sorry," he says.

Why would you say that? he thinks to himself, but renders no opposition. Kazan crosses over the melting shadows that frame the room and takes hold of her hand as he steps through the door.

Pulling her hand away, she says, "I am afraid to start!" She is playful and yet a little nervous about being alone with him when there is so much at stake. "That is the hardest part about this case, to know which stick to pick up without toppling the whole bloody mess. Jenga case management, I really can't stand it," she says.

The demands of a trial, Kazan imagines, are like planning an invasion during the war. You look for a safe and sheltered place to come ashore without suffering too many casualties, and he then rubs his forehead. He attempts to look into her eyes to detect her mood. The room smells of spice and wood smoke, and he feels the fear seeping out from her body just as she must be aware of his own lack of confidence. The moment he opens the door, the two of them have landed on the beach, open to friendly and enemy fire.

"You know, I am so glad you are on this case with me," he says, and then he smiles and a wave of confidence fills the room. "You know, I have been thinking, and I really think we have a shot at this damn thing."

Marianne extends her arm and embraces him. Her grip on him now extends beyond the pile of papers he has carried with him. They remove their coats and he places them by the banister overlooking the fire. At this point, he reaches for a bottle of wine, but chooses a scotch bottle he has secreted on the shelf overtop of the kitchen sink.

"I will take one of those too," she says.

"I thought you might," Kazan says, and he notices her become more relaxed with the notion that regardless of the outcome, they are in this mess together. "Misery loves company. Ice?"

She is reminded of the cry heard on the Titanic as it crossed the Atlantic.

"No need. I just want it straight up."

At this point, he knows she is not referring to the liquor. Drinks are poured and they make their way into the crowded dining room, where a large dark oak table welcomes the brief and papers that litter the file. She stokes the fireplace, and within ten minutes, the fire is raging against the black scorched brickwork inside the fireplace. The atmosphere is relaxed and the tension has escaped the room as if a draft has been ushered out by a window that remains open and with the fire intensifying. She looks around the room and then tugs at her woolen sweater, filling herself with the warmth of the room. He finally captures the look behind her eyes. The blueness of eye colour contrasts the greyness of the walls. Everywhere now are stacks of paper and file folders holding the contents of their case.

Kazan has never worked on such an important case with anyone before. He has been a lone wolf for so long, he struggles on how to balance the work with someone else. During his legal career, he would slip away to this place and work without interruption. Briar would call, but would never visit, so as to not venture onto the ice, for fear of adding just the right amount of weight to cause the ice to crack. It was a lonely existence, but he had thought that was the price to have a case properly prepared.

It is also the place where he saw his ex-wife for the very last time. She left him on a windy day on a beach in Tofino, and he only returned to this room to drink coffee in the weathered rattan chair that sat in the corner of the room. The chair was soft from the passage of time and weather, and had survived being moved from across the country. The chair must have been at least one hundred years old, and smelled like the beach and of old leather. He had carried it with him through the disintegration of every other aspect of his life. He refused to leave it behind. He watched his grandmother read the daily newspaper while drinking a gin and tonic from this chair. He can remember how her housecoat and white hair in braids would flow down the side of the chair. His mind wanders as he recalls the many women who liked to sit there.

"Who is this?" Marianne asks.

She is staring at a poorly focused photograph on the dusty mantle over the fireplace. He smiles, and admits that it is someone from his past.

"She looks happy."

"She was happy then. At least, that's what I was led to believe," he quips. "Just someone from the past! She is married now and lives in Calgary. She is like you, hates the east and thinks of herself as some kind of western convert who is better than those Bay Street boys she once dated."

"While they have left, I am right here now," Marianne says, striking a pose in the middle of the room. "So much for the past, my friend, we have battles to win and prisoners to take!"

Kazan does not look amused at how she is able to discredit his life so easily. It becomes apparent to her that she now occupies the room with several of the ghosts from Kazan's hidden past.

"Sorry, Kazan, I did not want to go down that twisting road with you."

Her dedication to the task at hand is admirable. It is he who has to tug on the rope, to help someone get over their past, now he is at the other end, navigating the daunting canyon wall. It is good that she is there, if not, he would be finishing the scotch bottle and putting on some scratched albums he had stored in the hallway closet. Marianne pushes her hair back. She is looking worried.

She spins abruptly and says, "I will put on some coffee. We need to get down to it."

It is time, and they both realize that the clock is ticking. He pulls out a chair from the dining room table. He wants to put his arm around her and calm her fears. He can't help himself. Something about the stress of a trial always causes him to fumble into a stupor or make him excited about the possibility of failure. She has made her way across the room and is standing beside his chair. He leans back in his chair and smiles at her. He feels the electricity between them, her mouth opens softly and before she speaks, he abandons his thoughts and returns to the task at hand. The dining room is now cluttered with even more paper, and the edge of the tablecloth is pulled up at the corner to reveal the dark oak wood underneath. Marianne gets energized again, looking to get the ball moving.

"Do you know Tom Attwell?" Marianne asks with a handful of papers against her chest. "I heard he was the lead investigator on this case. It is likely his last fuck up."

"This is awful good news," he says in a sarcastic tone.

"I thought they might attack the law on this one."

"Yes," Kazan says and repeats the overused phrase, "If the facts are strong, attack the law, and if the law is strong, attack the facts, and if both the law and the facts are against you, attack the bloody cops!"

She swallows hard and says, "It is hard to know where our case rests, Kazan. Maybe we should prepare for challenges to everything. God knows, they could be attacking Ms. Dawson on this one!"

"The arrow does not seek the target, the target draws the arrow. I know! I know!" he responds.

"We are going to have to find a sliver or a crack and exploit it, or create a fact, or create a cause of concern here. There is no margin or obvious edge to use. A new reality must be created!"

The firelight produces its own shadows on the wall. Kazan finds a crystal square glass and fills it with some single malt. His mind is also occupied with the case against Smith. He thinks about a case from his past.

"It is like the Corey Arthurs case. Arthurs had been charged with criminal negligence as a result of a party favor that had contained carfentanil and ended up in the hands of the deceased at one of his legendary pool parties in West Van. The case was a loser until they had found an ex-girlfriend who was more than happy to give evidence against Arthurs when he had dumped her the following morning after sleeping with her best friend. It came down to finding the needle in the haystack, or that one piece of cheese that the hungry rats must eat. Yes," Kazan murmurs, pouring himself a tall glass of scotch. "It will be fun to find what pebble will stop the machinery on this one."

"You need to find it soon," Marianne says, looking straight into his eyes.

"I think I have," Kazan smiles and greets the challenge with a nod of his head.

She is not sure if Kazan is talking about the Trinity Rivers case or his decision to go after Smith.

"Are you sure, or is this some type of ploy to make me stay?"

He remembers how it felt when he was a young lawyer, the thrill of finding that one piece of evidence that could turn a case. He ponders whether this is the right facts, the right issue, the one morsel of an issue that can dig him out of this mess. He is complicated by the sheer simplicity of the moment. He shoots her a confident smile. Marianne gives him a quizatorial look.

"You look like you are enjoying this," she says. "What is it that you have found, Kazan?"

It is an Occam's razor moment, when your instincts take over and reveal the obvious.

"It is in the details, isn't it, wouldn't you agree?"

"What on earth are you talking about?" she says. She shakes her head and scans the papers on the table. "I think I need that glass of scotch now."

HYMAN KAZAN
42
BRITISH COLUMBIA

THE BEDROOM IS dark and unkept. The pillows are scattered about the room, the windows are covered by shutters, the walls are painted ivory white. How this room reminds him of sleepless nights and failed relationships. His glass is three quarters full, Kazan sits on the edge of the bed. He places his cloudy drinking glass on the bedside table, and allows himself to fall back onto the bed. He closes his eyes and allows himself to drift into the space between dreams and memories. His feet remain on the floor while the upper half of his body cuddles the top of the mattress. His mind is like a photo album that is found in an abandoned desk drawer. He balances his expectations against the questions of what happened to lead up to his point. He remembers the love he had felt in this room. Where did it all go? And what happened? Did the work erode his sense of self? Surely, there was something left for him. A window pane of sunlight, a walk on the beach, a sense of self. What was it all for? Why was he thinking about this now? His focus should be on the damn trial. Did he not come here to marshal the evidence and take his preparation to the next level? The skeletons in the closet were now pulling at him.

He tugs at the bedside drawer and then unwraps the handgun he has secreted away. Oh, and what do we have here? The cold steel feels heavy in his hands. Why had he brought the gun here? A little reminder of the escape hatch from his depression and burdensome relationship with Briar. He wraps it tightly in his T-shirt and swallows a couple of diazepam with the leftover scotch. It calms him.

"Get it together, Kazan," his inner voice calls out to him. "You are the senior counsel on this bloody case."

Why he had wanted to pull Marianne into this case escapes him. Did he feel that she would rescue him from his mistakes? Was he attracted to her? Or did he want Briar to feel something again? He makes his way to the medicine cabinet in the bathroom. Behind the smeared mirror and dark image of himself, is a half-bottle of morphine. One or two tablets mixed with the booze and the diazepam ought to calm his fears. *Remember, Kazan, doubt kills warriors.* The combination of drugs cause his head to pound and he splashes cold water on his face to bring him back to the moment. He enjoys feeling the rush of the energy of the battle and the false confidence brought on by the combination of drugs and alcohol. He always has.

Suddenly his conscience takes hold of him. The need to ready himself is now like the rush of wind one feels as they stand at the opening of an airplane before making a skydiving jump. He props himself up by his hands and stares into the bathroom mirror. Yes, he needs the pills or numbness brought on by the combination of alcohol and drugs. *Take a deep breath, Kazan,* he thinks. He inflates his lungs and takes in the air from the Pacific Ocean through the five inch crack in the bathroom window. The wind is howling outside, and he has captured the sweetness of the sea kelp and sand from outside. He finishes the last of the scotch in his glass and pushes his hair from his forehead. Briar would never forgive the weakness he has shown today, not one show of emotion, or understanding of his pain. He would have done anything for her to be here with him now—anything. But now it is too late.

Sometimes, Briar thinks of him like an understudy or second string actor who plays out on the stage of her life. He has cameo roles and shows up from off stage when a significant thing happens in her life. Other than that, he is a chauffeur who drives her to her next relationship.

"You have to see what I see," she would say to him when they were in an arm's length embrace, eye to eye, with fingers intertwined in front of them.

Kazan has a narrow face, dark brown eyes, and a Cheshire cat smile. He often has a day two growth that frames his strong features. Briar is now feeling the loneliness of waiting for his arrival. Briar feels very strong and alone in her tawny-coloured field jacket as she walks the beach. Kazan has been late for some time. Smith looks at Briar and asks her if she is alright. She replies, of course, she is just tired from the day.

"He is fine, you know," Smith chirps in. "It is not like he did not know that things are likely going to end badly."

"Why would you say that? It is not like you know Kazan. He is trying to do something he believes in. You would not understand that," she offers up.

"What do you mean?"

The comment now causes Briar to glare. "I love him. I know we have had our moments, but you have to understand, he can be episodic. He is a very driven man and a good lawyer. His intelligence and sense of humour amazes me."

Briar is anxious now. She walks quickly back to the parked car. The sunlight catches the diamond necklace that hangs around her neck, a rainbow of light cascades across the front of her blouse and onto the ground in front of her. She misses Kazan. Briar stares at the blue Pacific Ocean, a sliver of foam appears against the dark sea.

"They are like window panes or stages of life, snapshots from a scrapbook," Briar says. "You can see them and you can try to touch them, but they are fluid with no edges. I have mood swings. I see art in the same way you do, not in a flat or non-angular way." She laughs and starts to lean back in the passenger seat of his car.

Episodes, pages of a book, it is a depression, it is an LSD dream. He is always leaving from somewhere or from someone, but never arriving anywhere. He tried to talk with a therapist about his manic depression, but they couldn't understand him. He dragged himself into a shrink's office who just made matters worse. They just don't get it. And then Kazan is in the room, on the balls of his feet, looking like a boxer waiting to enter the ring. Marianne feels the electricity that comes off of him.

"Sorry to have kept you waiting. Let's get this thing started!"

"You are unbelievable," she laughs. "What took you so long?"

"In the bedroom, drinking up the courage to start this blasted case."

"That's not all you have been drinking up."

"Right," he replies. "And what is that you cannot do as counsel?"

"You should never mix business with pleasure, or wine with wisdom."

Waiting and preparation are painful for her. Kazan fixes his eyes upon her. He wants them to do their best, and he wants her to do her best. You cannot change the facts or the law, but you can change how they are presented. You have to find that inner voice that allows you to change that which you expect or accept. You have to be prepared to change the way you work, the way you live, the beliefs you have, everything must be geared toward one simple goal. Changing perceptions. What is real, and what should be real, rests in the corner of the room, in the back of what might have been, where the best work is done.

Marianne is looking at Kazan. He smiles at her and seeks some reassurance that she is fully committed, but she knows she needs to prove herself to both him and herself before the next steps are taken.

"You have a bloodlust for a good fight, don't you?" Kazan asks. "And it means that battles are not won without losses."

"Of course," she replies.

"It means just that. At the end of this, Marianne, you will lose something. You will lose a friend, a lover, a way you look at something, or yourself! Maybe a belief. I admire those that can give of themselves, that can suffer loss to capture the obtainable."

"Kazan, please. This is not my first trial involving a serious case. They are all serious, and I get it. It will not be easy, and there is always a price to be paid."

"Good, I just do not want you to go bankrupt believing in something that just amounts to a hill of bullshit."

"Well, we are clear on that now, and we might as well start climbing the hill before we are covered in it."

"Too late, my friend, too late. I have always tried to be straight up with people, and I know you operate in the same manner," he says as she is walking back toward the kitchen.

Kazan is standing holding on to the back of a hoop chair. He looks pensive. He pulls the chair away from the table to ready himself for the work to begin. It is now real. Reality rushes into the room and time has eroded to a point of certainty. Marianne pours herself a glass of scotch and drains it. Within minutes, Kazan is working through the witness statements, transcripts, and pages of notes. She walks over to Kazan, stoops down and kisses him on the mouth. It is a soft but definite kiss of goodbye. The role of friendship is quickly cast aside. They are now partners with the focus on winning at all costs, regardless of the prices that will have to be paid.

HYMAN KAZAN

43

BRITISHCOLUMBIA

DRINKS WITH KOOGAN *can wait,* he thinks to himself as he fumbles with his cell phone.

"Hello, Briar. Are you there? I guess not. Just a call to say how much I miss you."

Kazan looks up and sees the retro square clock above the stove flashing. Time is escaping him now. It is 3:30 a.m. on a Thursday. Monday morning they will have to pick the jury. The much respected Braxton Rexwood is the beat reporter assigned to follow the trial. She is thirty something and is entirely focused on herself.

"Self-expression is so important," she waxes on.

Like her cohort, she is obsessed with offering her viewpoint on everything, with the view that she is in some way advancing social justice issues or misunderstood moral values that have escaped the popular consciousness. She is always about advancing those interests or groups that advance her own way of thinking. Her selfishness is undetected by her or her readership. It is the easiest thing in the world to feel you and the things that advance your viewpoint are at the centre of the universe.

Preparing for trial now morphs into a kind of weird torture for him. He wants to be at his best, and he wants to erase any doubt. The whole damn system is built on doubt. "Beyond a reasonable doubt" is the formula for both a conviction or turning the knob on the door to freedom. Counsel, who resembles a warrior who has doubt, then is easily killed in the arena. Doubt is everywhere, and yet like any other legal fiction, it is either ignored or left unexplained. Kazan files away any hint of doubt. To advance a case like this will take a different kind of courage.

He always forgets about how much work a criminal trial is. When he was younger, he could easily work around the clock, armed only with a 2HB orange pencil and a will to win. He now scratches out the faint outline of a game plan on a flickering computer screen. Once upon a time, he would have been able to work around the clock, marshalling the evidence, reading the cases, but now, when he does, he will daydream or his mind will wander. It is so hard to focus.

Eventually, he realizes that each case rests upon the evidence of one or two witnesses. The rest of the case is tangled up in the barbed wire of perception or misperception, depending on how it is to be played. Having resigned himself to this formula, he teaches himself to carefully cherry pick the flaws that many lawyers would miss. And he learns that there is a strategy in this. He breathes in the details of the case and with this, his confidence gets stronger and stronger. Now he feels the energy growing in his pounding heart, shooting electricity down the length of his arms. He would give anything if this feeling could grow, or more importantly, last.

When Briar would not return his calls and when he was alone in the war room in the past, he would stop on the way home and pick her up a small gift from her favourite jewelry store. And he would then painstakingly present it to her when she finally got home. Often it was a diamond necklace or a pair of earrings. The more clarity or sparkle the better. It immediately made up for the absence or long hours that he had spent brooding over some aspect of work. Staring out at the ocean, there is a faint subliminal alarm going off in his head. He has taken a moment to return home to surprise her. He holds the corners of the small velvet box in his hand that houses the diamonds. The key that he hopes will clear away the frost that covers their relationship. But now he is wondering how Briar will react to this feeble attempt to repair their union. With a sudden turn of a key, she opens the apartment door and can be heard kicking off her shoes. He stands there and closes his eyes, imagining her face before him, her smile beaming as she greeted him.

"Are you staying or just passing through?" Briar says with a grin.

"I guess that is up to you," he replies.

He is squeezing the box in his hand behind his back.

"What is that you are holding?"

"Sorry."

"Behind your back."

"A gift to make up for my absence."

"Nothing can be a substitute for you being here, really here, Kazan! It looks like you are attempting to escape," Briar says.

"I can use your help, Briar," Kazan says, swallowing his feelings of inadequacy.

He draws the box from behind his back, pushing it toward her, and places the corners into her small hands. He imagines her dress hitting the floor, her bare neck a blaze with the light from the sunlight hitting the diamonds. He draws her close and kisses her shoulders.

*   *   *

They are together again, if only in his mind.

The Saturday before the trial, the rain is coming down sideways, and the streets are flooded. All day long, thunderstorms rumble and there are flashes of lightning. The gloom of the day spins negative thoughts throughout his mind. The absence of light changes everything. Lawyers stare at boxes and boxes of file folders holding witness statements. Joy and anxiety compete.

Marianne, who had worked around the clock has now given in to exhaustion. She appears to be in some kind of a trance. The confidence which she had longed for, has escaped from her preparation. Witnesses start to blend into the black typed pixels on a printed page. Line after line, their faces become muted. Awareness of their strengths and weaknesses gives way to an inability to decipher their importance. Sleeplessness begins to take its toll. The only link between them and reality is their connection to the victim.

Witness statements are like historical postcards, they contain time frames, emotions and explanations connected to what happened. Perceptions, right or wrong, will be determinative. Everything turns on what you think you saw, or what your mind tells you, or what you expected to see. Perceptions and thoughts stop being time fragmented when they become pictures burned into your subconscious. The time is now to marry the thoughts and perceptions together, and have them brought to the surface. Witnesses are contacted and times are juggled to rehearse all that they have been committed to tape, paper or video. There is light at the edge of the waterway.

That tired weekend and for the few short hours left on Sunday night, the work took on a fever pitch. Sometimes they spoke, often they did not. Instead, they took on a bomb defusing role, quiet and painstaking, working side by side in the hopes of not crossing the wrong wires. Sometimes, they walked around holding coffee cups and pencils in a hush, as if nitroglycerin was hidden in the floorboards. Sometimes, they argued with each other with such energy that they felt a passion grow within themselves. Hidden answers to unadvanced dreams of success. They fed off each other. They found the groove between anxiety and boredom. The force of their arguments grew more and more palpable. It was so freeing to have no other focus but that of preparing for trial. Witnesses became chess pieces that could be easily shifted to squares of a shared history. Their strategy was mapped out. So tight, so ready for presentation.

In those days leading up to their opening before a jury, doubt became their friend, and disappeared, and they learned to trust themselves. Value and quality of evidence became paramount. They became transparent to each other. They responded to fears and issues that would have otherwise challenged their confidence. Briar, when she saw Kazan, could see the changes the time spent with Marianne had on his confidence. And this made her happy, and increased her admiration for him.

As the time grows near, Briar watches as the sunlight grows stronger, reflecting off the snowy caps of the North Shore mountains. *Time,* she thinks, *reveals all.* In their bedroom the night before the commencement of the trial, there is a calmness—a sense of purpose and no fear. They are entangled in the bedclothes and in every aspect of what is at stake for them. Briar reaches over from her side of the bed to find Kazan's blanket wrapped hand. It is tightly holding on to the duvet cover up near his chin. The room is cold and dark, and she struggles to place her hand inside of his. He rolls over, and lets out a heavy concentrated sigh.

"What time is it? I guess I should be getting up soon?"

They speak in short sentences when they finally make it into the kitchen in search of coffee. They struggle to adjust to the little bit of sunlight that is coming in. The waiting to get the case started has taken an enormous toll on both of them. They have lost time and each other. They have lost themselves. The stress has sliced open old wounds.

Day after day leading up to this moment, their home became transformed into a motel for strangers. A place to sometimes sleep while on the road to somewhere else, both of them behaving like guests unknown to each other on a distant highway filled with regrets. Anxiety infected all they were, or had been. They could not adjust to the change in pressure. The physical demands of trial advocacy was taking over. They lost sight of each other, and became enemies concerned with the most insignificant of things. Fractures grew and grew with the passing of each hour. Rapidly, and almost unpredictably, the power of now rose like the morning sun that rested in the vanilla scorched sky.

At home, he behaves like a lifer waiting to be executed. In the car, he becomes more and more self-absorbed. No one says anything. No one wants to be the one that adds fuel to the dry kindling. They depend on tomorrow, the passage of time, and the chance to be themselves again.

LIKE EVERY OTHER morning, it is raining. The Trinity trial is adjourned until Monday. The weekend is a time to regroup and refocus. Kazan struggles to find his footing. He's gotten very little sleep the night before, and he had been awakened by a throbbing headache. He limps to the kitchen in search of a cold glass of water. The wine he drank from the night before has left him dehydrated and exhausted. He reaches inside the fridge and grabs a bottle of Evian water from inside the fridge door. He swallows quickly the last quarter of the bottle while staring at the now empty refrigerator. He closes the fridge door, and makes his way to the shower. The steaming hot water cascades down on the top of his head and tired shoulders. Having showered and dressed, he picks up his cell phone and dials the number for Briar.

It is shortly after 7 a.m. and the weather outside is grey and cold. He waits for her cell phone to kick over to voicemail and decides to leave her a message about Smith. He is eager to unburden himself with the knowledge that he was responsible for the death of Simon Westfall. This would also signal the end of his painful involvement in the emotional triangle that has ensnared him. The idea of being free gives him hope. He thinks of moving back to Montreal or maybe Vancouver Island. Kazan stares out toward the ocean from his balcony and wonders how it is that nothing ever seems to work out for him. He feels defeated and lonely. The seagulls are gathering in the parking lot below, scattering at the sound of his sliding glass door.

He makes himself a coffee and goes over the scant mental notes he made and arguments he will present to Briar about how Smith had lured Simon to his hotel room, and how he had decided to drug him in the hopes of satisfying his twisted sense of sexual gratification. Kazan knows she will not be receptive to his disclosure of the evidence against Smith. He sits down on the weathered white Muskoka chair and drinks his coffee, hoping to find the right words to tell her what kind of man she has been involved with. He worries that his sense of jealousy will overshadow his presentation of the facts. He knows that the reporters from the Vancouver Sun will be soon showing up at her door, eager to ask questions and take pictures of the wreckage. He knows that there is no way of protecting her from the thunderous storm about to blow in.

He arrives back at their condo shortly before 11 in the morning in search of the gun, but the handgun is nowhere to be found. Kazan tries to pay attention to the time, but is over anxious by being back at the place that they had once shared. He attempts to calm himself by taking a seat on the edge of the bed in the bedroom, but he is overcome by exhaustion and stress. His mind is racing as to what to say to her. He feels both heartbreak and guilt. They could have been happy.

Arbutus, Oak and Alder, the tree streets fly past her fogged passenger side window as she watches the rain drops slide down her window. This driving with Smith to her former home with Kazan feels so strange to her. She begins to think about the many drives from the airport they had taken together when they were still living together. She cannot remember the last time she returned home without him. All the years they had laughed and loved together, and then the time suddenly escaped them. The streets become more and more crowded as they approach the Burrard Street bridge. Could she have made a terrible mistake by agreeing to meet with him at their former home? No, this tension between the three of them would have to be dealt with. She remembers what Kazan said about Smith and now it all seems like a lucid dream. A nightmare that has lasted far too long. Kazan has become bitter by their relationship and begins to make accusations about Smith that will jeopardize his job and her future. Kazan has to be reasoned with, made to understand that Smith had just been a witness to the death of Westfall, that he had taken no part in the tragic events that had led up to Simon's death.

Kazan finds a bottle of a discarded white wine in the refrigerator and pours himself a glass. He thinks of making one more call to Briar to see when she will arrive. A "where are you?" type of call, but then he thinks better of it. He grows more and more anxious with the passing of every second. Kazan is finishing his last gulp of wine when he feels the vibration of his cell phone. He sits back down on the edge of the bed and looks at the screen of his phone. He can see that it is Koogan calling, but decides to not answer the call. He is likely wondering why he did not show up for that drink they talked about. When he rises to his feet, his head begins to spin from the wine, and at that exact time, he can hear a key in the lock of the front door.

"What's going on, Kazan? You look terrible," Briar says. "Craig is with me, is everything alright?"

"No, everything is not alright, Briar," Kazan says. "Has Smith told you about how Simon died?"

He takes a step toward them and stares at Smith who looks startled by Kazan's display of disgust. The anger he feels whenever he is in front of Smith is now boiling over.

"You forgot to pick up the packet, Smith, didn't you? You know, the court exhibit laced with carfentanil. Time to come clean, Smith."

Smith takes a step back. "I don't know what in the hell you are talking about, Kazan! I thought we were here to talk about me and Briar! Why are you bringing this up now?"

"Because you killed a young man, Smith, and Briar has a right to know what kind of an asshole you really are," Kazan says.

"Briar, let's go, there is no point in talking to him when he is drunk."

"I am going to have the pleasure of seeing you in cuffs and taken downtown to answer some very difficult questions."

"He took the shit himself! I had no idea that he was bringing drugs to my hotel room. You have got nothing on me, Kazan, and we are not going to stay here any longer while you bring up such bullshit," Smith says.

"You never told me you knew Simon!" Briar says. "What were you doing in a hotel room with him? It is time to explain things to me."

Briar is now flushed and sweating at the ambush of emotions that are filling the room.

"Look, there is still time to figure this out," says Smith. "He just showed up at the hotel with the damn drugs. How in the hell did I know he was going to overdose."

"Well, he showed up because you invited him there, and the drugs have been traced back to you, Smith! Jesus, can you not tell the truth just once in your life?"

"I am telling the truth."

"Bullshit," says Kazan. "We have the hotel staff on video showing you checking into the hotel earlier and Westfall showing up later. We also have your DNA all over the little sugar packet found in your room."

He pushes past Briar toward Kazan.

"Look, you sick fuck!! You better just take a seat. The cops are on the way and this is about to get worse for you."

"No, Kazan."

"It is about to get very bad for you. Are you sure you want to play things out like this, Smith?"

"You have left me no choice, Kazan. Your jealousy is about to get you killed!"

"Do you have to always make matters worse? Briar is a big girl. She would have figured you out sooner or later."

"You think so, Kazan? Really, look how she wasted all the time she spent with you!"

Briar smiles a nervous smile and then takes a step toward the door.

"I don't want to be here when the police arrive. I just can't take this anymore. I do not know what to believe anymore."

After a few seconds, she gathers up her things and leaves Smith and Kazan in the living room awaiting the arrival of the police. Smith reaches into his jacket and draws out Kazan's handgun. His hand is visibly shaking as he points it in the direction of Kazan. He knows that there is no turning back from this desperate attempt at escape. The situation is getting quickly out of control.

"There is no way out! You stupid bastard!" he yells out at Kazan. "You had to tell Briar, God damn it, Kazan, why couldn't you just leave it alone?"

Now he has to make up some type of story to explain why Kazan has taken one more swing at suicide. Briar will be taking his side, explaining how the depression and the deterioration of their relationship had gone on for months. Smith is overcome with a sudden rush of adrenalin since he has pulled out the gun from the drawer a few days ago. He can't understand how things have gotten so out of control since the passing of Simon. He is convinced that Kazan must die. At this point, Briar is seated in the passenger side of his car with the radio on, waiting for his return. Reasoning with Kazan is not an option, there is no escape. His only hope is that the obese cops and other members of the bar will buy into his explanation of the tragic loss of Kazan. He prays his story will be believed. Trying to craft a believable story is now his only focus. He is tempted to take his own life also, but focuses on the rage that is brewing in Kazan's eyes.

"Smith, why kill me? Haven't you done enough killing? This is how you got yourself into this predicament. I am sure manslaughter will be on the table, you crazy fuck!"

Just as Kazan takes one step toward him, Smith freezes as he hears a small yellow sea plane outside of the window. His eyes water and grow wide as he glances outside and back to Kazan. His hands begin to shake and the sweat is now pouring down his reddened face.

"You always hurt the women that are in your life, Kazan. You never learn."

Kazan feels the pain of regret, wishing he was the one holding the gun. Kazan takes a deep breath

"For what it's worth, Briar never stopped loving you."

Smith points the gun toward the bedroom.

"Get away from the window. Time to go into the bedroom!" he demands.

Kazan shakes his head.

"Time for you to give me the gun. There is no way out."

Smith takes one step toward the bedroom and then motions for Kazan to step toward the dining room. Kazan follows. As they step away from the glass balcony window, Kazan's stomach tightens. He once again entertains the idea of rushing Smith, but abandons the idea as foolhardy. Kazan stands on the other side of the trestle dining room table from Smith. Smith tightens his grip upon the Beretta.

"You need to stop moving."

Smith is visibly shaking now at the thought of firing the gun. Kazan shakes his head and brings his hands up toward Smith, sensing the increasing danger.

He calls out to Smith, "You selfish prick, you don't know what love is! Why you had to ruin Briar's life as well as your own is a mystery to me."

"It is not like you saved her," Smith smiles. "But you could have saved her a lot of heartache if you had just learned to mind your own business sometimes."

Kazan takes one more deep breath and tries to prepare for what he can only expect to happen next. Kazan throws his hands up in front of his face, palms facing Smith, uncertain when he will hear the pop of the gun and feel the hot sharp pain of the bullet entering his body. Kazan leans over and grabs a dining room chair, uncertain if it is an attempt to steady himself or a feeble effort at self-defense. Smith steps briskly forward and savagely grabs Kazan by the upper bicep and pulls him closer to the wavering handgun.

"You bastard, you do not have to kill me," Kazan states definitively.

Kazan struggles to catch his breath and throws a right cross that catches the temple of Smith.

"Stop!" Smith barks.

The fist cracks so unexpectedly into the right side of Smith's face and Smith is staggered by the force of the blow as pain shoots through his round face. Despite the force of the blow, and agony that is caused, Smith lashes out, pistol whipping Kazan. The room goes dark and quiet, except for the muffled sound of Marianne pounding on the outside door. Kazan can taste the blood that is dripping down the side of his face and nose and into his mouth, and struggles in an attempt to get to his feet.

"Stay down!" Smith barks out again, and Kazan rolls over so that he can see where the next attack will come from.

Smith pushes Kazan to the floor using both hands while still holding the Berretta in his right hand. In the time it takes to swallow, Kazan will be gasping for his last breath as his mind is filled with colours and shapes and images of Briar smiling at him. For a second, Kazan feels like he is floating high above the room, like the yellow sea plane outside of their condo in search of a safe place to land. It is the loss of blood and opportunity that finally comes crashing down on a life filled with regret and misadventure.

HYMAN KAZAN

45

BRITISH COLUMBIA

MARIANNE FEELS FAINT as she bends over the body of Kazan spread across the dining room floor. His head is resting on the Persian dining room carpet as if he is listening to her call for an ambulance over her cell phone. They arrive in minutes with a gurney in tow and are followed by a hysterical Briar. In this case, they will not need to rush. Kazan's body is now absent of any signs of life. It is hard to believe that it once held the spirit of the man. He is lifted up and placed on the stretcher and taken to the emergency cube van parked on an angle in front of the building with its whirling blue lights lighting up the neighbourhood. The rain has finally stopped and the sun begins to peak out behind the dark clouds and coastal mountains. A lone seagull dips and flies overhead. A tired Chmura and two undercover cops arrive to investigate. Briar is shrieking with grief.

"Please take your time and try and describe exactly what happened here," Chumara says to Marianne and Smith.

"I heard the gun go off and then found him there," Marianne says and her eyes are laser focused on Smith who is standing cross armed in the kitchen.

"What about you?" The question is raised with Smith. "Where were you? What happened here?"

"He came out of the other room with the gun, and then without a further word, shot himself!"

"Shot himself?" Chmura asks.

"Yeah, right in front of a superior court judge."

"What? A judge? Why did he do that?"

"We had come to tell him that we are in love, and that his ex-partner would be leaving him. I guess it was all that he could handle," Smith says. "I was worried that he might have killed us both, but I think he must have been drinking and so depressed because he just pulled out the gun and shot himself."

Chmura takes a deep breath for a long second and then asks, "Was there an argument or a threat made to you or her?" He looks over at Briar.

"No, nothing. He just came out of the bedroom with the gun, and then it was all over," Smith says.

"Yes, he kept that handgun in our bedroom," instructs Briar.

"And why were you here mmmm... Justice? Smith is it?"

"To support Briar, his ex, and to talk to him about how it might look to the legal community."

"Did you expect that he would react this way?"

"No. He always seemed so in control, we thought it was better to clear the air with him."

"Okay." Chmura looks toward his two younger counterparts and then shakes his head and glances back toward Briar. "I guess you might have to come downtown and write out a formal statement."

"Can I come in tomorrow? She can go with you now," Smith asks.

Chmura shakes his head again. "No, we need you to go downtown right now and be interviewed by investigators."

"I am a superior court judge. I need to go to my office. I will have my statement emailed to you."

"I guess the rules are a bit different for you!" one of the young officers speaks up.

"So much for everyone being the same under the law," Chmura's agitated voice barks out.

Chmura reaches his hand into his jacket and pulls out his notebook and scribbles something down frantically. Chmura then nods to the other undercover officers and places his notebook into his back pocket.

"Alright, let's get out of here before Ident shows up to take pictures."

Chmura reaches for a patrol radio that has been placed on the dining room table.

"This is Chummy. We have 10-59 in North Van. We are requesting a Code 12 follow up on a Smith C. Need all available units to respond to a Code 3!"

He then tosses the radio to a young uniform officer who has just arrived. "Give them our 10-23 and the address."

When Chmura is about to leave, he moves to pick up a dining room chair that has been toppled over laying adjacent to the deceased body.

"Wait a second."

He reaches down to see a legal size envelope taped to the bottom of the overturned chair.

Chmura pivots and spins toward the other officers while holding up the envelope.

"I don't think Kazan left a goodbye note."

He turns to Briar who has not left the room yet and with a steely stare asks her if she knows what is in the envelope.

She turns her head and opens her mouth, "I . . . I . . ."

Smith has already left the room.

Chmura turns to her and with a smile says, "It is not like Kazan to leave a party without leaving something for the host."

Briar begins to lose her balance but falls back onto the sofa in the living room as the remaining officers encircle Chmura who is still holding up the large white envelope. Briar is completely overwhelmed by her feelings of sadness and regret. Her breathing is labored and shallow. Police form an impromptu scrum and make plans to arrest the absent party guest. Briar senses the flood of pain and sheer anxiety. The feelings of regret and her role in the death of Kazan race through her troubled mind. It takes all measures of any sense of self control to not pick up the Beretta from the living room floor and find a passport to freedom from the guilt that now presses down on her heart and soul.

HYMAN KAZAN

46

BRITISH COLUMBIA

JUSTICE CRAIG SMITH breathes a heavy sigh of relief as he settles into the quiet of his Mercedes SUV. He is still shaking from having pulled the trigger on Kazan's Beretta. He tries to focus on the simple act of driving while feeling content that he has now rid himself of the overwhelming pressure that has kept him awake for the last four days. Smith glances up at the nicotine stained rear view window and sees a smile begin to form on his face, confident now that he can resume his romance with Briar.

Smith has witnessed his share of traumatic events over the years. It is part of being a criminal court judge. All that is required is to abandon all empathy for those victimized by violence. But this time it is different as he is haunted by the calmness that Kazan exhibited as the bullet pierced his body, causing a crimson river flood onto the dining room carpet.

"Every suicide is a homicide," Kazan once said.

His voice and death now are ingrained in Smith's turbulent subconscious. Smith gags as the acid from his stomach reaches his cigarette bathed throat, causing him to gag while swallowing his guilt. *Thank goodness Briar and that bitch Marianne had not been in the room,* he thinks to himself. He wipes the drool from the corner of his mouth with his sleeve.

"If only Westfall had not come to my hotel room that night!" he shouts out in the empty car. "Fucking drugs! None of this had to happen. God damn it, Kazan got what he deserved."

He tries unsuccessfully to convince himself. Smith takes a deep breath and attempts to settle his shattered nerves. His mind races with the thoughts of whether or not there are any loose ends that he must tie up to avoid detection. An unexpected chime from his cell phone beeps twice and begins to unnerve Smith. The noise sounds again, indicating that his cell phone is connected to his answering system. Smith's eyes grow wide as he has come to the realization that his cell phone is in the process of receiving a message through his answering service.

Just as he is about to reach out for the small blinking red phone on his touch screen, he hears Kazan's voice and the sound of a gunshot. He feels a burning sensation in his chest, and he begins to sweat as he fumbles for his cell phone.

47

HYMAN KAZAN

BRITISH COLUMBIA

"PULL OVER NOW!" Chmura's voice thunders over the loudspeaker of his undercover black Ford Explorer, panicking Smith, who is in shock by the turn of events. "Stop the car now!"

Smith grabs the steering wheel tightly and swerves into the driveway of a local convenience store and dry cleaner. He thinks about running for a second, but realizes that this would secure his guilt.

"What the hell is happening? Did the other officers not tell you who I am?" he calls out to an unrecognized Chmura.

"You are under arrest for the murder of Hyman Kazan!" Chmura barks out through the radio. "Stay seated in the car and place your palms on the front dashboard!"

"This is ridiculous!" calls out Smith.

Smith jumps out of the car, leaving the driver's side door open and walks toward the stopped police SUV. He is both agitated and annoyed by the traffic stop. A crowd of young curious Asian men look on at the unfolding chaos. Smith puffs himself up in an attempt to deal with this unexpected scenario. In the moment leading up to this mayhem, Smith has failed to turn off his car, and he can hear the low hum of his cell phone and the recording of the gun being discharged into the upper torso of Kazan.

He reaches into his pocket and pulls out his cell phone in an effort to turn it off before Chmura reaches him.

"Hands where I can see them, Smith!" Chmura yells out.

Smith ignores the order and focuses on shutting off his phone, aware the incriminating evidence is also on Kazan's cell phone. He takes a second to digest the predicament he finds himself in. He lets out a heavy sigh at the sight of Chmura with his service pistol now pointing at him. A shadow of a person can be seen in the back of Chmura's car. An anemic Briar is slumped in the backseat of the police vehicle.

Chmura races over to Smith and forces him to lie face down on the black asphalt of the driveway with his hands cuffed behind his back. He cannot fight off the urge to place his arthritic knee between the rounded shoulder blades of Smith. The two other officers that have shown up at the condo have now arrived on the scene. Briar squats down in front of Smith and is holding Kazan's cell phone in her left hand. Her eyes are red and tear stained and her face is very pale.

"Can you hear Kazan's voice? He is saying you killed Simon?"

"I did not kill anyone! Briar, you are in shock, you do not know what you are saying. Kazan was angry at us being together, the gun just went off."

A wail of sirens is heard off in the distance. Briar is now coming to grips with what is happening, and begins to dial the number for Koogan. The young officer standing beside her reaches out and grabs the cell phone.

"This phone is now evidence. You can use a phone back at the station to reach a lawyer!"

The blood is now draining from Smith's face as he struggles to his feet. Briar watches as he complies with the instructions provided by Chmura. After a long pause, he begins the long walk toward Chmura's vehicle, limping from the aggressive takedown. Chmura shakes his hand as a small amount of blood drips from a small cut to the back of his hand. He tugs at the back of his belt and hikes up his pants, taking a second to wipe the flow of blood on the side of his pants. He smiles and nods to the other police officers who look on intently.

"You could have helped out with the arrest you know?"

"You looked like you were enjoying yourself," they respond while clutching their body worn cameras.

"I am too fucking old for this," calls out Chmura.

When Briar walks back to the police vehicles, she observes the two other officers placing Smith into the back of the Chmura's police car. As she walks toward one of the other vehicles, she looks back at Smith, who looks like a deflated shadow of a man. How did she get involved with him? She recalls Kazan asking the very same question.

AS A RELUCTANT sun slowly creeps over the snowcapped coastal mountains, Briar attempts to get dressed for court. Koogan, who is seated in the living room, sips his coffee, waiting for Briar to exit the bedroom. It has been almost a year since Judge Smith was found guilty of criminal negligence causing the death of Simon Westfall. The case was largely successful due to the work put in on the case by Hyman Kazan. Members of the RCMP from Kelowna are still investigating the death of Kazan, primarily based on cell phone records and recordings obtained by an over eager Vancouver police officer. It will be several more months before he will be finally charged with his death.

Koogan smiles as he glances at the black and white photograph of Kazan that still rests on the maple mantle above the fireplace. *He would have loved to see Smith in the prisoner dock awaiting to be sentenced,* thinks Koogan. Briar is sad and confused with her feelings about the day. Victims tend to prosecute themselves.

"I cannot believe he is gone, Koogan."

"Yeah, I still expect to see him outside of the courthouse."

Briar offers a nod and a courtly smile. She is still trying to process why and how Kazan died. She is weighed down with an unresolved guilt as to her actions that may have lead to his death.

"I am sure that this is just the start, Briar. If the cops did not find that envelope left by Kazan, we would have probably never arrived at today. The case is always in the details, those particular shards of evidence that form the ring around the accused . . . the particulars."

Briar is overcome with pain and sorrow as she reaches for her black leather shoes at the end of the sofa.

"I am sure that it will be standing room only at court, and the local bar will be talking about me in hush tones for years to come! I cannot believe this scandal will ever end."

"It will take some time, Briar, but unfortunately for someone else, there will be a death or a rape tonight, or something worse and a new victim will become the entertainment headliner tomorrow."

Briar begins to cry. "I never wanted this. We just wanted to be happy, Koogan."

"Happiness is very elusive, Briar. Moments, moments. Simon was looking for love and acceptance. Kazan was looking for justice, and you, my dear friend, thought you found both seated on the bench at the head of the classroom."

Briar looks down and then out the balcony window, not wanting to think about any role she might have had in the death of Kazan or in having a relationship with Smith.

"You just got caught in between two destructive forces, Briar," Koogan continues. "Kazan did love you, you know?"

Koogan's attempt to comfort her falls short.

"Yeah, I know."

Briar finds a bit of comfort from hearing that she was loved. She struggles with what she is supposed to feel about the sentencing of Smith.

Stirling and Fera are standing outside of the courtroom smoking cigarettes. Inside, the crowd is energized. Chmura and some undercover cops are also lingering on the damp grey steps to the courthouse. Chmura is tired, but there is a glimmer of relief in his eyes. Briar walks up the steps, passing them with her head down.

"How are you doing?" Stirling asks.

"Day by day, I guess," Briar answers back. "Just here to see justice done."

"Kazan would have told you this before, but you have come to the wrong place," Fera scoffs. "A jury of his peers would be hard to find."

"What do you mean?" asks Briar.

"Someone who completely does not give a shit," Fera says. "Lawyers feed the justice system, the justice system feeds the lawyers! But I know that does not include you."

Stirling shakes his head at both the rudeness and honesty of his comment.

"You just can't let it go, Fera, can you?"

"I am not running for public office like you, Stirling."

Stirling nods. "I am really sorry for you, Briar. You did not deserve to be pulled into this. I am sure you are having mixed emotions about being here today."

"Nobody will feel good about today: my brother, Craig, or even you, Fera."

The tormenting question is, how did it all turn out so wrong? It keeps ricocheting around inside her head like a 22 caliber bullet shot from close range. It's destroying her self worth, causing her anxiety and sleepless nights, and causing her to hide away from the public. She becomes like Kazan. She is slipping away. There are no warning signs or barriers to keep her safe from the bottomless pit of despair. Like Kazan, she has embarked upon a journey into the darkness, the open pit of her own fears and regrets. There is no light at the end of the tunnel, nothing to grip onto to prevent her from falling into a endless dark wintery season of depression. It is only the twinge of fear and anxiety that hold together the hairline crack of the person she once was.

Alone now, she plunges ahead, back into the courthouse, in search of some vague sense of direction in which to turn. After some awkward goodbyes and "I will see you there," Briar and Koogan head through the courthouse doors and over to the largest courtroom in the courthouse. They reach the doors outside of the courtroom and are greeted by security. Inside, there is a special constable seated by the doors who rises to his feet and ushers them to the front of the packed courtroom.

Craig Donald Smith sits in the glass enclosed prisoner's dock with his arms crossed. He has lost weight and looks defiant. His lawyer bends over to whisper something into his ear. He nods and smiles and appears to indicate that he wants to address the court himself.

"How dare those that have come to watch me, their local judge, be judged by some out of town hack!" Smith announces.

"Are you aware, Craig, you do not have to say anything? You have counsel."

"I don't care! I did not care! I did not kill anyone, I am responsible for nothing! Those vultures in the back do not give a fuck about justice, they are just here to see me hang."

A grimaced defense attorney nods. "Alright then, I will tell the court."

"It was a huge mistake to try and attempt to help those downtown gays. It was a mistake to show any kindness to them, a huge fuckup."

"You can't really mean that, Craig?" his lawyer questions.

"It doesn't matter anymore," Smith demands. "Who was Kazan, anyway?"

"Kazan? You mean Simon Westfall."

"Yeah. Simon Westfall. Just another dead east ender."

Counsel stares coldly at Smith. "You might just want to keep those comments to yourself."

Smith's face lights up when he catches a glimpse of Briar seated in the courtroom beside Koogan. He speaks to the special constable that is seated beside him.

"I told you she would come!" Smith proudly states.

Even though Briar is seated in the courtroom, she is miles away.

"A place of misery and regret," she muses aloud. "Nothing matters anymore, all this is just a show, for those who are not here to care."

"What do you mean?" Koogan asks.

Briar controls her panic as she thinks about the images of the senseless death of both Kazan and Simon in her head. It is like it was all for nothing, and then this final stage play. Panic begins to swell and subside like the tide on their many beach walks. How could this be? Why did this happen? How could this respected man in the dock now be about to be sentenced for taking a young man's life? How does this justice thing work? It was the same old set of questions of why? She recalls the many sleepless nights when she and Kazan would lay in bed and ponder those very questions before attempting to find some rest in the darkest of nights.

Whatever was going to happen today, whether it was months or years, it would not pull back the vicious lack of empathy that could have saved a life. Over the next couple of hours, Briar feels the infection has been lanced and is draining as the lawyers drone on and on. Then she hears his annoying voice.

"That is not quite right. That is not how it happened."

Blah, blah, blah. Instead of dropping her head and gazing downward, she stands straighter and sharpens her gaze out in front of her. She will no longer look upon him with anything but disgust. With no more inner voices calling out to her about what she did to cause Smith to be the person he has become, or do the things he was both charged or guilty of, her hearing of Kazan's voice gradually falls silent, bathed in his spirit of what might have been.

Outside, a light drizzle begins to fall. Rain—the weather is fine. It is called rain, layers of the atmosphere falling from the dark skies overhead, affecting how we dress, feel and respond to our surroundings. Like emotions and dreams, we all attempt to weather the current storms of our lives.

ACKNOWLEDGMENTS

*"Whatever is the lot of humankind
I want to taste within my deepest self.
I want to seize the highest and the lowest,
to load its woe and bliss upon my breast,
and thus expand my single self titanically
and in the end go down with all the rest."*

—Johann Wolfgang von Goethe, *Faust, First Part*

THIS STORY FIRST came into being when a local lawyer asked me one afternoon, shortly after I had returned from court, what I would do next. I attempted to explain that life is like a book with many chapters.

When I started to write this book, my focus was on the people in the justice system, rather than the outcomes. From there, I had the good fortune to draw upon the vast number of victims who shared their journey from rain to sunshine to rain again with me. Again and again the questions were raised: What is? What was? What matters? And why go on? A fictional meditation was started to explore the human condition of why venture down the road to our ultimate demise? Why bother?

Fortunately, I had a very supportive group of friends and colleagues who encouraged me to scribble a few lines on a yellow pad of paper to bring the lives of Kazan and Briar to life. I am tremendously grateful to all those who pointed out to me over the years that the greatest exhibition of humility equals untapped courage. In short, to choose that it is all about everything, rather than about nothing, to continue, and the sweet moments of life increase our tolerance to the bitter.

A special thanks to all those who have helped me along the way: Linda Elliott, Hunter Hamilton, Captain Don McKinnon, Jennifer Chapin, Bradley G Dempster, Joy Comendador, Matt Stanley, Timothy J. Trojan, Katie at Tellwell, J. A. Fera, Margaret J. Janzen, Jasper Hamilton, Patty Shifflett Rimonteil, Michael G. Soo, Justice G. Young, The YLD, The Write Portal, James Bay Stories, Behind the Scenes: Authors Journeys, EARL, The West Coast Book Club, and Benjamin at Tellwell for a great cover design.